Ember MEADOW

Ember MEADOW

ABIGAIL MORGAN

*For Samantha – the co-dreamer/plotting partner of
this wild and wonderful world.*

Lone Pine Ranch
Barn & Bunkhouse
Ember Meadow
Ranch House
Guest Cabin
Grazing Field
Old Cabin
Lone Pine Ranch
To Jackson Hole

Jackson Hole, Wyoming

Deloney Ave

Center St

Broadway

Ember Meadow Maps

Prologue
Miles

HOLLOW BROWN EYES STARE back at me in the window. The sand colored buildings of Salt Lake City, Utah blur behind my own reflection, glowing orange in the sunset. Even through the glass I can make out the bags under my eyes, my crumpled button up shirt, bolo tie hanging loose from my neck.

I look like I've been run ragged. It doesn't help that Parker and I were up at three this morning to drive all the way down to Utah for a cattle auction.

The beginning of Spring down here is much warmer than Wyoming. Back on Lone Pine Ranch, it's snowing right now. At least this year, we aren't presenting cattle at the auction. Instead, we are here to pick up a few head to strengthen our herd. When one of our fences broke, I figured we'd lost a good amount of cattle. But the final count last week was more than I expected. At least Walt will be proud of the amount we were able to wrangle up today.

"Miles," Parker yells from the other room of our hotel suite, "Hurry up. My buddy is waiting for us outside."

With one more glance out towards the glowing city windows, I turn around with a sigh. My bolo tie slides down my button up as I loosen it all the way. I already despise going out, I definitely don't care what I look like. Those days are over.

Running a hand through my messy hair, I throw on my baseball cap backwards and make my way toward the door where Parker waits, his entire focus fixed on sending a text. Seeing his phone makes me wonder where mine is. I haven't seen it since the drive down here.

"Ready?" Parker smiles, finally looking up at me. I feel a little underdressed compared to his perfectly styled chestnut hair, button down, and not-dusty jeans. But that just about explains Parker and I. We've been this way since the first day he walked onto the ranch looking for a job. It's probably why we are such good friends.

"I suppose," I reply.

"Oh come on," he laughs. "Live a little, will you? It's been over a year, man. It's time."

It turns out Parker's buddy who lives in the city has some other buddies that live in the city, and they all lead us down a couple of blocks to a rooftop bar at the top of some swanky skyscraper. I didn't even know Salt Lake had places like this. I almost never go out when I'm here. We usually just head to the auction, and maybe to dinner somewhere with a good steak.

The music is loud, the lights are shining above us, and I really don't fit in here. Parker, of course, fits in anywhere and already has a whole group of new friends to shoot the shit with. I shuffle towards the bar, finding an open bar stool to order a whiskey sour.

My gaze scans along the crowded rooftop as I take a swig of my drink. Girls in sundresses and heels, guys in button ups, some even with ties. Most people are laughing and paired up. It's a nice scene. I might even come back some time if I'm in town. The city lights glow all around us. The magnitude of the skyscrapers always takes me off guard. It may not be a huge city, but it's the biggest I usually go to.

My shoulders loosen up a little more with each sip of my drink, the warm air blowing across my arms. Maybe I should try to have a good time. Enough moping. Maybe Parker is right, it's probably time I try to live a little.

Right as I'm about to get up and head back over to Parker and his new posse, long crimson hair brushes across my shoulder. A blur of a woman rushes by before planting herself in the seat next to me.

"Four lemon drops please," she tells the bartender with a dazzling smile. She's wearing a skin-tight shiny, burgundy dress and a sash that says twenty-one across her shoulder.

But what catches my eye are her cowgirl boots. Real cowgirl boots. Not the fake kind you buy for twenty dollars on the internet. I'd be willing to bet she has actually seen a horse before. At some point, my brain catches up enough to realize I've been staring at this girl's boots for too long. I snap my eyes up to her face.

It must be the whiskey. She's the most beautiful woman I've ever seen. Her green eyes practically sparkle with mischief. Big, auburn curls frame her face, slightly flushed from running through the bar. The spaghetti straps holding up her dress are the most thin, ridiculous straps I've ever seen.

A spark ignites an ember in my chest when her pine green eyes catch mine. It's been a long time since I've felt anything like that.

I feel like I should run away, but I can't.

"Well hi," she says, her head tipping slightly to the side. I track the movement of her curls falling over her bare shoulder. "Who are you?"

Oh god. She's talking to me. What's my name? Shit. "Miles Autry," I manage to choke out. My full name? What are we, in kindergarten?

"Well, *Miles Autry*," she teases, "I'm Katie MacPherson. Pleased to meet you." She holds out her hand for a handshake. The second I grab her hand, an electric pulse runs through my arm and I'm drowning in her big green eyes again. Stuck in a trance.

"Hello? Anyone home in there?" she says with a laugh. I hadn't realized I was staring for so long.

"Yeah, sorry," I clear my throat, "I'm just a little tired. Long day."

"You can't be tired. It's my birthday, you know. Everyone must be awake and excited," she says. The bartender brings over her lemon drop shots and she flashes him another movie star smile. My chest constricts as envy bubbles up in my veins. Why does that guy get a smile?

"Oh yeah? Happy birthday. I'm guessing you're twenty-one," I say, gesturing to her sash.

"Why yes, I am. My first ever alcoholic beverages," she winks.

"Can I buy you a drink?" I offer, before a rush of anxiety hits me straight on. "I mean, you know, for your birthday. After you're done with those. Or now. Whenever, really."

"Only if you're drinking with me," she says. It's been a few years since I've done this, and apparently I'm way out of practice.

"Right. Sure. I can do that," I say. She runs off to her group of friends to deliver the lemon drops, letting me know she'll be back. I order us another round of whiskey sours, hoping she drinks that. I'm not creative enough to think up anything else at the moment. It's been, shit, a good amount of years since I've done anything like this.

She walks back over to a table full of girls about her age and one guy. I look over just in time to see them all tip back their shots, Katie the first one. If it fazes her at all, she doesn't show it. First drink, my ass.

She whispers something to her dark haired friend and they both look over at me before I can snap my head back to the drink I've been twirling in my hands. There's no way they didn't see me looking. I turn back to the bar with a deep sigh. I'm not made for this.

What am I doing? I'm a twenty-eight-year-old rancher from Wyoming who hasn't been on a first date in ten years. She's here with her friends for her twenty-first birthday. The last thing she needs is some older guy flirting with her. I shake my head, adjusting my ball cap.

Parker was wrong, I am definitely not ready for this. I'll just give her this one drink for her birthday, and go back to the hotel. Download that taxi app thing Parker has. No reason to ruin his one night out in the city.

I feel around for my phone in my pockets before remembering I didn't have it when I left the hotel room.

Shit. I'm screwed.

Katie startles me as she bounces back down onto the barstool next to me. "Alright, I'm ready, Autry. What are we drinking?" All thoughts of leaving fly out of my brain once I'm in her presence again. She called me Autry.

"Well, Mac," I smile, "Figured I'd see if you're a real cowgirl. Ordered a couple of whiskeys." I nod to her legs, "I like your boots."

"Thanks," she laughs, grabbing her glass, "My best friend lives on a dude ranch. We ride a lot. I guess I'm just used to wearing them now." I try not to watch her throat as her head tips back when she takes her first sip. "So what do you do?" she asks.

I clear my throat, running through any possible information about myself. It's hard to focus when my heart is racing like this. "I'm a cattle rancher up in Wyoming. My ranch hand and I are here for a cattle auction."

"Ah. One night only?" she giggles. Her laugh is like wind chimes in a summer breeze.

"Yep, just tonight. What about you?"

"Same. We just came to the city for my birthday. I live up in a small town called Juniper Ridge just barely inside of Idaho," she explains, taking another drink. Her cheeks turn more pink with every sip. I feel my leg start bouncing under my stool.

"I think I've been through there," I say, not wanting the conversation to end, "It's pretty."

In the next hour I find out she's here with her best friend, who's name is Hazel, and a few others from their small town. She just graduated college early, and started running her family's vacation rental properties around Juniper Ridge's Bear Lake. She loves it and wants to expand one day.

I tell her a bit about my family's ranch. It's an easy conversation, like we've known each other a while.

I can't help but stare at her. The way she gets so animated when she talks, throwing her arms all over the place. How the sparkle in her eyes glows brighter when she talks about her town and her friends. The slight spackling of freckles trailing across her cheeks. Her giggles when I order us another round.

She's like a magnet. I can't pull away, just keep moving in closer and closer.

"You know," she slurs, "Historically, I don't date cowboys. Not my type. Too flighty, always covered in sweat and dust," she makes a sort of 'ick' face before continuing. "But you... you're different. You're all smiley and kind and funny. And you smell like a cedar chest. I like you, Autry." She jabs her pointer finger into my chest with each point she makes.

"I like you too, Mac," I nod. She likes me? Why?

Two whiskey sours in, we are laughing hysterically at a joke I can't remember and my arm is tingling where her hand rests. I've forgotten about our age difference completely. I've forgotten we are strangers. I take her by the hand and whisk her away from the bar, over to where the band is playing.

Three whiskey sours in, we are dancing with her friends to a song I've never heard before, lights blurring around us. Her hands are around my neck and I can count the stars in her eyes. The warmth from her body radiates into mine when we are this close. She's like the sun. Warm and comfortable and keeping me close with a gravitational pull.

Four whiskey sours in, her soft lips finally meet mine and I feel the ember in my chest grow into a flame. I never want her to let go. Her fingers scratch on my five o'clock shadow, sending a shiver down my spine. I haven't kissed very many girls in my life, but I already know this is the best kiss I've ever had.

After that, I just have pieces of memories, mixed with heightened emotions. Leaving with her. Kissing her forehead as we walk down the city sidewalk through the melody of her giggles. Trying way too hard to unlock her hotel room door, and probably waking up the whole floor in the process. Ridiculously thin dress straps falling down her shoulders. Soft cotton sheets around us with nothing in between us. Hearing her little gasps in the dark.

I want to brand them into my memory.

Feeling my heart beating so hard I'm sure she can hear it. The flame in my chest igniting into a burning fire I've never felt before.

When I wake up the next morning in a bed that is not mine, sunshine pouring in through the window, head pounding, ears ringing, it takes me a few minutes to realize where I am. Memories come back in patches, and I can't help the grin that spreads along my face. I reach over to the other side of the bed to touch her again. I'm met with an empty pile of sheets. I panic, shooting up in the bed, cracking my eyes open to look around.

The room is completely empty. The fire in my chest extinguishes into a pile of smoking coals.

I reach for the nightstand, only to realize my phone isn't there. I forgot I didn't bring it with me. I groan, wincing as my eyes open all the way. It's far too bright in here. She not just gone, she's gone-gone. No trace left behind.

My heart aches as I remember her gorgeous, happy face, bar lights twinkling behind her. I turn over to the nightstand again and notice a small, folded piece of paper with Autry scribbled on the front next to the hotel writing pad.

The note reads, *Thx 4 everything. Had to jet. Call me!* I frantically turn it over, looking for a phone number, but there's nothing. Who leaves a note that says call me and doesn't leave their phone number?

Probably someone who doesn't actually want you to call them, Miles, I think to myself.

Standing up from the bed I run my hands through my hair. My face heats up. I can't believe I let this happen. Should have known. In fact, I did know. Parker knew I didn't want to come here.

It's only been just over a year. Fourteen months since *she* left without a trace, not that anyone is counting. And now, here, the first time I feel a tiny spark, the first girl I feel anything for doesn't feel the same.

That's it. I'm done. No more giving into feelings, no more letting hope tease me only to be ripped away. I'm glad she didn't leave her number. I was already too attached to Katie after one night with her, I need to stay away anyway. I'm not a one night stand sort of guy. From now on, I'm going to focus on the ranch and only the ranch.

No more distractions.

Letting out a frustrated growl, I pull my jeans and shirt back on, and head off to track down a cab to take me back to my own hotel. I'm sure Parker isn't worried in the slightest where I am, if he's even in our shared room, but I need to track down my phone, then him, then pack up to head out.

I go over the list in my mind a few times until I'm no longer thinking about Katie. No reason to. She probably does this all the time.

Plus, she lives in Idaho. It's not like I'll see her again anyway.

Chapter 1

You're Trespassing

Four Years Later (Katie)

I'VE LIVED NEAR MOUNTAINS for over a decade now. I see them every day when I step out of my house. I spend time near the peaks, I hike, I take pictures. But I've never seen mountains quite like these. The mountains passing on the other side of my windshield are another level from Juniper Ridge.

These are huge, award winning mountains. Olympic-level mountains.

When I decided to take on this project and head up to Jackson Hole, Wyoming, I'll admit I had high hopes. It's one place I've never been. My expectations have been far exceeded. It's gorgeous here.

It's the start of May and all of the snow has just about melted, save for a few places way high up in the peaks. Although, I have a feeling the snow never truly leaves the tallest points. The fields are green, the river is full, and the very first signs of summer are peeking through.

Sun reflects off of the Snake River as I drive up the most beautiful canyon I've ever seen in my life. Groups of families walk along the road carrying large rafts, wearing helmets and life jackets. Fishermen stand in the river casting flies into the current. Hikers trek along the rocky mountainside. It's pictur-esque. If I didn't know any better, I'd think all of this was setup as a tourist advertisement.

As I drive through town, the ad continues. Couples eating lunch on bistro tables outside of restaurants, rows of western themed shops in buildings that look like they're right out of a movie, and at the center of town, four huge arches in each cor-ner of the square made completely out of elk antlers.

My navigation app takes me a ways outside of the main town, towards the south end of Grand Teton National Park. I turn onto a well-groomed dirt road and pray my little car makes it without popping a tire or bottoming out. I pull up to a weather worn cabin and kill the ignition, pulling my wind blown auburn hair up into a ponytail. One deep breath and then it's time to get to work.

As soon as I step out of the car, I already love it here. The sun warms my face as mountain fresh air fills my lungs. It al-most feels like home. I live in the mountains of southern Idaho, almost Utah, so I'm used to this environment. The mountains may be slightly larger here and the town a bit bigger and fanci-er, but it's still a Rocky Mountain town.

I know all about those. I love them. We vibe well, the moun-tains and I.

Gravel crunches beneath my runners as I walk up to the cab-in. My wonderful parents bought a tiny cabin on the outskirts of Jackson Hole, and instead of coming up here themselves, they've sent me. I found out about it by email. They couldn't be bothered to call me on the phone. In fact, there's still a small chance I've come all this way for nothing if their email was hacked by a very convincing criminal.

I guess I'll find out soon enough.

"Please be do-able," I whisper under my breath, blowing a stray hair out of my face.

The Old Cabin doesn't look great from the outside. It's situated back a bit on a beautiful piece of land surrounded by a cattle ranch. There's a view of the southern bit of the Tetons behind it. The wood looks as though it was stained dark at some point and has weathered over time to be almost gray. To be honest, it's better looking than I expected when I heard it needed an entire summer to be fixed up.

I walk up to the front door already making a mental list of what to do first. Sand and stain the exterior, deep clean the windows, replace that one that's cracked on the second floor, power wash the porch. This is where I thrive. I'm great at problem solving. I'm a great vacation rental host. And, apparently a great cabin fixer upper.

Put me in an eclectic B and B and I'm in my happy place. It's why I'm still working for my parents despite our... interesting dynamic.

We have four large cabins in Juniper Ridge that I manage full time, along with remotely managing another thirteen properties around the west. All that belong to the MacPherson Enterprises empire.

I had to earn this job, despite working for my parents' company. They were harder on me than other applicants. But I'm great at what I do, and I can't wait to dig into this new property.

I spent the last month since we acquired the charming cabin researching the area. I've done so many virtual walkthroughs of this cabin I feel like I've been here before as I walk in the door. It's dark and dusty inside, filled with spiderwebs. But all I see is potential.

As soon as I make it over the threshold, a warm feeling envelops me. Like heat radiating off of a crackling fire on a winter's day.

I pull out my notebook to jot down all of the ideas running amok in my head. Rust orange couch, leather chair, restore the hardwood floors, cowhide rug, bright yellow curtains.

The rooms are in great condition for how old the cabin is, and how long it's gone unused. From what I could tell, it used to be part of the ranch surrounding us. The owners don't use the cabin, and are having some hard times so they sold it to MacPherson Enterprises for a pretty penny, advertising it as a perfect vacation rental property.

It came with a couple of acres, more than our other properties, and no surrounding buildings to obstruct the breathtaking view. Also included was the promise the cattle belonging to the ranch wouldn't come close enough to agitate guests, which is very helpful for me.

A smile breaks out across my face as I look around the living room area, complete with a fireplace, of course.

I've made it.

My first Wyoming property. In a proper vacation town. It's all mine. For the summer, that is. I have four months to fix this place up and have it ready for fall visitors. It would have been ideal to do this part in the winter to be ready for summer vacationers, but I've heard the winters here are brutal. I'm glad we started now. The most magical time of year in the mountains.

Out of nowhere, a warm breeze glides across my arms. It wraps around me, smelling like honeysuckle and making me feel at home. In my mind's eye, a crackling fire burns in the fireplace, splatters of orange, red and yellow trees on the peaks outside of the window. A fresh cup of tea warms my hands, the smell of mint filling my senses. A broad chest at my back, firm arms pulling me close.

Then, the breeze is gone and it all melts away.

Startled, I look around the cabin only to see all of the doors and windows are firmly shut. There's definitely not any air conditioning installed, and the heating shouldn't be on yet. It felt like... almost like I'm supposed to be here. I can't explain it. I must be exhausted or something.

Shrugging it off, I take another step, itching to check the rest of the place out. There's a spring in my step as I adjust my high waisted jean shorts and skip towards the porch. Stopping short of the front door, I notice an open window and a rich campfire smell wafting in.

As I take in the view, a small dirt cloud appears in the distance where the road keeps going past the cabin. It's a beautiful day outside. Not a cloud in the sky, golden grass blowing in the wind, red and orange leaves falling off the trees.

Hang on. Why are the leaves already changing?

That doesn't make sense, it's spring. I step up to the window to take a closer look. Sure enough, it looks like the middle of fall outside.

Movement catches my eye towards the back of the sprawling field. I squint my eyes to look closer. It's a deer. A buck with three antler points on one side and two on the other. He saunters closer to the yard. I've seen a lot of deer living in Idaho, but this one is different somehow.

Afraid to scare the deer away, I tiptoe to the front door and step out onto the wraparound porch. My boots barely make any noise as I creep over to the side of the house where the deer stood. But when I get there, he's gone. No sign of a deer at all.

I let out a disappointed sigh, sad I didn't pull my phone out and take a photo to send to my best friend Hazel. It looks different than it did from the window. A lot different. The trees and grass are green, not shades of yellow, orange, and red.

It looks like spring again.

I shake my head, trying to get a hold of myself. I'm clearly imagining things. That, or the windows have some sort of tint on them. But, I'll have to check that out later. Because now, a big dirt cloud on the road is heading my way.

If I remember my maps correctly, that's the road to the main ranch buildings. They're far enough I can just barely make them out. The dust cloud gets closer and closer until I can just make out the silhouette of a horse.

I run a hand through my hair. Someone from the ranch must be coming down to welcome me. The owner knows I'm arriving today, an older man named Walter. I never got a last name, just Walter. We spoke on the phone a few times, and he was so kind to me, answering all of my questions about the property and telling stories of his ranch in the old days.

The closer the horse gallops, the less sure I am that it's Walter in the saddle. Onyx hair falls out from under a cowboy hat, fading into a scruffy beard. The dark ink of a tattoo sleeve covers his left arm, poking out of his black t-shirt.

Another tell-tale sign this isn't Walter: he looks pissed off.

I pump up my smile a bit as the horse stops a few feet away from the porch and its rider dismounts.

"Hi," I wave as the man approaches. Honey always catches more flies than vinegar, as my Aunt Millie always says. I'll just kill him with kindness. There's no response beyond a gruff grunt as he approaches. His olive skin is darker from days out in the sun, hat covered in a thin layer of dust. He's wearing a set of black leather chaps that kickstart my heart rate a little bit. Huh. I guess I'm a chaps girl now.

Brown eyes pierce mine with a fire behind them.

He's really mad. And also extremely attractive, but that's beside the point.

"You're trespassing," he growls, his no-nonsense tone startling me. A strong cedar scent envelops me and draws me a little closer.

Holding out a hand for him to shake, I put on my best PR smile. "Hi, I'm–"

"I said, you're trespassing," he interrupts. My hand falls slowly back to my side. "This is Lone Pine Ranch property. There's a sign on the road. This cabin isn't for tourists."

Okay, guess we are skipping pleasantries today.

"As I was saying, hi," I start again. "I'm Katie. I'm here to renovate this cabin. My company just bought it a few months ago. This particular piece of land doesn't belong to the ranch anymore, which technically means *you're* the one trespassing." I grin wider, standing my ground. "Who are you?"

"I own this ranch, and yes, this is part of Lone Pine. I think I would know if someone bought the Old Cabin," he says, holding my gaze. Alright, guess he's not backing down. I'm stuck in place as he studies my face, looking like he's trying to piece something out. A spark of recognition passes across his expression for just a second but it leaves as quickly as it came.

"I spoke to a man named Walter, he should have all of the details of the purchase and my arrival today. Do you know anyone by that name?" I ask.

For a second he doesn't say anything. "Yes," he sighs, "I know Walt."

"Great," I clap my hands together and plaster on another smile, "Then surely you can call him up and confirm I am, in fact, the owner of the cabin. Well, not me personally. MacPherson Enterprises owns it. But I represent them and I share the name, so it might as well be me."

"Hold on just a sec– wait, what did you just say?" His eyebrows furrow as he searches my face.

"Walter. That's the man I've spoken with. Can you call him?" I repeat and his eyes widen a bit.

"No, no. The name. What did you say your name was?" He asks, suddenly paling.

"Katie. MacPherson. Of MacPherson Enterprises. Walter should know who I am," I say cautiously. This man looks like he's seen a ghost. After a few long seconds of silence I try again, "Who are you?"

He clears his throat, looking away. A dry laugh escapes his throat as he shakes his head slowly back and forth.

"I'll be damned," he mutters under his breath. Turning back to me, our eyes lock and I swear I've seen those brown eyes before. I just can't remember when.

"Miles. I'm Miles Autry."

"Nice to meet you Mi–" It can't be. Words fail me as I finally remember the last time I saw Miles. In a hotel in Salt Lake City over four years ago. The Wyoming cowboy from the bar. The one who never called. This can't be him.

My Miles was charming, funny, light-hearted, and smiled almost constantly. Yes, he worked at a ranch and they look alike, but there's just no way this man is the same Miles. I can't imagine Miles being gruff with anyone, much less me. It has to be a coincidence. Right? Unless...

"Oh my god," I stagger backwards a step as the realization smacks me in the chest like a semi truck.

"What the hell are you doing on my ranch, Mac?"

Chapter 2

Too Dusty

"**W**HAT DO YOU MEAN, *your ranch*?" My voice comes out a little shakier than I'd like. Am I being punk'd? There's absolutely no way my one night stand from my twenty-first birthday in Utah owns the ranch surrounding my new vacation rental property.

There's a zero percent chance of this happening.

Okay, so maybe there's, like, a twenty percent chance.

And he did say he worked on a ranch in Wyoming, so add another twenty percent.

And the universe generally hates me, so maybe add another twenty percent. But that's only sixty percent. There's still another whole forty unaccounted for.

I look a little closer at the cowboy standing before me. The beard is new. If he shaved, I could see the resemblance. Possibly. It isn't until I catch his eyes again that recognition starts to creep into my bones.

"This can't be your ranch. You don't own a ranch. You're, what, twenty-seven? Eight?" I croak, "This is Walter's ranch, *he's* as old as a ranch owner should be. Where is he? I'd like to talk to him."

"Technically, yes, this is Walt's ranch–" he starts.

"Hah!" I exclaim, pointing a finger at him.

"–But Walt isn't exactly in working condition at the moment so I've taken over ranch duties for him. None of that matters, though, because you can't be here. There's no reason you need to know about anything that goes on here. So pack up your tiny car and get back to Idaho," he says matter-of-fact. As if he can just tell me to leave and I'll go. Not likely.

"Yeah, not going to happen, Autry. My company bought this property fair and square. I've signed the paperwork. In fact, I have it with me. I'm not leaving. If you would be so kind as to let Walter know I've arrived out of courtesy, that would be wonderful," I plaster another smile onto my face, shooting darts Miles's way with my eyes. "In the meantime, I'm going to continue my walk-through of the cabin then head to my hotel for the night. It's been a long day of traveling and the last thing I need is to continue this asinine argument with you. Cowboys aren't my type, anyway. Too dusty." I wave him off with a hand.

The more I smile, the redder Miles's face turns. I can almost see the smoke coming out of his ears. Very different from the last time our paths crossed. That was, what, four years ago now? He had seemed so calm, cool and collected. It was one of the reasons I let him buy me a drink that night in the first place.

He was quiet, yet commanding. In charge, yet careful.

He smiled from ear to ear all night long. I think he may have even had dimples when his smile got big enough. Today, I haven't so much as seen the corners of his mouth twitch in any direction other than down.

His eyes have hardened since that night, and his demeanor is colder. If I saw him at a bar today, I'd probably avoid him and wonder what he was even doing in a fun place like a bar anyway.

Didn't he have that one friend with him all those years ago? The well-dressed one? I wonder if he works here too. Maybe he'd be more understanding.

I'll call Walter as soon as I get back to my hotel. If one of his employees is going to treat my guests like this once we get the rental up and running, it could ruin my business. Where does Miles Autry get off thinking he's in charge of me? He's not even in charge of the ranch. He just works there.

What an ass.

"Look, I'm not trying to be an asshole," he says. *Apparently he's a mind reader too.* "I just haven't heard anything about this and usually everything that happens at Lone Pine goes through me. Last time we had an uninvited trespasser, we had two acres on fire and I lost two head of cattle. I'll check with Walt and see what's up," he pulls out his phone and dials.

Fire? That's intense. Even so, he shouldn't assume everyone that steps foot on Lone Pine Ranch property is a pyromaniac.

"Okay great," I reply with a smile. His face remains stoic.

"Walt? Yeah this is Miles," a pause while he studies the sagebrush near his feet, "Yeah, sure is. Look, I'm out at the big cabin and there's a woman here. Says she talked to you about being here?" He seems to get cut off by the man on the other end of the call. His face goes from neutral and professional to angry again. Great, the fire eyes are back. "What do you mean?" he says through gritted teeth.

Uh-oh, I think to myself, *someone didn't communicate with their ranch hand.*

Miles runs a hand over his short charcoal beard. I catch a glimpse of a playing card tattooed onto his forearm. It's a cowgirl queen of hearts, big wispy curls with a cowgirl hat on and a wink in her eyes. The top corner of the card is on fire, black flames licking his skin. His veins push up against it, ink darkening his tan skin even further.

Even though his other arm is covered in a sleeve of tattoos, this one catches my eye.

Suddenly, the urge to reach out and touch him overwhelms me. I have to physically stop my arm from reaching out to him. Like a moth to a flame again. I clasp my hands behind my back so tight I can feel my knuckles turning white.

"You can't be serious. We talked about this, there has to be another way–" he turns around, pacing. Not sure what to do with myself as awkwardness washes over the scene, I rock back and forth on my heels. This is just my luck.

Not only do I run into an old one night stand (top five at least if I'm being honest), he also happens to work at a ranch we just bought property from. There has to be a way to spin this situation into a positive one. I weigh out options in my head, but can't seem to land on a good solution.

"Okay, Walt, I'm coming up there to discuss this with you in person. Yeah, see you soon." Miles hangs up and turns back around to me. At first, I think he's going to yell at me again, but he doesn't. His jaw ticks once and he takes a deep breath.

"It's good to see you again, Mac," he says, still without a smile. My stomach does a weird flip thing at the nickname. That's twice he's called me Mac and zero times he's called me Katie. I don't like how much I like it.

"Yeah you too," I say, shaking the unwanted leftover feelings off.

"I'm going to go see what all this with Walt is about. Just don't start anything until I straighten this all out, okay?" He seems sincere. I really don't want to ruffle any feathers right off the bat.

"Sure," I agree with a polite nod. "But I've got a crew coming soon for renovations," I say, hoping he'll catch my hint. I'm doing this with or without his approval. There's no legal reason I can't.

He nods again, turning back to his horse. Okay, maybe the unwanted feelings don't go away immediately. There's just something about a big cowboy mounting a horse and riding away. And Miles is definitely a big guy. He has to be at least eight inches taller than me, and I'm a somewhat tall girl at five foot seven.

He's not super jacked like a man that goes to the gym every day, rather he's built more practically. Like he spends his days working outside on a ranch. I imagine him hauling a barrel of hay across an open field at sunset, horses in the background, sweat dripping down his face.

Stop it, I whisper to myself the second the butterflies are back in my stomach.

I cannot be lusting over a one night stand right now. I have important things to do. Even if he looks like a walking wet dream.

I stand up from the dusty porch bench, brushing off my shorts. I look around at the cabin one more time and clap my hands together. Time to get to work. I haven't been this excited about a new project in a while. Everything with the ranch cabin seemed to line up so perfectly. Now that I'm here, I love it even more.

After checking a few more things off of my list at the cabin, I lock the lockbox up again and pull out my phone calendar. All that's left to do tonight is check in once more with my vendors on the packages I had sent to the cabin, and check into my hotel in town I'll be staying at during the renovation.

I've got this, I think to myself. Angry cowboy or no, I'm going to rock this renovation.

Chapter 3

New Miles

THE CASCADE INN IN downtown Jackson Hole looks more like a motel from the outside. It's adorable. Marigold yellow paint peels off the corners of the wood siding. A white metal railing runs across both floors, rows of light brown doors lined up all in a row. I drag my suitcase up to the second floor, and into room thirty-three. The room is quaint, but cozy. The first thing I notice is the balcony on the other end. I walk past the bed, parking my suitcase near a chair.

The balcony overlooks a street that connects to town square. I have a straight-on view of Snow King Resort, a ski resort overlooking the city. Large ski paths covered in lush summer grass cut through the pine trees and I can just make out a gondola heading on a steep path up the mountainside. The sun shines from the west, almost to the horizon. The buildings surrounding the Inn have just started to turn their lights on for the night. I can't believe this place is real.

I take a photo with my phone of the scene and send it to my Aunt Millie, letting her know I got to my hotel okay. She immediately responds with a heart-eyes emoji. I can picture her laugh like waves crashing onto a shore, standing in her brightly colored living room in New Mexico wearing a bright pink, flowy sundress, red hair wild like it always is.

Working on one of her short-lived projects, painting murals with a mop or crocheting rainbow colored gloves and scarves. Laughing to myself, I put my phone back into my pocket and lean against the balcony railing.

I don't bother letting my parents know where I am. They likely already do. Callum and Florence MacPherson own MacPherson Enterprises, the company I work for. Their true favorite child. It's definitely not me. My parents sent me to live with my aunt when I was ten years old to 'better focus on their empire.'

Apparently I was too much of a wild child for them to handle. Ever since then, everything between us has been a business transaction. In the end, living with Aunt Millie was probably the best thing that happened to me.

I loved moving to Juniper Ridge, and I made lots of lifelong friends. Though, Juniper Ridge has never been quite the same since Aunt Millie moved away.

I head back into my hotel room and plop down on the bed next to my laptop. Might as well go through my checklist. Since I started managing my parents' rental properties back when I was nineteen years old, I've grown from one cabin on the lake in Juniper Ridge to twelve total. I climbed my way up in the company until I was in charge of all properties in Idaho, Utah, Colorado and now Wyoming.

At first, it took a couple of years to gain my footing as a host, but now it's just like clockwork. I may be disorganized in my personal life, but I know what is happening at all times with all MacPherson properties I'm in charge of.

Aunt Millie was skeptical at first of me working for my parents' company, but honestly, I probably talk to them less now. There are plenty of people in between my parents and I, including my manager. Plus, just like I've always known, my relationship with them is much better as business anyway.

Just as I'm about to set my phone down, a text comes through from an unknown number.

UNKNOWN

> Hello, Katie. This is Walter from Lone Pine. I'm glad to hear you made it to Wyoming safe and sound. My wife, Isabella, and I would like to invite you to breakfast at our home on the ranch tomorrow morning. Please let me know if you'll be able to make it.

I can't help but smile at the text that reads more like a written letter. At least one person in this town is kind. I type back a response (yes of course I'll have breakfast at the ranch) and breathe a sigh of relief. A big weight is lifted off of my shoulders as my chest deflates. Hopefully, Walter explained everything to Miles and I won't have to deal with him again. I can be polite and cordial from a distance, even if we do have somewhat of a past.

There's no reason for Miles and I to interact much all summer.

Standing up, I look at myself in the mirror on the wall. My hair is already practically standing straight up from my head in a mess of big barrel curls, fly-aways fanning around my head like a messy halo. I kick off my favorite pair of cowgirl boots with the pink stitching and head into the bathroom to clean up.

As the scalding shower water runs down my face, a vivid, four year old memory pops up in my head. Strong hands in my hair pulling me closer. Lips crashing into mine, heat tingling all the way through my body.

The blur of twinkling city lights around me as I fall deep into a vortex. Waking up in a tangle of limbs, a sinking feeling in my gut. *Beautiful,* he whispers in my memories, so clearly it's like he's right in front of me.

I reach for the shower knob, turning it to cold, jolting myself out of the memory. This is probably the worst time to be remembering my one night with Miles. We were two different people back then. I can't have old memories seeping into my interactions with him now. It's time to do what I do best and compartmentalize.

Old Miles is a distant memory, fading from view. New Miles is my grumpy neighbor who does not want me here.

I nod to myself, repeating *New Miles* in my head until I can shake the feeling off. I can totally get my shit together before work starts on the new cabin. I'll go to breakfast at the ranch tomorrow and make sure Walter and Isabella love me, finish my plans for the cabin decor, and by then, my renovation crews will have arrived in Jackson to start work. Miles will get used to the idea of me owning the cabin and all will be right with the world.

The main house at Lone Pine Ranch is breathtaking. As much as I love my best friend's ranch back in Idaho, Connor Ranch, this takes the cake. The house is made of gray rocks that look like they were sourced from the surrounding mountain ridge, held together by a bone white grout.

Steep peaks jut out of the roof, covered in deep red tin. The front door is a deep red as well, bordered by two large logs as posts for the porch. I think they might just be whole trees, stained with a cherry finish.

It's a little intimidating, if I'm being honest. I was expecting an older, ranch style home similar to Connor Ranch. This is a western mansion. I can already imagine a wall of tall windows on the back of the house facing the Teton Range. Stepping out of my car in the gravel drive, I take a few deep breaths before walking up to the door.

My long, tan, floral skirt ruffles in the wind as I step up to the door. I went with my trusty cowgirl boots again, paired with a cropped pink shirt and black jean jacket. My hair is pulled up into a thick bun on the top of my head. As I was leaving the hotel this morning, I felt a little overdressed. Now, I feel the exact opposite.

Before I have a chance to knock, the door opens revealing an adorable older woman dressed in head to toe denim, dark hair peppered with gray pulled up into an updo, eyes crinkled with joy. I'm immediately pulled into a tight hug.

"You must be Katie," she exclaims, pulling away but still holding onto my arms. "You're adorable! I'm Isabella. We are so excited to have you here." Her accent is so slight I almost miss it.

"Thank you, it's so nice to meet you," I smile. "Your home is beautiful. Like, wow."

"Oh I can't take credit for it, it's been in the family for generations," she shrugs. "Come on in, we are just about ready."

Isabella leads me into a foyer with a large staircase leading up towards the left, and a hallway leading into a bright room lit by the morning sunlight. I follow her into the room, which turns out to be the kitchen. Rich wood cabinets line the walls, a white breakfast nook sits in the corner of the room with plates set for four, and food already fills the countertops.

Taking some strips of bacon off of a griddle by the stove is an older man who I assume is Walter. He's the picture of a rancher, worn blue jeans and a dark green plaid button-up.

Isabella introduces me to Walter and we exchange pleasant-ries. He's just as sweet as she is. They're the kind of people I feel instantly at home with. They remind me a bit of Aunt Mil-lie. Kind and very welcoming.

As we talk, I take in the rest of the room. It's gorgeous here. Just the right amount of homey and lived-in. Framed photos of the ranch and the Grand Tetons scatter the walls, to-do lists cover the front of the refrigerator, and mail piles up on the cor-ner of the counter.

"So," Walter asks, "How are you liking Jackson so far?"

A grin covers my face as images of my drive into town dance around in my head. "I love it. I can't believe how beautiful the mountains are here."

"We're partial to them too," Walter chuckles. "You'll have to ask my son for some pointers, he hasn't been out and about much lately, but I'm sure he'll have some recommendations of things to do while you're up here."

"That'd be wonderful," I say. I wonder how old their son is. They're definitely a bit older than my parents. Maybe they have cute little grandchildren. I bet Walter would be a fun grandpa.

On the opposite side of the kitchen island sits a few pho-to frames. One of Isabella and Walter together, one of Walter in his younger days with a few horses, and one of them with a young man on the porch of the ranch house.

I squint my eyes a bit to make out who they're posing with in the photo. Is that who I think it is? It can't be. Dark hair, tight smile, jean jacket. Just missing a beard–

My thoughts are interrupted by the sound of the front door opening again. Boots clunk against the wood flooring of the hallway, stopping at the entrance to the kitchen.

"Oh that must be Miles," Isabella says, turning around.

Of course. Of course it's Miles. Of course he's here. I think to myself, plastering a smile on my face once again as he rounds the corner into the room. Miles smiles at Isabella, giving her a quick hug as she peppers him with questions about a cattle drive yesterday. He looks happy, relaxed. Until he turns and looks at me. His smile falls and I swear I can see lightning crack in his eyes. Apparently neither of us was told about the extra company at breakfast today.

My breath leaves my lungs when his gaze pins me. His deep brown eyes pulling me closer as my heart whispers, *Miles.*

"Mac," he says in that deep voice, nodding a hello at me. Why does he always look at me like I've stolen the last piece of pie?

"Autry," I reply, matching his greeting. Two can play at this game.

"Howdy, son," Walter says from the stove. *Wait, what? Son?*

The photo I saw before Miles walked in. How Miles acted like he ran the ranch. My heart races as I scan around again for any other clues, and that's when I see it. Over in the corner near a pile of paperwork on a small desk is a framed newspaper article, headline reading *Walter Autry, local rancher, inducted into rodeo hall of fame.*

Autry.

Oh my god. Walter and Miles are related. Miles really is in charge of this ranch. He's not just a ranch hand. I'm totally fucked.

"Sit, sit everyone, let's eat while it's still warm," Isabella says, waving us over to the breakfast nook. We shuffle over to the big U-shaped bench, Walter and Miles scooting into the back section leaving each side for Isabella and I. Isabella sits by her husband, leaving me the seat closest to Miles. Great.

"So, Katie, how are you liking Wyoming so far?" Isabella says as I sit down.

"I love it. It reminds me a lot of where I'm from in Idaho, just with slightly bigger mountains," I smile and reach for the biscuits, bumping into Miles's arm with my hand. Sparks pass between us like a firecracker, shocking my wrist. We mumble half-hearted apologies and he lets me have the first pick of the biscuits, pulling his hand away so fast it's almost like it never happened in the first place. Funny how now that there is company around, he's suddenly a gentleman.

"Walter says you run vacation rentals on Bear Lake, tell us more about that," Isabella says, taking a bite of eggs. Everyone looks at me expectantly. I make brief eye contact with Miles, but he's the first to look away.

I clear my throat. "I do. MacPherson Enterprises has four properties around Bear Lake. I've lived there since I was ten, so I'm really lucky to be able to stick around. It's very much a vacation town so you have to be in the vacation business to live there for the most part. My best friend Hazel actually runs a dude ranch. Not anything like your ranch of course, this is amazing. Her's is amazing too, but you know, just different." I take a breath. I'm used to rambling. I do it all the time, in fact. But for some reason, I'm a little self-conscious rambling in front of these people. I think I might actually care about what they think of me. That's new.

"It's turning into a similar story in these parts, I fear. The tourism industry is definitely taking over," Walter sighs. "Sure doesn't help out us ranchers. Visitors come here and want a high-end experience."

"I can definitely see that from looking around town. Although, MacPherson is kind of counting on that for the new rental property. The goal is to test out the area to see if we can grow here. I'm pretty lucky I get to lead this up, actually. It's a very desired area in the business," I say.

"Yeah, that's what we need. *More* high-end rentals," Miles growls, looking down at his plate.

"Actually, looking at last year's statistics, tourists mentioned not having a wide enough array of accommodations in

Jackson Hole. Hotels are on either end of the pricing spectrum with not a lot of options in the middle, and there really aren't very many vacation rentals in the area. Especially not ones that allow visitors to get out into the mountains outside of the city for a semi-affordable price," I retort.

If this man thinks I didn't expect some pushback from locals, he's dead wrong. My entire job is dealing with pushback. I don't back down once I've decided on a project.

"Well I for one am very excited to see how the Old Cabin comes along," Isabella says cheerily. "Walter and I looked over your previous work and we were very impressed with your designs, and especially, the way you incorporate the local feel into each one. It takes a special eye to be able to do that. And, the Old Cabin is a very special place." Isabella looks over at Walter, a knowing look in her eyes. He winks back at her.

Something warms my chest as I try to find words. I don't think I've ever heard such a sweet, positive critique of my work. "Thank you, Isabella. I really appreciate that," I say sincerely.

Walter hums a sound that might be an approval and exchanges a look with Isabella I can't read. She smiles at me and asks how my first night in Jackson was. During our conversation, Miles is suspiciously quiet. He doesn't so much as look in my direction. But, I know he's listening and considering everything I'm saying.

His face gives away that much.

I pull my attention back to Isabella's story about her first time in Jackson Hole. As much as I'm trying to pay attention, Miles's attention is resting on me as heavy as a hundred pound weight. Everytime he readjusts himself my eyes scream at me to look over and see what he's doing. By the time I'm almost done eating, my head is pounding.

I excuse myself to use the bathroom once we've reached the point in the meal that breakfast has been eaten and we are just chatting. Splashing some cold water onto my face, I sit on top of the closed toilet seat for exactly four and a half minutes before deciding it's time to head back out.

Even the bathroom at the ranch house is comforting. The teal tiles are bathed in soft golden light coming through the small window. I smooth my hair down in the mirror, fixing my makeup a bit. I know I'm letting him get to me, and I know I shouldn't be doing that. It's just so hard to ignore Miles.

I get just about to the end of the hallway when Miles's angry drawl stops me in my tracks, sending my stomach into a tailspin.

"...just don't understand why you're doing this. She's just like the developers. You heard her, they're looking to expand. We can't need the money that badly. I'll get a second job if I have to. I'll find the time. There has to be a way out of this deal," he's practically growling. I don't know what to do. I can't just walk in there right in the middle of this, they'll have to know I heard some part of it. My feet stay cemented in place.

"Miles, it is not for you to decide," Isabella says confidently. "With the cattle losses we've experienced this year and the property taxes the way they are, we had to sell that parcel. It was time. Let someone else enjoy it. Her company paid a pretty penny for it, and I think it'll all turn out fine. Not to mention, you don't have *time* for any other jobs. We need you here. I don't think Katie is the type to pull anything behind our backs. I like her." My heart beats faster, and I shift my feet around nervously in my boots.

"I like her too. I think this will be good for the area, Miles. And, to be frank, I don't care what you think. It's time to let that cabin go. I wouldn't have sold it to her company if I didn't think it was the right thing to do. It's what's best," Walter says, voice stern and unwavering.

Miles sighs. "I don't like this. And I don't like her or her family's company. Don't come to me if this all goes wrong and they're pressuring you to sell the rest of the ranch. I've seen how these things happen around here, Walt. It's not good," Miles argues. I hear some shuffling, then, "I'm heading out. I need some fresh air. Thanks for breakfast, Mom." More shuffling, quiet goodbyes, then silence.

After a few beats to collect myself again, I step out into the room. Walter and Isabella are standing at the kitchen island giving each other a knowing look. Walter's brow furrows as he takes Isabella's hand on the table. Something passes between them.

I shouldn't have come out yet. I'm clearly interrupting something. I turn on my heels to head back in, but before I can make it all the way around, my elbow crashes into a pile of books on an end table.

"Oh, don't worry about that, dear, I can get those," Isabella says as I bend to pick up the books I knocked over. *Very smooth, Katie.*

I set them back on the table with a nervous laugh. "I'm so sorry, I've always been pretty clumsy."

"Miles had to run, he said to tell you goodbye," she says with a sweet smile. *Yeah, right.* "We won't keep you here, I'm sure you've got lots to do with the cabin. Please come and have dinner with us on Sundays. We'd love to have you around. It's not often we have visitors, and we always have way too much food."

"I just might take you up on that," I say. With the exception of Miles, I love being around the Autry's. Plus, it's not like I know anyone else around here. "I better head back to my hotel and work on a few things today. My crew is coming up on Tuesday to start work on the cabin. I'll make sure they don't cause any disturbance to the ranch, but please let me know if they do."

"Where are you staying?" Walter says.

"Over at the Cascade Inn in town."

"Well," Walter starts, pausing to look over at Isabella across the table. She nods. "How would you feel about staying in our smaller guest cabin on the ranch while you're here? It'd have to be just you, it's pretty small, but it's closer to your cabin than the Inn by far. That way you wouldn't have to drive all the way out here from town every day."

These people have no obligation to be this nice to me. I open my mouth to turn them down out of instinct, I wouldn't want to impose on their lives any more than I already have. But, it does sound pretty nice. I'd love to be on-property to watch over the renovation, and it's so beautiful out here. Maybe this is just what I need.

"You know what, that actually sounds pretty perfect. Are you sure I wouldn't be imposing?" I ask.

"Never!" Isabella exclaims, clapping her hands together with a grin. "Oh, I am so excited. You will love it here. And the little cabin is far enough from us you'd never be bugging us. I'll have one of our ranch hands head out there and make sure it's ready for you. Is tomorrow morning okay?"

Plans are made, and I'll be moving into the little cabin in the morning. From what Isabella explains, it sounds like it's a cozy one bedroom with a bathroom and fireplace. Perfect for me, and a lot better than the overpriced hotel I'm in now. Obviously, I plan on paying the Autry's for letting me use their cabin, but I'd much rather that than a hotel in the middle of town that has no problem selling out every night in the summer.

It's not until I'm in my car on my way back to town when I consider what Miles will think of this. A smile forms on my face when I picture his reaction, especially after what I overheard today in the kitchen.

The supposed enemy, on *his* ranch twenty-four seven. The knowledge this will piss him off makes me more glad I agreed to it. I can't wait to see the look on his face.

Chapter 4

Nice Boots

THE SUN SLINKS OVER the horizon between two towering mountain peaks as I unlock my hotel room door for my last night staying in town. After the roller coaster of emotions that was breakfast at Lone Pine Ranch, I spent the day working on my laptop from a cute western-themed coffee shop downtown called Altitude Coffee Co.

Now that I'm absolutely positive all of the other rentals I manage are taken care of, I can finally relax a little bit before the crew arrives for the start of the renovations on the ranch cabin. I'm buzzing with anticipation. This is my favorite part of every project. When there's so much potential I can feel it starting to take shape.

My fingers run over the lasso imprinted on my to-go coffee cup for the hundredth time. I blink a few times, my eyes drying out from looking at the screen.

I haven't managed to set down my leather work bag yet when my phone starts buzzing again. I pull it out of my pocket and breathe a sigh of relief when Hazel's name flashes across the screen, instead of anyone from MacPherson.

"Hey, babe," I answer, walking out to the balcony. Might as well spend as much time out here as I can.

"Hi!" Hazel answers way too loudly and out of breath. "I haven't heard from you in days, just wanted to make sure you're still alive."

"Sorry, it's been a little crazy since I got here. But yes, I made it okay, Mom," I tease. I run a hand through my hair absentmindedly. "Did you just finish a ride or something? You sound like you just ran a mile."

"Yes, very busy around here and all that. Start of the busy season. You know the drill," she says.

"I sure do," I laugh. "It's a bit like that around here too. It actually reminds me a lot of Juniper Ridge. Very touristy, very beautiful. The mountains are unreal. You have to come up and visit while I'm here. Bring Wadey while you're at it."

"I'll run it by him tonight, I'm sure he'll want to," she says. Wade is our shared friend, although he's much more Hazel's than mine. They've been best friends since before I moved to Juniper Ridge, although I've always thought there was something more between them they haven't admitted to themselves yet. They're my favorite people in the world, next to my aunt. "So, how is it? I need a recap of your arrival. Is the cabin amazing?"

"The cabin is gorgeous. The ranch surrounding it is a dream. The view is just unmatched, I don't know who wouldn't want to stay there. I can't wait to jump into renovations," I smile.

"I'm sure you'll rock it, as usual," she says. I hear a horse whiney in the background, letting me know she's in the barn.

"If angry cowboy will let me, that is," I say with a sigh, twirling my hair around my finger.

Hazel is quiet for a moment, and I can practically hear her confusion. "Yeah, you're going to have to elaborate. I have no idea what you're talking about."

I let out a dry laugh. I didn't think about it until now, but she has actually met Miles before, and will definitely have an opinion on this. "Well, it turns out Walter has a son who isn't super thrilled MacPherson Enterprises bought some of their land. He let that be known to me very loudly the moment I arrived."

"You're kidding," she exclaims. "Nice old Walter has a son? Does he know the deal is already done? He doesn't have much of a say now."

I rub my face in my hands. "That's the problem, I don't think he knew about it at all." Honestly, I get where Miles is coming from. I'd hate finding out about it the way he did. But he had a chance to redeem his bad behavior today, and he didn't. He doubled down.

"Well, that's kind of shitty. What did he say to you?"

"Just the usual, that I'm not supposed to be there, as if I was trespassing on his land vandalizing it. He was so mad I thought he was going to blow a fuse. But that's not even the best part," I say.

"What do you mean? Something else happened?" she asks. There's a loud crash behind her and she mumbles a few swear words under her breath. I'm used to this kind of thing with Hazel, she cannot stop working for five minutes. Not even for a phone call.

"Well, as I was talking to him I was thinking, 'Man, this guy looks so familiar. But there's absolutely no way I'd know him,' right? Until he recognized me. He wasn't super happy about seeing me again, by the way. But it took me a minute to figure it out, until he introduced himself. As Miles Autry," I say, waiting for her to freak out like I did.

"Am I supposed to know that name? Help me out here," she says, confused.

"Miles. Salt Lake City on my twenty-first birthday." I wave my hands around listing descriptive details as if she can see me through the phone. With how close Hazel and I are, she probably can. "Dark haired cowboy, worked on a ranch in Wyoming—"

"Oh my god! No way! Sexy Cowboy!" she yells. My mind flashes back to four years ago when she first whispered that nickname, pointing him out to me in the bar. He looked so sad, sitting by himself lost in thought at the bar. I wonder what he was thinking about then. "Well, that's a good thing, right? You two know each other, a little bit at least. And he was so sweet. You got along so well."

"Yeah, not the case anymore," I let out a dry laugh. "Sometime in the past four years he's acquired a huge stick up his ass. He hates me, Hazel. For real. He was so angry, even after he recognized me. Honestly, it took me off guard."

"What a jerk," she says.

"If you can believe it, that's not all. His parents invited me over to their house for breakfast this morning. Beautiful ranch house by the way, it's right out of a movie. Anyway, while I was there I accidentally overheard him talking about me when I left the room and he literally said 'I don't like her.' Straight up. I don't even have to assume. He's scared MacPherson is going to come in and take over their whole ranch," I explain.

"Wow. He is an asshole. Has he not met you? You're a delight. How can anyone dislike you?"

"I know, I'm a ray of sunshine every waking minute," I joke with a smile. Hazel and I both know she is the ray of sunshine. I'm more of an extremely loud tornado.

"I'm so sorry, Kate. That's crazy. What are you going to do?" she asks.

"Honestly, nothing. It's not my problem. I bought the land, there's nothing he can do about it. I'll be cordial to him, and nothing more. Hopefully I won't have to see him much anyway," I say.

"Well, that sounds fine to me. His loss, you're an awesome person to be around," she says.

I laugh and take another sip of the coffee I brought home with me. It's starting to get cold, but I'm desperate for the caffeine. "Thanks. The Autry's invited me to stay at their small guest cabin on the ranch since it's close to my cabin during renovations, so I have tonight in the hotel then I'm packing up and heading out there. It'll be convenient to be so close."

"Oh that's nice of them," she says, "You know, you should go out since it's your last night in town. Take advantage of the bars in walking distance. It'd probably do wonders for your stress levels."

"That's not a bad idea," I say. I have no problem going out by myself, I do it all the time back home when Hazel and Wade are busy. "I'll see where I get on the renovation prep."

"Stop it," she reprimands suddenly.

"Stop what?"

"Stop working. You've worked enough I'm sure. I don't have to be there to know that. Get out of your hotel room and have some fun."

I sigh and look out towards the street. It's twilight now, the glow of lights illuminating the row of buildings. I can hear voices and laughter below, visitors stepping out for the night. Jackson Hole does have some famous western bars. Hazel is right, if I'm going to check them out, tonight is the night.

"Okay fine, I'm going," I say, standing from my chair.

"I'll leave you with some advice you've always given me in situations like this: wear something slutty!" She yells.

"Yeah, yeah. Talk to you later," I hang up the phone and head inside. Might as well have some fun here while I can.

I can't help but smile as I step past the wooden saloon swinging doors and walk into Alpine Rose, the bar right across the street from my hotel. The big neon rose glowing in the dark starry sky pulled me in, and now that I'm here, I never want to leave. It's a pretty big bar with rows of pool tables, bar stools made of real saddles, every type of alcohol known to man in elegant wooden shelving behind the bar, and it's already hopping in here.

All kinds of people, at all levels of tipsy, and almost everyone is wearing cowboy boots and hats. This is my new favorite place.

My boots click against the hardwood floors as I walk over to the bar, find an open stool, and order a whiskey sour. They've been my favorite since I first had one with Miles all those years ago, and I'm not about to give them up now just because he's a jerk. He can't take whiskey from me.

"What can I get you?" A polite voice says from behind the bar. I glance over to a woman about my age shaking a cocktail. The name tag on her black shirt says "Codie" in big, swoopy letters. Raven hair falls out of her braid, framing her face.

I smile back, leaning in a bit so she can hear me over the loud music playing. "Whiskey sour, please."

"A woman after my own heart," she laughs. "Coming right up."

She pours the drink from her mixer into a glass, sliding it over to a guy at the end of the bar. When she comes back over to where I'm sitting, she has a bottle of Jack Daniels in her hand.

"So, are you new here or just passing through?" She asks, measuring her whiskey pour.

"I'm here for the summer. For work. I live in Idaho."

"Welcome to Jackson then," she smiles. "I'm Codie."

"Katie," I reply. "Is that the new Willa Gray book?" I nod towards her apron, where the corner of a book is popping out just slightly.

"It sure is. You read romance?"

"Who doesn't?" I joke.

"No one sane, that's for sure," she laughs.

"I love her books," I gush. "I read them all in, like, a week last year. I've been waiting for that one to come out, but I totally forgot it's already May."

Codie grabs the book from her apron pocket, handing it to me. I turn it over and read the back, even though I've already read the teaser a few times online.

"No one can write a perfect book boyfriend as well as Willa," I shake my head.

"Ain't that the truth. If you haven't found it by the time I'm done, you can totally borrow my copy. I'm a third of the way through, and I'm addicted to it." Codie finishes mixing my whiskey sour, pouring it into a glass and placing it on the wood bar top in front of me. I hand her back her book, which she tucks back into her apron.

"Thanks, that'd be great," I smile.

"Of course. I'm here on weeknights if you ever want to talk books."

"I might take you up on that," I say. Codie smiles, turning to the other side of the bar which has filled up pretty quickly.

With a sip of my drink (very strong, I might add), I survey the room. The live band is setting up in the corner, and some folks are already dancing to the music coming from the speakers. A bachelorette party plays darts on the opposite wall, and a group of actual cowboys I can only assume are locals stands at a tall table in between. There are a few couples scattered throughout, and plenty of excited tourists taking photos.

Next to me sits a couple of guys who I assume are from out of town, but aren't dressed up like they're an extra in a wild west drama like some of the other tourists. One of them glances my way and smiles. His dark, curly hair peeks out from underneath a worn ball cap. He's dressed pretty casually, wearing a plain black t-shirt and jeans with boots. He's cute enough to know it, and he gives off a sort of country frat boy, non-commitment kind of vibe.

Just my type.

How do I know all of this so quickly after seeing him? Well, I'm kind of an expert on fuckboys. I am one with fuckboys.

A fuckgirl, if you will.

I'm not exactly looking to get into a long term relationship either, so it works out for both parties. Like my Aunt Millie always says, men are like expensive wine. Best enjoyed in moderation, on special occasions.

I turn towards mystery guy and smile back, tossing my wide curls over my shoulder. This gets his attention. It's way too easy, like clockwork.

"Hey," is his great, captivating pick up line. *Come on, dude, you can do better than that,* I resist from rolling my eyes.

"Hi back," I say. "Nice boots."

"Thanks. Right back at ya," he says, nodding towards my boots. I went with the heeled, bright pink suede boots tonight, visible under my short, black ruffled dress.

"Oh these old things?" I tease, kicking my leg up. That earns a laugh. "I'm Katie."

"Dean," he says, shaking my hand. "Are you from around here?"

"I'm from a little town in Idaho, but I'm here for the summer. You?"

"I'm from Star Valley, about forty-five minutes south of here," he says. "My buddies and I come up here every once in a while for the live music." Perfect. Not a tourist but also not a local I'll have to see all summer.

We flirt a while longer and I learn Dean is twenty-seven years old and works at a lumber yard. I tell him about why I'm in town, and he seems at least a little interested in my managing vacation rentals. It's more than I can say for most guys I talk to.

His friend eventually joins a few other guys at one of the pool tables, but Dean stays back at the bar and orders us another round. I'm having a good time for the first time in a couple of months, and it feels great. I'm laughing at his jokes, he's smiling at me. The start of a magical night out. Hazel was right.

It almost stays that way, but out of the corner of my eye movement catches my attention as two more cowboys enter the bar. One with a megawatt smile, curly chestnut hair, and eyes so blue I can see them from across the room. But it's the one in the black cowboy hat next to him with the perma-frown on his face that makes my stomach drop.

And after it drops, it flips a couple of times at the Wranglers hugging Miles's backside. Of course he's here.

I don't understand my luck. Out of all the bars in this town, on all of the nights, Miles Autry just walked into this one that I happen to be enjoying myself at. I should have known. I swear, sometimes my life is one big cosmic joke.

"Katie? You good? You look kinda pale," Dean's hand lands on my thigh, sending goosebumps up my arms. I pull my gaze back to his.

"Yep, sorry, I'm great. What were you saying?" I try to appear interested as he continues his story about kayaking drunk down the Snake River last summer, but I can feel Miles across the bar. I watch him out of the corner of my eye as he and his friend walk over to a table near the band.

I hate that his presence has already ruined what was going to be a great night in Jackson Hole. But does it have to? There's no reason I need to pay any attention to him at all. I'm done with Miles sucking the life out of every interaction I have. Just because he hates me, doesn't mean I need to put any more energy or brain cells into figuring out why. There is absolutely no good reason anyway.

I'm going to have fun tonight despite him almost ruining my day. I won't let him have that power over me. A cute boy is touching my leg and telling me about falling into a river. Dean *wants* to talk to me. He thinks I'm funny. I don't need Miles Grumpypants Autry's approval. In fact, I'm going to delight in his disapproval.

"Do you want to dance?" I interrupt Dean.

"Sure," He agrees and walks me over to the dance floor. The band is playing Patsy Cline and quite a few people are dancing now. I resist the urge to look over at Miles, who I'm sure has seen me by now and has probably left so he doesn't have to be in the same room as me. Dean is so fun. We dance for a while, eventually giggling through a line dance neither of us knows, but we are determined to at least try.

I finally catch my breath when the music turns slow. Dean's hands are around my waist, mine are in his hair. We sway to the song, a little tipsy, all smiles. Movement catches my eye behind his head, and I look past only to lock eyes with Miles.

Shocker, he doesn't look happy.

His jaw clenches but he holds my gaze, fire behind his eyes again. I wonder if he realizes how mad he always looks. Is it just around me? Does he hate me so much that he can't even bear to smile?

Not one to back down, I don't look away. We are trapped in an awkward staring contest neither of us can break away from. I can't imagine what it looks like to an outside observer. His stare passes over me like licks of a flame. I can already feel my body temperature rising.

Annoyance and something else angrier flashes in his eyes, watching as I dance with Dean. I look away, reaching up to play with Dean's hair and whisper in his ear about how much fun

I'm having. Taking my hints, he pulls me in, our bodies clamped together as close as we can get.

I push away another flashback to Salt Lake City, when Miles and I were this close. I still remember the heat radiating off of Miles, almost burning me on contact. He's like a magnet, when we were together I never noticed how drawn I was to him until I pulled away. Unfortunately, that feeling is hard to shake.

I feel a prickling on my shoulder. Looking up towards Miles again, I find him still staring a hole right through me. If looks could kill, I'm sure I'd be long gone by now. His jaw ticks in frustration. So dramatic.

I throw him a saccharine smile I know he'll hate. The bigger I grin, the more his scowl grows. If he's going to glare at me all night, I might as well have some fun with it.

The stare-off finally ends when his friend claps him on the shoulder, leaning in to tell him something. Miles breaks eye contact with me to nod and reply to his friend. They both get up and head over to a pool table with a few other guys.

"I'm a little thirsty, do you mind if we grab a drink?" I say to Dean. Now that Miles is here, I'm going to need one. We head over to a table near the bar and I start to fall into a stool. I'm a bit dizzy from drinking without food on my stomach. Rookie mistake. Before I can sit, Dean whisks me over to his lap, nuzzling into my neck. Giggling, I lean into it. He's a nice enough guy and I need some fun.

"Can't have you falling out of your chair, can we? I think you're much safer over here," Dean laughs, "Do you need some water? Food?"

"Water would be great," I tell him. I gulp it down as soon as the waitress brings me a glass. I'm already feeling much better now that I'm out of Miles's immediate orbit. *Don't think his name,* I tell myself. *Focus on Dean.*

Dean's friend, who's name I cannot seem to remember for the life of me, comes back after his game of pool is over. Dean's hands travel up and down my back as they talk, giving me goosebumps again. We are alone again when his friend heads up to the bar to order another drink, Dean catches my eye and smiles.

"Can I kiss you?" he asks. I smile and nod, excited by this fun little turn of events. Kissing a stranger in a country bar on my first night in town. Hazel will love hearing about this.

His lips gently brush against mine, testing the waters. I kiss him back, inviting him to go further. It's a bit awkward, and he pulls away way too soon. There's just not a spark.

The second I lift my head, I feel Miles's gaze on me again. Sure enough, I look up in time to see him white-knuckling a glass of beer. As soon as I catch his eyes, he looks away quickly. Nice try, bud. I can practically see the steam rolling off his shoulders.

For someone who pretends not to care, it sure seems like he cares a lot about what I'm doing. I don't know what I did to make him hate me so much, but I could really do without his judgment of my every move.

"You know what," I start to say to Dean. "I'm gonna grab us another round. Be right back." I hop up out of his lap before he can protest and walk over to the bar, Miles trailing me as soon as I stand.

Playing right into my hand, Miles shows up next to me at the bar just as I've thanked the bartender, drinks in hand.

"Double fisting drinks tonight, Mac? Why am I not surprised?" He grumbles, brushing my shoulder slightly with his arm. I ignore the goosebumps, lifting my chin up in the air. This asshole is not getting to me.

Then, he does something I'm not expecting. He surveys me from head to toe, his eyes lingering a beat too long on my lips.

It's not anger in his eyes this time, it's just heat. The weight of his gaze leaves a trail of sparks on my skin. I'm not sure if he even knows how obviously he's checking me out. I smirk at him and he immediately looks away.

"Just trying to have a good time while I'm in town," I say, hoping I don't sound too breathless.

"You know, there is such a thing as having too good of a time."

"Is there some problem you have with me, Autry? Got your panties in a twist?" I ask with another smile, turning towards him. It's answered with another frown. He turns to face me as well, but it seems absentminded. Magnets, and all that.

"No, do you?" Miles shoots back, taking a sip of the new beer that showed up in front of him. My gaze lands on his throat, just below his beard, as he takes a drink.

"Not wearing any," I quip. Miles chokes on his beer, eyes wide. "See you around," I wink, walking back over to Dean.

Knowing he's still watching me from the prickling on the back of my neck, I set the drinks down on the high top table next to Dean and plant an exaggerated kiss on his cheek.

"Come here, girl," Dean laughs, grabbing my hand and pulling me around to the front of his stool. "Next time, I'll buy. My momma wouldn't let me live down the day I let a lady pay for my drinks."

"You bought the first round, it's only fair," I say. *How very 1950's of him.* I think as I lift the glass to my lips. I'm standing between his knees now, a fairly comfortable position.

Two drinks and one country swing dance that I don't know any of the moves of later, I feel myself hitting a wall. I've had fun tonight, but right now, all I want is to curl up in bed and read until I fall asleep.

Dean pulls me into his lap at our table, and I can't quite get comfortable. I glance up, wondering where Miles went off to.

He's got a comfortable shoulder. If he wasn't such an ass to me earlier, I'd love to curl up and fall asleep on him.

Woah, Katie. Do not go there, I scold myself. I've only had a few drinks, but they're going to my head already.

"Listen, I think I'm going to get going. I've got an early day tomorrow, I should get back to my hotel," I say to Dean as politely as I can after a few more minutes of listening to the band.

"Right on," Dean says with a genuine smile. I breathe a sigh of relief. Apparently the spark wasn't there for him either. "Can I walk you outside?"

"Sure," I say thankfully. I'll miss Dean, what a nice guy. He reaches for my hand to walk me out, and I take it, threading my fingers through his. We are almost to the door when I bump into a rock hard shoulder.

"Oh excuse me–" I start, looking up only to bump right into none other than Miles Autry. His neutral expression melts right back into anger as he looks down at me and nods politely.

"Sorry man," Dean says from ahead of me. Miles doesn't say a word to either of us, but his gaze slides over to Dean. If possible, he looks even angrier than usual, towering over Dean. Dean doesn't seem to notice, he is already walking ahead pulling on my hand.

"Kay bye," I mumble to Miles sarcastically as I turn away.

We stumble out of the bar and onto the sidewalk, noticing the long line that has formed outside of the entrance. I guess it's lucky I got here when I did.

"It was nice dancing with you tonight, Katie. Thanks for making me laugh," Dean says, pulling me into a side hug as we walk down towards the Cascade Inn.

"It was a good time for sure. I needed it, I think," I nod.

We say our goodbyes outside of my hotel and I head back up to my room. As I close the door, I lean back against it and fall to the floor. Just like breakfast this morning, if I just remove Miles from the equation, I had a great time. But, I can't. He was there, glaring at me. Judging me, I'm sure.

I send Hazel a quick text letting her know I got back okay and crawl into bed. Tomorrow is a new day. Hopefully a Miles-less day. And yet, despite all that he's done today, Miles's smiling face four years ago is the last thing I see in my mind before I drift off to sleep.

Chapter 5

I Don't Care

SUN HAS JUST STARTED to peek through the curtains of my window when the worst sound in the world wakes me up. Groaning, I reach over to stop my alarm.

It's Monday. My first day of work at the Old Cabin. And I need to get an early start to stay motivated. I pull on my leggings and sports bra, throw my hair up into a ponytail and head out the door for a quick run, Shania Twain blaring through my headphones.

The quiet, empty streets swallow me up as I jog through town. A few coffee shops and cafes are awake, with the smell of coffee beans wafting out of windows cracked open to let in the morning mountain breeze. On the other hand, bars and night-time restaurants are eerily still, chairs stacked on tables, neon lights switched off.

Aunt Millie and I used to go for runs most weekday mornings when I was a teenager. We'd run around her small neighborhood, on the shore of Bear Lake, on trails through the mountains. I remember thinking that's what I wanted to be when I grew up. Running care-free through the mountains every morning, and coming home to a fresh pot of coffee. It sounded like a dream.

Now, I do that almost every day.

My aunt passed a lot of things down to me in the years I grew up in Juniper Ridge. Her love of chips and salsa, all of her many hobbies like crocheting and yoga, and her infinite wisdom on relationships. I've cried and sniffled through many a heartbreak on her couch with a bowl of ice cream, listening to her recount stories from her younger days.

Once, when I was seventeen and had just lost my first love, Aunt Millie picked me up from my bed, pushed me into her car, and drove me out to the far end of the lake. She marched me down the beach until we were a ways out from anything or anyone else and picked up a rock.

"Here," she said, "Write his name on this." I took the sharpie from her hand and did what she told me without a protest, wiping the tears off of my face.

"Okay. Now on the count of three, I want you to throw that rock out as far as you can. Take all those sad, angry feelings and throw them out with the rock too. Once it sinks to the bottom of the lake, it's over. No more crying over a boy who isn't giving you two thoughts."

I threw the rock, and surprisingly, it really did make me feel better. Whenever I thought about him afterwards, I remembered standing on that beach throwing all thoughts of him into the water to sink forever. We made it into a tradition, heading out to the lake everytime I had a bad breakup, a crush that didn't reciprocate my feelings, or even a really tough test in school I got a bad grade on.

Now, I look back on all of the little ways Aunt Millie tried to make my life a little bit easier and see someone who was thrust into parenthood for a kid that wasn't hers, making the best of the situation. But back then, she was a goddess. There's no one I love and respect more than my Aunt Millie.

She shaped me.

After my morning run (and a stop into a coffee house, naturally), I head up the road to the ranch cabin with all of my bags packed in the back seat and get a sense of deja vu. Hopefully this time, no angry cowboys come and yell at me when I get out of the car. The mountains are glowing with morning light, dew on every blade of grass.

I turn down the short dirt road from the main ranch road to the cabin, and immediately slam on the brakes. Black, mooing blobs speckle the land all around the cabin, including on the road directly in front of me.

Cows.

Everywhere.

There has to be an easy way out of this. If I honk my car horn will they move? Or will they trample me? I look ahead, assessing the situation. They are everywhere I look. Dozens and dozens of cows, trampling the empty flower beds, eating the grass around the cabin, pooping in the road.

My gaze slides to the left, where a few more are gathered by the back wood fence that goes around the cabin, separating the small yard area from the rest of the property. Well, what used to be the fence. Now, it's gathered on the ground in a pile of logs. Perfect.

I pull out my phone and dial Walter. Surely, he'll have some cowboys come and take care of this, right? These have to be his cattle. He answers on the first ring.

"Well hello there, young lady. How is everything coming along so far? Did those boys get the guest cabin ready for you? They better have." I can hear his warm smile through the phone.

"Actually, Walter, I haven't made it quite that far yet. I was heading up to the Old Cabin to take some photos for my interior designer, and when I got here... well..." I search for a polite way to describe my current predicament. "There are sort of a few... cows. Dozens of them. Blocking the road, standing all around the cabin. I think some might have trampled the fence too. They wouldn't happen to be your cattle, would they?"

"Ah shoot. They're mine, alright. So sorry about that, I'll get someone out there real soon to take care of it. There's not too much damage is there? Damn cows, they kinda go wherever they please I'm afraid," he says.

"No, nothing too bad, just the fence. Thanks for the help," I assure him. If it was anyone else I might be a little mad, but I just can't be mad at Walter.

"Don't you worry about that, we'll get it fixed too. Sorry again," he says.

I pull out my laptop after saying goodbye to Walter, hoping to get a little bit of work done while I wait for someone to come and get the cows. It's not like I can go anywhere anyway, I'm blocked in by cows on all sides now.

The familiar sound of a horse galloping towards me pricks my ears. It's only been around fifteen minutes. My laptop shuts with a snap as my attention is dragged away. Two cowboys on horseback ride towards me with a cattle herding dog following closely to the side of the first horse.

They surround the cows on one side, pushing them back towards the back right of the cabin yard. The cows in front of my car run off to the side, clearing my path, but I'm too wary to move quite yet. The horses move so quickly, cutting sharp corners, working with the cattle dog to move the cows into a pile in the back corner of the yard.

It's a flurry of hooves, dust, cowboy hats and whistles.

One of the cowboys hops down and unlatches the small gate in the fence. Cows pour through it like water through a funnel. I'm so in awe of it all I can't look away. They were so quick, the cows just listened to their movements and gathered like they were just waiting here for instruction.

After the last of the cows is through the fence and they're running off towards the ranch again, the cowboy that hopped down to open the fence closes it again and claps his hands, dust coming off of his gloves like a cloud. The second cowboy hops down from his horse and I can hear a murmured conversation. Feeling a little safer to move, I start my car and pull forward into the drive of the cabin.

I move to gather my things, ready to hop out and thank the two cowboys that saved my morning, when there's a quiet tap on my window. I look up, right into bright brown eyes and a bearded frown. Miles.

Of course it's Miles.

He steps back as I open my door, climbing out of my car with my laptop under my arm.

My eyes slide from his face down to his arms, on his hips. I don't think he even realizes how powerful his stance is. If I was anyone else, I'd be scared to mess with him. His biceps bulge in his sleeves, his tan forearms peeking out from beneath his rolled up, black long-sleeve shirt.

"Sorry about the cattle. Won't happen again," he says with a nod.

"No problem. Thanks for coming so quickly to take care of it." Good. This is exactly how things should go from now on, cordial, short and sweet.

"Walt insisted that I was the one to come out here, so you weren't dealing with a stranger," Miles explains, as if he can't stand I'd think he'd *want* to see me. Point taken.

"Okay," I say.

"Hi," a much happier voice says from behind me, "I'm Parker."

I turn around to the smiling face of Miles's friend from the bar last night, his curly hair hidden under a straw cowboy hat. He still feels familiar to me, but I can't quite place it.

"Hi Parker, I'm Katie." I shake his outstretched hand. At least someone that works here knows how to greet a stranger.

"Your name's Katie? That's so funny, one time Miles– ow!" Parker is cut off by Miles punching him in the arm.

"She doesn't want to hear your rambling, Park. She's got a job to do," he says.

"That actually hurt, man," Parker mumbles at Miles, still holding his arm where Miles punched him.

Turning back to me, Miles's face goes stone cold again, "We'll get out of your way."

"Actually I was just thinking about how nice it is to have someone around that wants to have a conversation with me in full sentences," I say with a sarcastic smile. I just can't help it, jabbing at him is so fun. His ears turn red within seconds.

"Don't mind him," Parker smiles. "He's just gotten senile in his old age. He used to be a lot more fun, trust me. Now, I'm the only fun one around here." Miles mumbles something under his breath as he rolls his eyes.

"Good to know," I say.

"What exactly are you up to out here?" Parker asks. Miles adjusts the cowboy hat on his head, turning to look somewhere off in the distance.

"Well, my company bought this cabin so I'm renovating it to turn it into a vacation rental," I explain, unsure how much Parker has heard about the sale. Miles hadn't heard anything apparently. "Today is actually my first official day of work on the cabin. Tomorrow my crew will arrive and we'll start on some of the major projects."

"Oh right on," Parker says, "Miles told me about that. Sounds like it's gonna be quite the project."

"The hope is we'll get it done by the end of the summer, ready for guests in the fall and early ski season," I say. "Although it might be a few days longer now that half of the fence is down."

I tilt my head towards the destroyed fence in the back. Both men turn to get a look at the fence, then share a look for a few seconds before meeting my gaze again.

"Yeah, Walter mentioned that. He said to let you know Miles is going to fix the fence for you while the rest of us are branding cows this month," Parker says, looking amused.

"Did he now?" I try to keep my polite smile on, but I can feel it slip just a bit. Now he's going to fix the fence? Hopefully it's an easy repair.

"Speaking of branding, I better get back. We've got the first group all ready to go. The guys will kill me if I flake," Parker says, tipping his hat down at me. What is it with all of these cowboys being so tall? "It was a pleasure to meet you, miss. Hope I see you around."

I find myself alone with Miles again once Parker rides off with the cattle dog, back towards the ranch. He's looking at the ground like he's trying to figure out what to say, shifting his boots in the gravel.

"So," I make an attempt at a conversation, "Did you have fun in town last night?"

"No," he says, meeting my gaze. I expect him to continue, but he doesn't. His stare hardens as we stand in a faceoff.

"Oh I'm sorry to hear that. I thought Alpine Rose was pretty cool. I've never been to a bar so big before. And everyone is so nice up here," I say with a smile.

"I don't know if I'd call the guys you were with nice," he grumbles. "Those guys come up here every couple of months to hit on stupid tourists and leave."

"Are you insinuating I'm a stupid tourist?" I tease, trying desperately to lighten the mood. His frown remains strictly in place.

"No," he starts, looking down again. "Just saying is all. If you're looking for a hookup, I'd avoid those assholes."

I can't believe what I'm hearing. Mood officially killed. "What makes you think I'm looking for a hookup?"

"You left with one of them," he says, arms crossed so tightly his veins start to pop out a bit. His jaw ticks.

"So, what? How is it any of your concern? Why do you care what I do anyway?" I say, voice raising.

"I don't care!" Miles exclaims. His whole face is turning red now. My body is confused, torn between anger and attraction. That frustrates me even more.

"Seems like you did last night. And now too, apparently." I stand my ground, arms crossed, mirroring Miles.

"Well, I didn't. I mean don't. I still don't. You can do whatever you want. I'm going to get started on the fence," Miles declares, walking away. "I'll have to leave Claro tied up out front."

As if she understands, Miles's chestnut horse blinks once, turning her head towards me.

I'm frozen where I'm standing, once again working on catching my breath as he trails off to the back of the house to look at the fence. Air rushes out of my lungs, cold like the morning mountain air.

I don't know what's going on with Miles, but it sure seems like he's mad about something and taking it out on me. There's no reason for him to be upset with me over something so inconsequential. He was way out of line. Unless he really is just an asshole. He'd better be ready to apologize next time he wants to talk to me.

I'm no stranger to random outbursts of anger. It happens a lot when you have a family like mine. But I'm determined not to let Miles get under my skin. If he wants to insult me and try to get my goat, so be it. I won't participate.

I don't have the extra brainpower to fight with my neighbor right now, even if we kind of know each other. Okay fine, we know each other enough. But it's not like we were in a relationship or anything. It was one night.

A really amazing night, but still just a night.

Not wanting to waste any more precious time before my crew arrives, I fish my laptop out of my bag and get right to work. I don't have time to think about Miles right now, that will have to wait until later when I'm relaxing with a glass of wine reading a book. The corner of my mouth twitches up at the thought of having a tiny cabin all to myself at last.

Chapter 6

Mi Cielo

"THIS WALL WILL NEED to go to make room for the new walkway, and I want the door taken out of this doorway. It needs to be open. Maybe an arch. Can we do an archway?" I ask Ralph, the foreman of my tiny crew for the renovations.

"We can," he nods, making a note on his clipboard. "That should go well with the rounded upper windows in the entryway."

"Great. Everything else stays according to the blueprints I sent over a few weeks ago. We can get started right away, as long as the supply shipments were on time," I say.

"Got it all out in the trailer," he replies, nodding towards the front door.

"Great, let's get to it then."

The crew of three arrived this morning, and I've been buzzing with excitement ever since. This is my favorite part of every project. The beginning. When everything is all mapped out and ready, and we finally get to start to dig into the work.

There's so much potential.

Ralph and his two crew men are freelancers out of Idaho we hire for a lot of my projects. Since I focus on small vacation rentals like the cabin, not big apartment buildings, it only takes a few crew members to make it happen.

After they do all of the big jobs like knocking down walls, installing flooring, painting, and major repairs, I take over from there. I design each rental to fit in with the local feel of the area along with my signature style, and add all of the finishing touches. It's a great system.

For the next few weeks, I'll oversee Ralph and the guys, while working on smaller tasks that don't require their expertise. Today, I'm digging up some flower beds along the edges of the cabin. My vision for the yard is outdoorsy and natural to Wyoming. I'll be planting local wildflower seeds in the flower beds, along with a few perennial bushes that will pop up each summer.

Once the crew gets started inside, I grab my shovel and head out back. Thorn covered weeds are sprinkled throughout the backyard, the former flower beds overgrown with morning glory vines. Long cheatgrass has already started to sprout along the fence. There may have been a lawn at one point but it has blended with the rolling fields surrounding the property, wild and untamed.

With my gloved hands on my hips, I take in the view. *It's a lot of work now, but in a few months, you won't be able to tell it ever looked like this,* I think to myself. Letting out a hopeful sigh, my shovel sinks through the top layer of the flowerbeds.

When I was a teenager, Aunt Millie and I spent a lot of time out in her garden. It's probably why I still do the landscaping for my vacation rentals. It relaxes me. She used to buy me a new pair of patterned garden gloves every year.

Sometimes they were flamingo print, other times they were bright yellow. I'd go outside and plant flowers, harvest peppers from the garden, replant tomatoes every spring, pull weeds, or sometimes just sit and listen to the birds. Then, by the end of the summer, my gloves were caked in dirt and covered in holes.

As I got older, I planted more fruit and vegetables in the garden and used them to cook with Aunt Millie. I still remember the year we had an abundance of strawberries, and had to use them in pretty much everything so they didn't all go bad. We had strawberry smoothies, strawberry pie, strawberry jam, strawberry cake. I didn't eat strawberries for a year after.

It felt nice to have something I could take care of. Something I could focus on when I was down. My parents might have sent me to a brand new place in the middle of nowhere, they might forget to check-in weekly, Aunt Millie might have a busy week and be gone a lot.

But, I always had the garden to escape to. No matter what.

I'm so lost in my thoughts I don't notice I'm no longer alone outside until I hear a thud from behind me. A figure looms over by the back fence, collecting the wooden logs that have fallen onto the ground into a pile. *Miles.*

My heart skips a beat as he lifts a fence post that was lying on its side. He's wearing a long sleeved button-up shirt today, but he may as well be wearing no shirt at all with how tight it's hugging his muscles.

A backwards baseball cap covers his inky hair as if he has psychic powers and knows that's my weakness. Damn backwards baseball caps.

He must sense me staring, too, because as soon my eyes slide back to his arms, he looks right at me. My cheeks betray me, immediately heating up. Maybe he'll think I'm flushed from shoveling out the flowerbeds.

I smile and wave, and to my surprise, he nods politely back at me before continuing to move the fence posts. He actually acknowledged me. He didn't just ignore me, or worse, scowl in my general direction.

We are making progress, people.

By the time Miles leaves in the afternoon, I've just gotten all of the flowerbeds dug out and he has finished removing the knocked down fence posts. Now the fence looks like it has an intentional break in the back corner instead of cattle damage. Who knew fences could be trampled by cows so easily?

The crew has just finished packing up their tools to call it a day when I feel another warm breeze inside the house. This time, I don't have any weird imaginings. All I feel is a strong pull towards the fireplace again. Maybe that's where a draft is coming in.

Nothing seems out of place on the fireplace. The smooth, gray oval stones that make the fireplace are the only thing in the entire cabin that seem brand new. I don't know how I didn't notice before, but it seems like this fireplace hasn't been used at all.

There's no soot anywhere, no dirt or dust on any of it. It's pristine. Whoever was taking care of this place for the ranch must have really loved this fireplace.

I reach out and touch one of the stones above the opening, and immediately recoil. It's hot. As hot as an oven door when it's on.

The warm breeze is long gone now, it's actually starting to feel a little cold with the sun going down. But somehow, the fireplace is warm enough I'd expect it to have had a fire roaring in it all day long. Maybe I missed something. Maybe the crew had some sort of machine close to the stones and they absorbed the heat.

Suddenly, a tiny bright light twinkles from inside. It's gone just as quickly as it came. *Am I going crazy? I have* been working myself into the ground lately. It's possible my brain is playing tricks on me. I just can't shake that feeling that I've had both times unexplainable things have happened here. The feeling of belonging, of love. Warm and tingly. Like a hug.

Another twinkle snags my gaze. This time, I can see where it came from.

Reaching down towards the back corner of the fireplace, some sort of paper sticks out from between a couple of rocks. How is there paper in here? It must have been left there after the last time a fire was lit.

My fingers snag on the corner of the thick paper. I work the paper out from between the stones carefully, making sure not to rip it.

I turn the paper over in my hands, reading the words written on it. It's a postcard. A really old postcard. The front is a yellowing, faded photo of red rock cliffs that remind me of southern Utah. But in big, bold letters, the name Villavieja, Colombia paints the top of the card.

Written on the flip side of the postcard is a letter addressed to, "Mi Cielo" written in Spanish. Signed, "Abuela."

On the wall of the fireplace, right where the postcard was, there's some sort of symbol. I kneel down further to get a better look. It's almost like a brand, burned into the stone. The shape of a longhorn skull is carefully drawn in black soot. The curvy "L" brand of Lone Pine Ranch etched onto its forehead.

This had to have been placed here on purpose. It's so delicately drawn.

Chimes ring through the air so loudly, I jolt and almost fall over. My pocket buzzes to the familiar sound of Aunt Millie's ringtone. I haven't spoken to her in a few weeks, save for the occasional text.

"Hey kiddo, whatcha up to?" Her comforting voice sends bursts of warmth throughout my chest. Everything in my world could be up in flames, and just hearing my Aunt Millie call me kiddo would fix it.

"Hi Aunt Millie," I smile. "Not much, just started on the first construction day at the ranch cabin." *The weirdest cabin in the world.*

I glance back over to the longhorn skull inside of the fireplace but it's… gone. How is that possible? I lean back into the fireplace, and sure enough, there's nothing there. I must be dehydrated or something.

"Not much? Knowing you, you put in more work than you should have. How is it looking up there? Still beautiful as ever?" she says.

"Yes, it's gorgeous here. I love the ranch. We are tucked right into a valley full of rolling green hills with a view of the Grand Tetons. You'd love all of the wildflowers," I say.

"Sounds heavenly. Everything is going okay so far?"

"Yep, all good so far. Although, I'm sure there's still time for something to go wrong," I joke. "I don't think the rancher's son likes me very much, though. I think he's upset that a company as big as MacPherson Enterprises is buying a section of their ranch." I conveniently leave out the fact we kind of know each other. The less she knows about that the better.

"Well he can suck it," she laughs. "They shouldn't have sold if they didn't want to. It's not like you came and forced their hand. Knowing MacPherson, they got a great payout too. I'm sure he's grumpy about everything." Oh if she only knew how spot on she was.

"Yeah, probably," I chuckle. "How's Albuquerque?"

"Hot," she says with an exasperated sigh. "I'd tell you to come and visit me, but I wouldn't wish that upon my greatest enemy so I'll come visit you next."

"Not even Greg?" I tease. Aunt Millie and her old neighbor in Juniper Ridge were always in an all out war. They fought over property lines, sprayed toxic weed killer on each other's rose bushes, and Greg let his dog poop on Aunt Millie's lawn so many times she gathered it all up one day and promptly dumped it right on his welcome mat.

"Why would you ruin my day by invoking the name of the devil?" Aunt Millie scoffs. "Now all I can see is his ugly, wrinkled face. Thanks for that."

"My pleasure," I hum, picking at the leaves on a tree in the backyard. "Well, if you called to check and see if I'm still alive, I am. For now. Until the rancher's son whacks me over the head with a shovel and drops me into the river."

"Alright, good to hear. If you could also check in with your folks before you get knocked out, that'd be great. Your mom has already texted me twice asking about what you're up to," she says.

"Why are they asking you? Are they not aware I'm not thirteen years old living with you anymore? They know exactly where I am and what I'm doing. I literally work for them." I bristle. My parents always go to Aunt Millie before me, and it never ceases to upset me.

"You know the deal, kiddo. They've never been great at the whole parenting gig. Just shoot them a quick text, let them know you're good. I know they know where you are, I think they're probably just curious about *how* you are," she says.

"Fine, but only because if I don't, they'll keep blowing up your phone."

"I don't care what the reason is, just get it done. Hey, I've got to run. Shelley just pulled up outside for Paint And Sip night at the downtown art gallery. I can't miss my monthly drunk painting."

"Okay, have fun, bye," I call out, lingering on the last syllable for a while before I hang up.

My phone stares silently back at me as I hover over the text message thread between my parents and I. It hasn't been used in so long I can practically see dust collecting on the little green bubbles of words.

The last texts in the thread are a couple of very generic *happy birthday* messages, almost identical.

It reminds me of all of the birthdays I'd sit by the phone when I was younger, waiting for them to call. Most of the time they would, sometimes they wouldn't. It almost worked out better if they just forgot to call altogether.

At least then I could make up some sort of event they were at, or the reason their phone wasn't working. I wouldn't have to hear the absentminded tone of my father, barely paying attention to the conversation. Or the way my mother not-so-subtly digs at my appearance. I could make up a new conversation where they were interested in my life in Juniper Ridge. I could tell myself they wanted to hear about my favorite class, or what Hazel and I did over the weekend.

The memories make it hard to want to reach out now. I'm not in that place anymore, I've long since moved on from the hurt they caused me. But still, now that I've seen how amazing my aunt was at stepping into their roles, even unprepared, it's hard to give them the time of day. Somewhere deep down I feel like they don't deserve me.

I click on the message icon, typing up a text to let them know I made it to Jackson safely and started work on the Old Cabin. If I don't want to do it for me, I can at least send it for Aunt Millie. It's the least I can do for her after all she does for me.

Chapter 7

The Damn Oven

THIS TIME WHEN I step into the Autry's home for Sunday dinner, I'm prepared. Prepared to stand my ground with Miles, not react to his disdain, and smile no matter what happens. No more being caught off guard. He may not want me here, but I'm here to stay. At least until the cabin is finished.

I walk through the short hallway to the kitchen, following the soft, warm glow of lights and smell of roasted chicken. Walter sits at the counter watching Isabella take a dish out of the oven, 1960's country music playing quietly on a small radio, the kitchen island completely covered in all sorts of sides from rolls to salad.

This time, however, there are two additions. Miles stands in the other doorway perpendicular to mine, leaning up against the door frame as Parker grabs two beers from the fridge.

I immediately feel too dressed up in my yellow, off the shoulder sundress and heeled boots. Miles and Parker are in dusty jeans and t-shirts that look like they've been baking out in the sun for a few years. Smoothing down the sides of my dress, I dig deep for a confident smile and step into the kitchen. I make it exactly one step before Isabella yells out.

"Katie! There you are. We are so glad you could come, with your busy schedule," she beams.

"I wouldn't miss it," I smile. "I'm so grateful you asked me back."

"Oh of course, of course," she says, taking off her oven gloves. "I think the boys are just watching the baseball game in the living room. You're welcome to join them. I'm afraid Walter and I won't be very interesting company today." Walter looks much more subdued than last time I saw him. His eyes droop a bit like he's tired, and his breathing is a little labored.

"Okay, sounds good," I say, turning to Miles and Parker.

"Yeah, come sit with us, Kate," Parker says, grinning. "We'd love the company." I try my hardest not to look over at Miles, but I can feel him standing in the doorway, looking at me. I nod at Parker, who grabs another beer and transfers them all to one hand.

"Mac," Miles offers as a form of greeting. His voice is low and gravelly. His shoulders are slumped, and I can just make out dark circles under his eyes. And yet, fireworks still pass between us the second he utters his nickname for me.

Parker offers his arm to me to escort me into the living room, so I take it. By the time we turn to the doorway to the living room, Miles is turned around. I breathe a sigh of relief.

"So, how goes the cabin construction? No other wildlife related obstacles, I hope?" Parker asks, sitting on the long leather sofa. I sit on the other side, while Miles opts for the chair furthest away from me.

"No, no more animals barging in. Although, I wouldn't exactly call ranch cows wildlife," I say, relaxing a little into the couch. I'm not sure what it is about Parker, but I feel like I can let my guard down a little bit. It feels like I've known him for years. I get the feeling he's everyone's best friend around here.

"They're pretty wild. And they are definitely alive," Parker shrugs.

"That's possibly the dumbest thing that has ever come out of your mouth," Miles grumbles from his solitude, fighting back a smile. It almost makes me smile too, hearing him joke for once.

"Hey, don't act like you're not the dad joke king over there," Parker snaps back.

"Oh really?" I laugh. "King of dad jokes, huh? I'm not sure I believe that. I don't think I've seen him so much as crack a smile since I got here."

"Well see, you've got to catch him in the right mood these days. He likes family dinners, so he lightens up a bit. Trust me, he used to be much less of a stick in the mud in his youth. You and I are still young and spry, much more fun than senior citizen Miles and his get-off-my-lawn ways." Miles rolls his eyes as Parker laughs at his own jokes. I've got to say, I'm a big Parker fan after our last couple of interactions.

"They say it comes with the AARP membership," I joke, earning another cackle from Parker. I look over at Miles just in time to see the corner of his mouth twitch ever so slightly. Got him.

"So Katie, you hail from mighty Idaho?" Parker takes another swig of his beer, eyes still glued to the baseball game on tv.

"I do," Miles must have told him where I'm from. I wonder what else he said about me. Nothing good, I'm sure. "I'm from a small lake town called Juniper Ridge. On Bear Lake."

"I've heard of it. Never been though, always wanted to. Is it true the lake is clear and turquoise?" Parker asks.

"Yep, the rumors are true. It's my favorite place in the world," I say as flashes of Juniper Ridge light up my mind. Turquoise lake, purple mountain wildflowers, blue skies.

"Is that where your family is?" Parker asks.

"Um no," I fidget a bit in my spot. "I actually moved in with my aunt when I was 10. She's my only family there. My parents are in Tennessee."

"Right on," he replies, setting my nerves at ease. No follow up questions. Good.

I look over at Miles, laying back in the chair watching the game. His dark hair pokes out through the bottom of his baseball cap, and my brain sends me an unwanted memory. My hands raking through his hair as he pushes me up against the hotel room door, his hands on my hips. I clear my throat, letting the images vanish from my mind.

As if he can see my thoughts, Miles catches my eye with an intense stare. I can't pull my eyes away, trapped in his gaze. My cheeks heat, giving me away again. His jaw ticks once and he turns away, taking a swig of beer. Suddenly self-conscious, I tuck my hair behind my ears, smoothing out the ends.

"What about you, are you from Wyoming?" I turn towards Parker. His bright blue eyes seem to smile.

"Nope, I'm from Whidbey Island. Tiny little place in Puget Sound up in the Pacific Northwest. I found my way out here by accident and stayed," he says. I smile and nod as Parker talks a bit about his hometown, coming out to Jackson Hole for the rodeo, then staying to work on the ranch years ago. I can't concentrate. All I can think about is Miles, sitting in the same room as me, not saying a word.

Four years ago we were laughing together, his lips on mine, his hands on my waist. It feels like a lifetime ago, but then again, it also feels like yesterday. Now that he's here, in the flesh, I remember it all so clearly. I'm not quite sure why it has stuck with me after all this time.

"Miles, would you come help me with the damn oven?" Isabella shouts from the kitchen, a series of clanging ringing through the air. Miles gets up from the chair, shoots me one last glance, and walks through the doorway to the kitchen. I accidentally let out a small sigh of relief and hope Parker didn't catch it.

"Listen," Parker starts, leaning towards me speaking softly. "I'd never tell you what to do or anything, but I'd suggest giving Oscar the Grouch a bit of a break. He's been a little extra grumpy lately. Lots of not so fun things going on for him lately. For the past five years, if I'm being honest. But worse this year." Parker gives me a sympathetic smile. "All I'm saying is, I know he can be an ass sometimes, but he means well. He's a good guy. Doesn't deserve the hand he's been dealt. Just have a little patience with him and he'll come around."

"Yeah, okay," I stutter. I'm a bit taken back by Parker's little speech.

What does he mean by lots going on for Miles lately? And for the past five years? We met four years ago and he seemed fine. Happy even. What could possibly be so bad for Miles that Parker feels the need to apologize for him?

I set my questions aside for now. I can't get too invested into this. I'm here to do a job, not investigate Miles's problems. When Miles comes back into the living room, it's all I can do to not analyze his mood.

He catches me staring once more, but instead of looking away flustered, I force myself to give him a small smile. He nods back at me, then turns to the game once more. I suppose I can be civil.

Dinner at the Autry's is a series of stories told by Isabella, comedy sprinkled in by Parker, and many, many questions about my plans with the ranch cabin. I'm not used to discussing a project with outsiders while it's still in construction, but I find myself sharing some of my design ideas, stories from the first week of construction, and even taking suggestions from Isabella on paint colors.

They're an easy group to talk to. I find myself wondering if this is what it's like at real family dinners.

Walter is pretty quiet compared to the last time I was here. But, he's smiling almost constantly, nodding along, listening to all of us talk. He radiates a warmth I didn't know was possible for a person to have. I wonder how it didn't rub off a bit on Miles.

Miles, on the other hand, sits quietly across from me at the table barely touching his food. To my surprise, all of the men took their hats off before dinner. Something about a no hats at the table rule on the ranch.

Miles has a touch of hat hair, but for the most part looks annoyingly better without the baseball cap. I didn't notice before, but his beard has been trimmed short since I saw him last leaving just a bit of stubble.

"–do you think, Katie?" Isabella is saying as I snap out of my trance. I drop my fork like it's on fire, tearing my gaze away from Miles as quickly as I possibly can.

"Sorry, what were you saying?" I ask, eyes wide. I hear a muffled chuckle from Parker to my right.

"Oh I was just wondering if you think we could contribute a few items that have been on the ranch for a few generations to your cabin. It could add a bit of history to it. It would mean a lot to Walt and I to have a piece of our family in the cabin even though we don't own it anymore," Isabella smiles.

"Of course," I say. "Yes, I'd love to. Send me a few photos of what you're thinking of including and I'll find a spot, I promise." Now there's a good idea. I can mention the cabin includes original decorations from the ranch in the listing too, of course.

"I'm just so excited to see the old cabin come to life again. I'm afraid we let it go unused for far too long," she says, tucking a piece of silvery hair behind her ear.

"Katie's doing a great job with it so far, Mom. Just this week she replanted the garden in the back. You'd be proud," Miles says. The sound of his voice makes me jump a little bit. Did he just compliment me? He has spent this entire dinner sulking, not eating, not talking. And now I'm doing a great job with the cabin? The same one I heard him tell his parents he didn't want me to have?

"Maybe I'll stop by and see it next week," Isabella says, clearly not noticing anything unusual about her son's sudden change of heart. "If that's okay with you, of course." Everyone turns to look at me, waiting for my response.

I nod, "Of course. Come by anytime."

Walter asks Parker about the recent cattle branding days, and the conversation switches gears. I look up from my plate to find Miles looking at me already. This time, his stare isn't cold or intimidating. It's more neutral than anything, with just a hint of understanding. One side of his mouth twitches upward in a tiny, half-smile before he looks away.

I'm not sure what just happened, but maybe Parker is right. Maybe I should give Miles a chance. After all, I've seen what he's like when he's happy, and I liked it. A lot. Somewhere underneath the gruff exterior, I'm willing to bet that guy is still in there.

A bright ball of light forms in my chest, forcing a smile onto my face. It starts out like this, just a little glow.

Ready to grow with just a little bit of a push.

Hope.

Chapter 8

Yeehaw

I WAKE UP TO GOLDEN rays of early morning sun shining through the tiny window across from my bed in the small cabin. This is one of my favorite places to wake up. The cabin is so cozy. The walls are made of warm, stained logs with white grout in between. The twin-sized bed has one of the softest, most perfect mattresses I've ever slept on. It's like being hugged by marshmallows all night.

The red plaid sheets make me feel like I'm at summer camp up in the woods. My view is of a wide open field with rolling hills as far as the eye can see, eventually dramatically rising up into gray, rock-covered mountain peaks, permanently covered in a layer of snow. It's breathtaking. When I get home, I'm totally stealing some inspiration from this place.

I rip the covers off like a band-aid, knowing it's the only way I'll get out of bed, and drag myself to the bathroom to get ready for another day on the ranch. Today, I won't be very busy. The crew will be taking care of rerouting some of the plumbing, which I can't help with, and everything else has to wait until the plumbing and heating systems are completely finished so we can build around them.

I've finished the garden in the back and landscaped the front as much as I can for now. My plan is to bring my laptop and get some work done while I have the time. Go over the 3D designs I've made for the inside and see if any changes need to be made. Isabella sent over some photos of a few vases, a quilt, and a lamp for us to use in the cabin decor, so I'll add those items to the renderings and see how everything looks.

Two coffees and a granola bar later, I'm jogging the mile and a half trail over to the ranch cabin. It's a short enough distance I can roll it into my morning run without being tired all day long. Plus, I'll be wearing workout clothing at this stage of the remodel anyway. My ponytail bounces behind me as I slow to a stop at the porch, catching my breath.

I'm used to high elevation in Idaho, but even the small distance has me breathing heavier than usual.

I end the workout tracking on my watch and head inside the cabin, pulling my backpack off to grab my laptop. Before I can sit at the makeshift work table I had the crew bring in, another 'sparkle' like yesterday glows in the fireplace. A small speck of light twinkling for just a second in large bay windows in the back of the house.

I'm on my feet in moments, rushing over to catch it before it goes away. Like before, the sparkle is gone in the blink of an eye, but I can't help but notice it's warmer over by the windows. Normally, I'd attribute that to the summer sun shining through, but it's still morning and now I'm a little bit spooked by this place.

In the corner of the window sill, something catches my eye. There, burned into the wood in black, is an outline of the Grand Tetons. I recognize the famous local mountains immediately. The peaks are shaded very realistically, and at the bottom sits Jackson Lake next to a forest of tiny pine trees. I run my hand over the brand, but there isn't any indent in the wood.

Movement catches my eye from out in the backyard. My head snaps up as Miles, dressed in his usual cowboy attire of jeans, boots, an old black t-shirt and backwards baseball cap walks along the fence. I sneak a little closer to the window to see what he's up to this early. I'm always the first one here in the mornings. I like it that way, nice and quiet.

Miles crosses his arms, looking at the fence with disdain. He steps back and shakes his head. All of a sudden, as if he can feel me looking at him, his gaze snaps up and meets mine through the window. Caught again. He raises a hand up in a sort-of wave, and I wave back. I'm not sure why, but I feel the need to go talk to him and see what's up. I can tell something is bothering him.

Opening the sliding glass door to the back porch, I step out into the cool morning air once again. Miles's gaze is heavy on me still as I walk towards him at the fence. Stopping about a foot short of the remaining fence, I smile at him on the other side.

"Hey," I say.

"Hi," he nods. I clasp my hands together, rocking forward a bit. What a shock, Miles isn't a man of many words again today.

"How's it going back here?" I say, hoping I'll get more than a one word answer this time.

"Fine," he says. So much for that.

"Okay, well, great. See ya," I turn on my heel to head back to the house. I don't have time for this. If he doesn't want to talk to me, that's fine.

"Mac, wait," he says. My stomach does a little flip when I hear him say that nickname in his deep voice. I internally scold myself for having a reaction at all. "Sorry, I'm just trying to fig-ure this thing out. The entire fence is rotting pretty bad. I'm not sure how long it'll even last once I replace the boards that the cows knocked down."

"Oh," I nod, turning back around. "I can let my crew know and maybe we can move some things around to make room in the budget for a new fence. If it's as bad as you say."

"No, no, that's not what I'm trying to say. I can still fix it," he says, shaking his head. "It should have been replaced before you bought the property. This fence is older than dirt. Look, we have some extra fence boards in the barn. If you're okay with wooden slats instead of logs like it is now, I can take all of this down and start on a new fence. It shouldn't take too much time." He reaches down and grabs a log from the ground that used to be part of the fence. "See this? It's practically falling apart in my hands." The inside of the wood is indeed crumbling, turning gray from years of weather.

He wants to fix my fence for me? Not just fix it, but build an entirely new one? I can't exactly say no to that. I wouldn't have to compromise on anything budget-wise, and my crew could stay focused on the cabin.

"Okay, sure. If you want to fix my fence, I won't complain. The slats will look better with the cabin's siding anyway," I say, flashing him a soft smile. I swear for just a second his cheeks turn pink.

"I'll finish taking it down today, then tomorrow start digging for the new posts," he says decidedly, analyzing the rest of the fence. His forehead crinkles in thought, and I can imagine him going through the day's plan in his head.

"Thanks, I really appreciate you doing this," I say. "And thanks for talking me up at dinner the other night."

He turns back towards me, catching my eye. "I just told the truth. The garden looks good." Another half smile.

"It was nice meeting Parker the other night. Does he join you guys for dinner every Sunday?" I ask.

"Not every week, but most of the time he's there. And, you've met him before. He has gone with me to Salt Lake City for the auctions every year since he started here."

"Oh," I say, flustered. This time I know it's me turning red. "Right. I guess I don't really remember."

"Right," he nods, looking at the ground, obviously disappointed. I want to tell him the reason I don't remember anyone else is because I only remember him. His laugh, his smile, the way he made me feel. But, I can't do that without making things incredibly awkward, so I leave it alone.

"Do you think he remembers me?" I whisper, suddenly in a panic. I really hope Parker doesn't remember me as the girl his friend had a one night stand with. I'd be mortified.

"No, I'm sure he doesn't," Miles says. I nod, but I'm not convinced.

We're interrupted by the sound of a horse galloping towards us. Miles steps away abruptly, startling me.

He reaches up to adjust his hat and my eyes immediately go straight to the small sliver of skin showing when his shirt lifts up. There on his side are faded black lines, hardly visible against his tan skin. He's still looking in the other direction, so I narrow my eyes looking closer.

It's a tattoo of something. I can make out legs, the body of some sort of animal, and... antlers. Yep, that's what that is. It's a deer.

A buck. With three antler points on one side and two on the other. It looks so familiar to me, but I just can't place where I've seen it before. It's a great tattoo. Whoever did it drew the deer very realistically. It's like I can see it in the field in front of us.

Holy shit. That's what I know it from.

The deer I saw on the first day I came to the cabin looks *exactly* like Miles's tattoo. Scarily similar. It's like someone took a photo of that deer and drew it right onto his skin.

I snap my eyes up as soon as Parker stops a few feet in front of us.

"Howdy Katie," Parker drawls, a bit exaggerated. He tips his hat towards me and I nod back with a smile. Parker turns his gaze over to Miles, smile dropping slightly. "Miles, we need you up at the corral to sign off on the last group for branding. The guys are already hootin' and hollerin', ready to be done, so I'd hurry if I were you before it turns into an early celebration."

Miles chuckles a bit, taking off his leather gloves. I try not to notice his forearms flexing as he does. "Finished early, did ya?" he says. "We'll have to see about that."

I like this new side of Miles. It's closer to, well... the old side. Parker seems to notice as well, shooting me a wink from atop his horse. I look away quickly, not wanting to be caught by Miles, conspiring behind his back.

"Speaking of celebrations, will we see you at Branding Night?" Parker says with a knowing smile.

"Whatever is Branding Night?" I ask, seeing right where he is going with this.

Parker gasps sarcastically and brings a hand to his chest. "Did Miles not invite you? Well I'm glad you asked darlin'. You see, Branding Day is a day of, well, branding cows. But Branding Night is a night-long celebration that branding is over for the year," he explains. Miles is already shifting uncomfortably where he stands, pretending to kick down some dirt with his boots. "There's a bonfire, music, booze, and of course, I'll be there." Another wink.

Without a side glance at Miles, I smile up at Parker. "Sounds like a great time, I'll be there."

"Yeehaw," Parker yells, kicking his horse up and turning back towards the ranch. He's gone as quick as he came. The only difference is, when he got here, Miles was a whole lot happier than he is right now.

"You really don't have to go to Branding Night," Miles grumbles, not looking me in the eye. "It's just a bunch of drunk cowboys and a few of their girlfriends. I only go because I have to."

"I wasn't lying, it sounds like fun. I want to go," I say. "Is there some reason you don't want me to go?" I bat my eyes innocently at him when he looks up at me. If Miles has a vendetta against me, I'm not letting him get away with pretending he doesn't.

"No," he says slowly. "I suppose there's not."

"Great," I say louder than I mean to, clapping my hands together. "I'll see you then."

Turning on my heel, I head back towards the cabin again. Only this time, Miles doesn't stop me. I close the back door behind me and slink onto the ground, letting out a big sigh. I have a lot of work to do. And my to-do list isn't getting any shorter.

But what's one night off to spend time up at the ranch? I'll just come in earlier tomorrow.

Plus, I can't say no to another opportunity to annoy the heck out of Miles Autry. It's just too much fun.

I take a deep breath as I stare at the familiar name on my phone, buzzing away on my countertop the minute I lock myself away in the guest cabin for the foreseeable future.

Florence.

Not Mom. Never Mom.

Florence is Florence. My boss, the one who signs my paychecks, the queen of MacPherson Enterprises. The woman who sent her own child to live with her sister-in-law instead of raising her.

I swallow the anxiety crawling its way up my throat, and press accept on the call.

"Yes?" There's more bite in my greeting than I intended, after the tension I've felt all night. But, I can't find it in me to feel guilty.

"Hello, Kathrine. Is this a bad time?" Florence's monotone voice crackles on the other end of the phone. Stone cold, as usual. I twist an imaginary phone cord in my hands. One that hasn't existed in a few years, but old habits die hard.

"No, it's not. I just walked in the door."

"Ah. That explains the short greeting, I suppose. How is the property coming along?"

As used to it as I am, a knife still twists in my gut when my parents ask about their business before their daughter. Nowadays, the pain just goes away a lot faster than before.

"It's going well." I switch my tone to business, stifling out any remaining warmth. "We'll be moving onto phase two this week. The crew has been great. And the cabin is very beautiful. I'm confident in its marketing potential."

"Wonderful. Be sure to check in with your father, I'm sure he'll want a progress update as well. We haven't heard anything from you since you arrived in Wyoming."

"Can't you just tell him?" I roll my eyes. The lack of communication between them is astounding.

She sighs, as if I've asked her to make a powerpoint presentation for him. "Katherine, you know how busy I am. Please don't argue with me."

The line is silent as I shoot daggers into the wall next to me with my eyes. I take three deep breaths, my usual coping strategy for phone calls, much less effective in person.

"Is there any other reason you called?" I ask, separating the conversation from my mother in my head. *She's just your boss. Be firm, but accommodating.*

"No, I just hadn't heard from you about the property all month. Do you know how it looks to have to go to my daughter's manager for updates on her project because she won't send a quick email?"

"I'll email you a brief every week if you'd prefer."

"That'd be preferable. Thank you, Katherine."

Once polite goodbyes are exchanged, I collapse onto the wool couch, staring up at the wooden planks on the ceiling. I don't notice I'm crying until my hands meet the wet trails down my cheeks as I cover my eyes.

It isn't often I still cry after a phone call with either of my parents. I've become numb to it all. Separated them as my bosses. Distant relatives instead of my mother and father. Every once in a while, though, my emotions get the best of me. And after the confusing dinner I had earlier with Miles, I'm far too exhausted to hold it together.

So, I let the tears fall. Give myself permission to sit in my feelings a while longer in the hopes that tomorrow I'll be fine again.

It's not often I wish I had a partner in life. I'm fine on my own. I'm independent. I've never needed anyone. I've had a job since I was fourteen years old. I travel solo often for my work. I can cook dozens of different meals for one.

But on nights like this, I just wish I had someone to share a tiny bit of the burden with. Someone to grab me and curl me up into a hug. Whispering it's going to be okay in my ear until I start to believe it myself. A person to lay with me in the darkness so it doesn't swallow me whole.

I tell myself I can do it all on my own. And, I can. But just once, it'd be nice not to have to.

Chapter 9

Two Whiskey Sours

A s soon as I arrive at Branding Night, I realize Miles and Parker downplayed this event by a lot. There are literally hundreds of cowboys here, and the bonfire Parker mentioned is closer to the size of a small forest fire. Before I got here, I was ready to have some fun with the only people around here that I know. Now, I'm feeling so far out of place, my heart is practically beating through my shirt.

A few cowboys I overhear by the makeshift bar mention that Branding Night isn't just Lone Pine Ranch, it's all of the local ranches coming together for a celebration.

It's held at Lone Pine each year because Lone Pine is the oldest running ranch in Jackson Hole. Another detail I wasn't aware of. One I found by googling it on my phone as quickly as I could while sitting on a wooden barrel at the end of the 'bar.'

The 'bar' is really just a collection of worn pallets and barrels that have been setup in a sort-of rectangle shape near the big barn. There's one very quiet cowboy behind the pallets serving drinks without a word. I heard someone yell, "Walker" at some point so I'm guessing that's his name. I'm just about to ask Walker for a drink when a familiar warm breeze wisps across my arm. Turning around, my elbow makes contact with a hard chest.

"I told you you didn't need to come, Mac," Miles grumbles from above my shoulder.

"Nice to see you too, Autry," I counter with a smile. He answers with a sigh, as if he just can't put up with me any longer. Can't wait to test that limit, because I'm not leaving for his sake.

"I just mean it's a lot of rowdy cowboys acting like children until all hours of the morning. I'm out of here by eleven at the latest," he says, placing an elbow on the pallet bar. Always leaning on something like he's exhausted.

"Wow, grandpa, you sure eleven isn't too late? Isn't your bedtime nine sharp?" I ask, eyes comically wide.

He rolls his eyes, scoffing at my comment. It almost looks like he might smile, but he doesn't. "Ha-ha," Miles deadpans, his eyes piercing into mine. "Very funny. You'll see soon enough, come eleven o'clock you'll wish you were leaving too."

"We'll see about that." I wink at him just as he's turning to order his drink.

"Two whiskey sours, Walker," he says with a polite nod.

"Double fisting it tonight, are we?" I tease, throwing his words from before back at him.

"Actually, smartass, this one's yours," he says, handing me one of the mason jar drinks. I try to hide my surprise, tapping his glass back when he nudges his towards me with an almost inaudible "cheers."

Miles holds my eye contact as we take a sip, which feels much more intimate than it should. I feel stripped down when he looks at me. Like he can see all of me, my insecurities, my thoughts, my real feelings. There's no small talk with him, no fake conversations. It scares me a bit. I've never met anyone that so easily rips through my walls of confidence and self-assurance.

I'm the first to break eye contact, looking down and clearing my throat. "Not much of a late night drinking kinda guy anymore?" I ask, trying to break whatever tension is floating around us.

"Never was," he answers. "That was a special occasion in Utah."

"Oh, were you and Parker celebrating something?"

"Not really," he stumbles over his words, looking down to his boots. "It's kind of a long story."

"Okay," I say with a nod. If he doesn't want to elaborate, that's fine. I'm not going to make him share anything with me he doesn't want to.

His lips part as if he's about to explain himself just as we're interrupted by a holler from right behind me.

"Katie! You showed up!" Parker yells, pulling me in for a side hug by my shoulder. Even sitting up on my barrel, I only come up to Parker's stomach. "I was hoping the old man wouldn't scare you away. I promise the rest of us are a lot more fun than Miles." A flash of annoyance dances across Miles's face, his jaw ticking once as he turns away from us.

"I don't know, I think under that tough guy exterior he's secretly a maniac," I laugh.

"I wish the two of you had never met," Miles grumbles. He grabs his drink and stands from the barrel.

"You're just bitter because Katie likes me better than you," Parker shrugs. Miles rolls his eyes, walking away from us.

"You shouldn't antagonize him so much, he's bound to pop that vein in his neck one of these days," I say to Parker once Miles is out of earshot.

"Oh, it's good for him," Parker smiles, nodding towards Miles. "He's too serious, that one. Wound up so tightly all the time. He needs a few dozen chill pills." I nod in agreement. "Have you been here long?" Parker asks.

"Nope, just got here. Looks like a good time."

"Well in that case, I'd love to introduce you to the rest of the guys from the ranch." He points over to a group of cowboys standing near a corral fence. "They're all dying to meet the new owner of the Old Cabin, especially after Walt described you as a 'pretty young lady' the other day."

"Wow, I'm honored," I laugh. Taking his outstretched hand and bouncing off of the barrel, I let Parker lead me over to the other guys and introduce me. A couple of them have girlfriends that ask me about my boots and tell me I should go out for coffee with them sometime.

"Hey, new girl!" A voice says behind me. I turn around and come face-to-face with Codie, the bartender from the Alpine Rose.

"Hi!" I smile as she pulls me in for a hug. "Oh my god, I can't believe I actually know somebody here."

Codie laughs, her bright green eyes sparkling in the twilight. "Look at you, already fitting in at a ranch party."

"I might have to visit for Branding Night every year, this is quite the ordeal."

"Cowboys do like to play hard," she nods. "What brings you out here?"

"My company actually bought a piece of property that used to belong to Lone Pine," I explain. "That's what I'm in town for this summer, to fix it up and turn it into a vacation rental. Parker Bailey invited me tonight."

Codie takes a swig of the beer in her hands. "Now that sounds like a really cool job."

"I can't complain," I laugh.

"How are you liking Wyoming so far?"

"It's gorgeous. I can't stop looking at the mountains, it doesn't feel real."

"I know what you mean. I grew up here, and I still can't believe it sometimes. Especially this time of year when everything is so green," she sighs. "I love summer."

"Me too," I agree. "Although, I am a little sad to be away from home. I'm missing the peak horseback riding season back home with my best friend, Hazel."

Codie's eyes light up. "You ride? I used to jump growing up! You can totally find a place to go riding in Jackson, that's like, our number one tourist activity in the summer."

I laugh, rubbing my fingers along the edge of the cold glass in my hand. "I should. I love touristy things. I don't even care if that makes me cliche. Give me all of the cowboy themed shops and wild west photo booths. The cheesier the better."

"You know," Codie tilts her head. "If you're into touristy things, you can't miss getting a custom cowgirl hat made for you. I work at a shop in town that makes them, I can probably swing a discount for you. It's called Sage and Felt."

"You work at the bar *and* at a custom hat shop?" I ask.

Codie shrugs. "I like to mix it up a little. I volunteer on the elk ranch in the winter too. Keeps my life interesting."

"Maybe I'll have to stop in sometime. That does sound like fun," I say.

"Oh hey," Codie nudges my arm, "I finished that new Willa Gray."

"No way, how was it?"

"Five stars, no notes," she smiles.

I sigh, a bit dramatically. "I knew it. She could never write a bad book."

"If I knew you were coming tonight I totally would have brought it for you. If you come by the shop, I'll give it to you then. You *have* to read it, it's so good. The love interest is my new favorite."

I laugh, "Awesome, I can't wait. I've been dying to read it, and I definitely have some free time up here at night."

After a while of talking about romance books with Codie, Reed, the one with the shoulder length brown hair under a straw cowboy hat interrupts. Codie wags her eyebrows at me as soon as he approaches.

"Would you like to dance with me?" He drawls, hand outstretched.

I nod, taking his arm as he leads me over to the field where there is a large speaker setup and a whole lot of people doing a line dance I've never heard of before.

"I thought Parker was just being Parker when he said that a beautiful girl bought the old cabin on the ranch, but man, did he under-exaggerate," Reed says with a wink as he spins me around to the beat of the music. He has the swagger of a rodeo cowboy. I can already tell he's a favorite with the ladies. "Are you planning on moving up this way?"

"Technically, my company bought it, I'm just here to renovate and then manage it after," I clarify. "I'll probably be coming back up every once in a while to check on it, but right now, I'm okay in Idaho."

"Just okay?" He furrows his brow. "Doesn't sound too permanent."

"I'm not sure where I want to end up," I say truthfully. I never considered leaving Juniper Ridge until my Aunt Millie moved away. Now, the only things that keep me there are my vacation rentals and my best friend. I don't think I'd be opposed to moving somewhere else, just haven't found a reason to yet.

The song speeds up a bit, causing me to majorly lose my footing a few times. I stumble into Reed, laughing. Who knew line dancing in a field in Wyoming could be so fun? We're spinning around in the twilight surrounded by dozens of cowboys, no one caring about what they look like or what tomorrow will be like.

"Well while you're here, I'd love to take you out sometime. Show you how much fun we have up in Wyoming," Reed says with a wink.

I laugh, spinning again as he leads me through all of the moves of the song. "Sounds like fun." I like Reed, he's a blast. Maybe he would take my mind off of a certain stick in the mud standing over by the barn by himself.

I look over at Miles and immediately regret it. Why does he always have to look so attractive? It's infuriating. Tonight he's sporting his signature look of a black button-down shirt, Wranglers, and boots. But, he's forgone a hat. His raven hair is combed back, and shines just a bit in the orange sunset glow of the sky. He's talking to another man, who I assume works for him by his body language. Miles is all take-charge around the cowboys. I wouldn't want to piss him off if he were my boss.

Thank goodness he's not.

"Let me buy you a drink," Reed drawls, reaching out his hand. I hesitate for just a second before taking it. I don't know why, it's not like he's proposing marriage. I just wish I could shake the feeling of being around Miles. I feel like I'm constantly pulled towards him. But, he clearly doesn't want to be around me. He'll pretty much talk to everyone but me.

I let Reed lead me over to the 'bar,' standing off to the side a bit since all of the barrels are spoken for. He brings a couple of beers over, handing me one.

"Hey, is there anything going on between you and Miles?" He asks before taking a sip, as if asking my favorite color. I'm taken aback, like a bucket of ice water has been poured onto me.

"Definitely not, what makes you say that?" I'm a little breathless from the shock of that question. Miles clearly dislikes me. He hasn't been near me since I first got here. He's not paying me any attention.

"Oh just because he doesn't look too happy about me buying you a drink," Reed says. "Wouldn't want to step into something between y'all. I'm not looking to get on his bad side."

My gaze slides over to Miles, still over by the barn. He's still standing where he was before, but now he's alone and he's looking right back at me. He's also clutching his drink for dear life, knuckles turning white. And Reed is right, he does not look happy. Seems pretty typical for him, though. This isn't the first time I've been the object of a Miles glare.

I smile as big as I can back at him, giving him an enthusiastic wave. That catches his attention, bringing him back to reality. He covers his mouth like he's clearing his throat as he looks away, walking into the barn.

"Oh that's just Miles," I assure Reed. "I don't think he likes me very much. In fact, I think I annoy him just by existing. We are definitely not together."

"If you say so," Reed mumbles. He doesn't sound all too sure, but I can't force him to believe me.

We exchange numbers and head back over to Parker and the group. They're a fun bunch, joking around with each other, telling stories of the ranch and rodeos. The kind of people you want to be friends with. I've never had a big group of friends, only a few really close friends. I like it that way, but being here makes me think this could be fun too.

The ranch hands are gathered in a big circle around a hay bail that has a plastic bull head staked into it. Parker stands across from the bull, swinging a rope around his head. He throws the rope with a holler, and I barely have time to see it land on the hay before he pulls it tightly around the horn of the bull.

"Alright, who's ready to test out my aim on a moving target?" He asks the group that has gathered around.

"I ain't drunk enough yet to let you rope burn me, Bailey," a cowboy across from me shouts.

"Aw, come on now, it's tradition," Parker yells back. His gaze lands on me and I swear his eyes twinkle just a bit. "Katie, would you like a turn?"

"I'm used to horses, not cows. I've never roped before," I say.

"I'll teach you, step right up." Parker grins, and I'd be willing to bet he usually gets what he wants because of that smile. What's the harm? I might as well be fully immersed into the ranch lifestyle while I'm here. When am I ever going to learn how to rope a cow again?

"Knew I could count on you, Idaho," Parker says as I walk up to him in the middle of the soft dirt.

"I hope you're a good teacher, because I've never done anything like this before," I say.

"It's easy, trust me. You'll get the hang of it real quick." He hands me a stiff rope, rolled up into a coil. It's mostly white, with a few other colors mixed in. The colors remind me of the sunsets behind the Tetons, orange, red, and purple.

Parker steps in front of me to direct my hands to the right spots on the rope.

"Hold the rope right here. Yep, that's it. It's already coiled up for you, so you're all ready to rope. You're gonna slide the rope through the hondo there, until you've got a big enough loop."

"Is that good?"

"That'll do. Now point your finger right down the center of the rope—"

"And just what in the hell are you doing?" Miles's voice comes from behind me, kicking my heart rate up to a level I'm not proud of. I look over my shoulder to see him stalking towards us, arms crossed over his chest.

"Right on time," Parker says just low enough for me to hear.

I'm about to ask Parker what he's talking about, but Miles interrupts my thoughts.

"Would you leave this girl alone and go rope some of your drunk friends like usual?"

"She's never roped before, Miles. She wants to learn," Parker smiles.

Miles sighs. "You teaching anyone how to rope is like Walt holding a class on computers."

"Why don't you teach her, then?" Parker says, holding a hand out for Miles to take his place.

Miles rolls his eyes, opening his mouth to respond, but I cut him off. "C'mon, Autry, show me what you've got. How many chances does a girl get to be a cowboy for a day?"

Miles finally looks over at me, assessing my words. After a moment, he nods. "Alright, if you want to learn how to rope, you may as well learn the right way."

A couple of cowboys around us hoot and holler as Parker steps back into the crowd. Miles comes over to take his place in front of me. "Alright, what did he tell you?" His voice is softer now that it's just us.

"The last thing he said was to point my fingers down the center of the rope," I say, holding the rope up.

Miles nods, "Yep, that's perfect. You've got a good natural grip on it. Are you ready to try it out?"

I nod.

Miles reaches down, adjusting my hands a bit on the rope, moving closer to me. Having him in close proximity is always distracting, but now that he's in my space completely it's practically impossible to focus. The scent of whatever cologne he put on tonight wraps around me. I drop my gaze to the rope in my hands as my cheeks start to heat.

"You're gonna swing the rope over your head in a circle. Just twist your wrist nice and easy." He steps back, showing me the motion with his arm. I copy him, letting the rope swing around my head with a *whoosh*. It catches on the back of my hair, whipping it over my shoulder.

"Now keep your eye on the tip of the rope, right there on the end of your loop. That's what's gonna hit the target," he instructs. "When you're ready you can go ahead and throw that rope. Make sure you follow through."

The rope flies from my hand when I throw it, landing miraculously on top of the bail of hay. A smile breaks out across my face.

"Now pull on the rope to tighten it around Mr. Bull there. That's it, great aim." Miles says from behind me. I don't get it right on the horn like Parker did, but my rope is pulled tight around the plastic bull head and for some reason, I feel like I've won something.

"Oh my god, I actually did it!" I exclaim, turning back around to Miles. He's smiling down at me as the crowd of rowdy cowboys around us claps.

"You're a cowboy, Mac," he says. His espresso eyes crinkle at the sides, and I feel myself being pulled closer by some invisible force.

His gaze drops to my lips as I stop an inch away from his chest. My heart beats thrum in my ears, faster by the second. I drown in the way he looks at me, his emotions painted on his face in a way I've never seen before. Gone is that stoic, unaffected frown. Right now he looks like he's half a second away from throwing me over his shoulder and getting out of here.

And the worst part is, I *want* him to do that.

"Told you she'd learn quick!" Parker yells from the crowd. Miles steps back from me as Parker walks towards us, the air growing colder in the spot he vacates.

I smooth down my pants in an attempt to collect myself. Parker's arm rests around my shoulder as he tells a story about his first time roping, but all I can hear is ringing in my ears as Miles turns away to return to the barn.

For a minute there, it almost seemed like it was just us. I wish it were.

Eventually, Parker excuses himself to help lead a drunk cowboy into the bunkhouse without falling down a hill. He hasn't had a drop to drink all night himself. I would have pegged him for the fun party guy, not the designated driver.

I take that as my cue to leave too. As much fun as I'm having, I should head back to my cabin and get some sleep. It's one in the morning and it's been a long week of working on the renovation. I'm exhausted.

Luckily, it's not too far from here, just about two miles, so I walked over. I love going on long walks and runs in the country. Especially at night when the stars are out and everything is quiet.

My favorite part of summer nights in the mountains is looking up at the sky. Especially when I can just barely make out the faint outline of the peaks, the Milky Way bursting out from behind.

I don't get very far before I hear footsteps approaching. I swallow a quick burst of fear and turn to face the sound, only to find a familiar cowboy dressed in black, looking like he's headed home from a funeral instead of a ranch party.

"You know," I say with a small sigh of relief, "some people would consider this stalking."

He huffs a laugh, catching up to me. A shiver breaks out across my arm as the soft fabric of his shirt bushes against me. I could blame it on the warm midnight breeze but I'm too tired to lie to myself. Miles Autry has an effect on me.

"Some people would consider it more dangerous to walk out into a field in the middle of the night alone." His voice is low and rough, a fog of sleep just sneaking in.

"Yeah well, some people don't know how to live a little," I joke, bumping my elbow into his arm.

"What are you doing out here, Mac? Where's that tiny car you drive? Did it finally break down?"

"The car is back at my cabin, since I walked here," I say. We are walking at the same pace now, in sync. Far enough away from the party that I can only hear a faint whisper of the music. It's so dark I can barely make out the annoyance on Miles's face.

"You walked here? It's at least three miles to the guest cabin, why the hell would you walk?" His voice raises a bit, cutting through the quiet of the night.

"It's exactly two miles, and I wanted to walk. I like long walks. I walk all over at home. It's fun," I explain. "Although 'fun' seems to be a foreign concept to you these days, so I understand the confusion."

"That's too long to walk," he says, ignoring my sarcasm. "What if you were murdered out here? There's no one to hear anything. What if you were bit by a snake?"

"Aw, Autry, are you worried about me?" I say, voice dripping with fake flattery. I bat my eyelashes a bit at him. He turns away, clearing his throat.

"I don't want to have to clean up a dead body on my ranch because you decided to walk two miles at one in the morning," He grumbles.

"If you think I can't walk around here at night when no one is around, maybe your ranch isn't safe enough. Sounds like a you-problem, if you ask me."

He sighs, mumbling something I can't hear. I make out the words *woman* and *death of me.* I can't help but chuckle. "If you insist on walking, I'll walk with you. I could use one anyway."

"Not having fun at your own party?" I ask, kicking a rock in front of me as I walk.

"It's not *my* party. Everyone just shows up here every year, whether I like it or not." I can practically hear his frown. "It's just a tradition that no one ever lets go of. I'm the unlucky one that gets to set it up and be in charge of it."

"But didn't you ever have fun at a ranch party? I used to love them when I was younger. Everyone is happy, having a good time, getting drunk off their asses and throwing up into the weeds. It's great."

He laughs at my joke, which I think might just be a first since I arrived. It reminds me of that night four years ago when he laughed with me for hours.

"Branding Night just doesn't appeal to me these days," he says.

"Is it because it doesn't start until after your bedtime?"

"Oh fuck off, Mac," Miles chuckles. "Part of it is because it seems loud and unnecessary. We just did all the work, the last thing I want to do is more work supervising a bunch of rowdy cowboys. I'd much rather hang up my hat, head home and sleep for a few days after branding. And the other part is I haven't fit in with this crowd the past few years, and if that's because I'm old and boring, so be it." I can tell he's trying to pass it off as a joke, but he sounds a little too earnest for it to work on me.

"There's nothing wrong with that," I say with a shrug. "I prefer to cuddle up with a good book after nine o'clock most nights anyway. But it's good of you to set all that up for them." I nod towards the flicker of a bonfire, slowly fading into the night behind us. "You're a good boss."

"Hang on, can you say that one more time? I've got to find my tape recorder."

"Don't push it." I shoot him a warning look in the starlight. "Only someone of your age would own a tape recorder," I mumble.

We walk in silence for a little while, but it's not an awkward silence. I can tell that Miles isn't the type of person that needs to fill every space with words, and I appreciate that. Sometimes it's nice to have company but still be able to think.

"How old are you?" I blurt out.

"What kind of question is that?"

"You clearly know how old I am, since we met on my birthday. It's not that weird for me to want to know how old you are. I know you're older than twenty-five and younger than fifty, but that's about it," I say. I have always wondered. I never asked him that night. I always just assumed he was a couple years older than me.

Miles gives me a pointed look. "You think I could be forty-nine years old?"

I shrug, looking ahead at the dirt road. "You have the personality of a disgruntled sixty-year-old. You're not old because of whatever age you are, you're old because you act like it."

"If you must know, I turn thirty-two in September," he murmurs.

Okay, so more than just a couple of years older than me.

"Well then, happy early birthday, Autry," I say. "Speaking of your bedtime, I thought you never stay at a party past eleven?"

Miles chuckles. "I had a reason to tonight, or I would have been home hours ago."

"Oh yeah? What's that?"

"Just wanted to make sure you made it back safe."

Oh. "Oh. That's... considerate."

Miles nods in the dark cover of night as my heart beats a little faster.

As we get closer to the guest cabin, I can feel a change in the energy between us. The air is buzzing. Questions pop up in my mind. Is he going to walk me to my door? Does he want to stay and talk? Why would he want to walk me back, knowing this might have an awkward ending?

Why am I thinking all of these things about him in the first place?

My thoughts are interrupted by Miles's low voice. "Did you really not know this ranch was owned by Autry's?"

"Of course not. Do you think I faked not knowing you worked here? That's a little insane, even for me," I say, a bit annoyed. Seems to be a regular feeling around Miles.

"I was just wondering, is all. We have a website with all of our names and photos. I figured you had to have seen it."

"No, Miles, I didn't look at your website," I sigh. I'm picking my battles wisely with this man, and this is not one of them. "If I knew this was your family's ranch... well I don't know what I would have done. But I probably would have been a lot more prepared to see you than I was. Don't worry, I'm not some creepy stalker going after a one night stand from years ago. I just want to do my job, and move on."

I turn to look at him, and catch a flicker of a softer emotion on his face in the moonlight. It's gone before I can determine what it was, replaced by his usual scowl.

"That's not what I meant," he argues.

"Well what did you mean then?" I demand.

"Nothing."

"Okay, well, if you don't mind, I'm going to excuse myself from your lovely interrogation and head inside. It's been a long week and I need some sleep," I say, pulling my curls up into a ponytail.

Miles tracks the movement of my hands as I tie the scrunchie around my hair. He seems to have trouble swallowing.

Eventually, he nods and shuffles away, leaving me at my doorstep without so much as a goodbye. About thirty seconds later, his boots stop walking as I'm unlocking the door. When I turn back, he's already looking at me with that quiet intensity I've come to know. The air feels a whole lot thinner in the dark night.

"You called me Miles," he says, breaking the silence.

"So? Isn't that your name?" I ask.

"I liked it."

Chapter 10

Your Elbow Is In My Ribs

ANOTHER WEEK WORKING ON the renovation has come and gone. Another week of Miles working on the fence outside and avoiding my glance at all cost. I've buried myself in paperwork this week, and helped out the crew with a few projects when I can.

Our biggest jobs are just about finished. New plumbing is installed, the wiring has been checked and fixed in a few spots, and it looks completely like a construction zone. Which means everything is moving along well. We've had a few issues, but nothing out of the ordinary for an old cabin.

After all, according to Walter this was one of the original ranches of the area. I'm actually surprised with how well it has been taken care of.

Miles is about a quarter of the way done with the fence. He wasn't around at all at the beginning of the week. I assumed he had things to do at his actual job like roping cattle or whatever he does up on the ranch. But he made good progress yesterday and today. The fence looks even better than before.

I still don't know what to make of him walking me home on Branding Night. It seemed so out of character for him. Or rather, out of character for the new Miles. I feel like old Miles definitely would have walked me home. Maybe he's warming up to me. Finally.

Taking off my gardening gloves, I wipe the sweat from my brow. It's later in the evening on Friday night, and the crew has gone home. I've spent a few evenings out tending to my little side project, planting some new flowers and weeding.

After Branding Night, the ones I had planted already slowly started to grow just a bit taller and fuller. Now, when I look out at the garden, it's a beautiful mix of reds, purples, and whites.

I grab my trowel, my gloves, and the tin watering can I found on the side of the cabin yesterday and head back into the cabin. It's quiet when I'm the only one around, but it's kind of nice to just sit with my thoughts. I set the supplies down by the backdoor where I usually keep them, and head over to wash my hands.

I still haven't heard from my parents, which is troubling. When they're this quiet while I'm out on a job, it's usually a bad sign. I'm much more comfortable with their unrelenting criticism. At least then I know I'm doing something right. Now, I'm not sure what's going on. I talked to Aunt Millie this week who said they're probably just busy, but I have a sinking feeling in my gut it's something else.

Pushing stray hairs out of my face, I walk to the kitchen table and pick up my laptop. It's one of the only pieces of furniture that was in the house when I got here, and I used it to make the kitchen my sort-of office for now.

I can see almost the whole house from here. The back door on the far side of the kitchen, the dining room right through the door, the living room through a window in the other wall.

As I look around the house, I feel it again. That warm, belonging feeling from before. As still as a statue, I look around the house. Everything's in place. There's no indoor breezes, no ghosts floating around in the rooms, no glints of light.

My phone vibrates in my pocket, startling me so badly I almost jump out of my skin. The warmth fades as I catch my breath and see who's calling. None other than Walter Autry.

"Hello," I answer, voice shaky.

"Hi there, Katie, it's Walter Autry, from the ranch," he says loudly into the phone.

A chuckle slips past my lips. "Hi Walter, what a pleasant surprise to hear from you." I haven't seen Walter or Isabella in a bit and I'll be honest, I've missed them.

"Right back at you, young lady," he says. "I'm calling on Isabella's instruction to let you know we'd be happy to have you over on Sunday night for dinner, along with every Sunday for the foreseeable future. At least while you're around. She was a little bummed you missed it last week, but she wouldn't want me to tell you that."

My smile grows. I was so tired from staying out late at Branding Night on Saturday I didn't even think about dinner at the Autry house.

"Of course I'll be there," I assure Walter. "You're both too kind to keep inviting me over to your home."

"As long as you're living on the ranch, you're family," he says. It's not often I feel like part of a family. Usually only with Hazel's family and my Aunt Millie. Walter has no idea how much that means to me.

"Thanks, Walter." I choke back the emotion in my throat. "Is there anything I should bring?"

"Just your charming personality," he chuckles. I almost wish I weren't leaving at the end of the summer. I've only been here a few weeks and I'm already falling in love with this place.

The way the sun sets on the ranch setting mountains aglow, the beautifully historic cabin I get to turn into something people can visit and love as much as I do, the wildflowers growing in the open fields like paint splatters on a canvas. The kind people who live here and have taken me in as one of their own when they surely didn't need to.

The front door hinges squeak open in a sudden gust of wind. Dust kicks up into a cloud in the hallway, shining in the sunlight pouring through the windows and revealing some sort of symbol drawn onto the glass.

I walk over to the front windows. Who would be drawing on my windows? One of my crew members? As I get closer, I can make out the design a little more clearly. It's a crisp, clear outline of the Wyoming symbol, the Bucking Horse and Rider.

It's drawn so well, I'm not sure I could ever recreate something so perfectly with just a little bit of dust on a pane of glass. There's nothing else written, just the cowboy and his horse.

When I make it to the door to shut it again, Miles's pickup truck is parked next to my car in the gravel drive. The top of his backwards baseball cap barely pokes over the top of a leafy plant he's hauling down from the tailgate.

He gets the potted plant down onto the ground, and snaps the tailgate shut. He hasn't seen me yet, so I take that as my one opportunity to really look at him. His onyx hair curls around the sides of his baseball cap, a few strands poking through the hole at the front. As he reaches up to test the tailgate latches, his black t-shirt lifts up at the bottom just enough for a sliver of his tan skin to show.

I can make out a tattoo on his back hip. The top part of what looks to be a longhorn skull, horns stretched out along the muscles of his back.

My face is on fire. His arms flex as he walks past the front porch to the side of the house with the huge potted bush.

"Whatcha got there?" I say, still leaning against the door frame. He jumps a little, looking around to find where my voice came from. His eyes spark as they settle on mine.

"Oh, hey," he says, turning towards me and setting the pot on the grass.

"Hi," I smile.

Miles makes his way up a few of the steps until he's right in front of me, looking at me with those dark eyes that make my heart do somersaults in my chest. "I brought you a Gaillardia bush. You can plant it out back with the other flowers. You like plants, right?"

My chest tightens. It's a thoughtful gesture. One I've seen Miles do for other people, but didn't think I'd ever have directed at me. The flowers on the plant look like a sunset. Dark red on the inside, then fanning out to orange and eventually yellow on the ends of the petals. "Yes, I like plants. I garden all the time back home."

"I noticed you had a big open spot out back, and I thought I'd bring this by. If you don't like it, I can take it back," he looks down for a second. If I didn't know Miles better I'd think he was sort of nervous. But he's not the nervous type.

"That's really thoughtful, Autry. Of course I'll take it." I take a step towards him, down one porch step until there's only one between us. Being this close to him is almost intimidating. He takes up so much space, the air is thin between us. It's intoxicating.

Miles stands his ground, holding my gaze. "Alright." His voice is so low it's almost a whisper but not quite.

One minute I'm staring at him trying to think of something, anything, to say to break up this tension between us, and the next, the whole world is tilting.

The stairs beneath me tilt forwards, causing me to fall right onto him. Miles staggers backwards too, but catches both of us before we tumble to the ground.

Right until the ground lifts again, effectively causing us both to lose our footing and fall straight to the ground.

The orange sky flies around me as I get my bearings. "What was that?" I mumble.

"Almost felt like an earthquake," Miles says from below me. *Miles is below me.*

I look down to find his nose about an inch away from mine. His arms are wrapped around me, holding me in place, and mine are tucked into his firm chest. The magnetic force that has been pulling me towards him since I stepped foot on this ranch only gets stronger now that we are closer than we have been in years.

An electric current passes between us. Miles's hands tighten around my waist, and instead of pushing me away like I expect him to do, he grips me slightly tighter. Suddenly I'm back in that bar four years ago, hoping he'll want me back.

My hair falls around us, glowing fire red in the light of the sunset. My fingers itch to touch him, to move across his chest, but I'm pressed up against him too tightly to move my arms.

I'm entranced. I couldn't pop this bubble if I wanted to. I could stare at him for hours, lost in the swirl of brown in his eyes. Electricity flows between us like a river, pushing and pulling us together.

"Hey, Katie?" Miles whispers.

"Yeah?"

"Your elbow is in my ribs."

I fall out of the clouds and back into my own head. "Shit, sorry. I should probably move."

The ungraceful way I stumble off of him and onto my feet is a testament to my current state of being. My thoughts are jumbled, trying to work out what is happening between us. I brush off my shorts and fix my hair as best I can as Miles pushes himself up to his feet.

"Did the stairs... move?" I ask, voice wobbly.

Miles brushes off his arms, covered in dust from the dirt walkway. "It sure felt like it."

"Weird," I breathe. Logically, I know the floor can't just move out from under you. But, barring an earthquake that didn't seem to affect anything else, I'm not quite sure what happened. I'd blame it on my own clumsiness if Miles hadn't felt it too.

"I'm gonna set this guy out back. Any place you're thinking of planting it?" Miles gestures to the plant on the porch, forgotten in the chaos of what just happened.

"I'll come with you," I offer.

We walk back to the flower bed up against the back of the cabin. One side contains my marigolds and other flowers I've planted that are thriving in the new soil. I'm proud of them. But on the other side of the back porch, there's an open spot I haven't gotten to yet. I always meant to find something for that spot, I just haven't found the right plant.

"Right there," I point. Miles sets the pot down in the grass next to the flower bed.

"Roger that," he says, picking up the shovel I left leaning against the cabin. With one swing of his arm, he plants the shovel in the ground, starting on the hole for the Gaillardia to be planted in. "This one is called Arizona Sun. I think the name matches pretty well."

"You're planting it now?" I ask.

"Yeah," he responds, digging a few inches into the soil, "is that a problem?"

"No, no problem at all. I'll stay and help."

"You don't have to stay, I'm sure you have things to do," he says.

I laugh. "What else do I have to do? This is it right here. Plus, this is the fun part. It's the painting and drywall that gets tedious."

We work together planting the bush of flowers. Digging the hole, spreading some of the potting soil I bought before lifting the plant out of the pot and into the ground. Watering the soil to pack it down.

We don't talk much, just sitting comfortably in each other's presence. I find myself laughing a lot more than I do when I'm gardening by myself. Miles does too. Especially when I go to pat the dirt down only to have it spray back up into my face.

"It looks so much smaller than it did in the pot." I clap my gloved hands together, sending a small dust cloud out into the night.

Miles nods, picking up the last of our gardening tools. "It'll grow."

"Thanks for doing this for me. I don't think anyone besides my aunt has ever given me a plant before." I take my gloves off, setting them on the cement back porch.

"It's really not that big of a deal, it's just a plant," Miles grumbles, but the smallest sparkle glints in his eye.

Arizona Sun Gaillardia.

It may be just a plant, but it's my new favorite plant in the entire world.

Chapter 11

The Amelia

SATURDAY MORNING IS TOO sunny, too beautiful outside to sit around working in the cabin. I've been waiting for a good time to take Codie up on her offer to visit the custom hat shop she works at in town, and there's just no better day than this.

I'm in desperate need of a break.

My boots clunk on the boardwalk in downtown Jackson Hole as I get closer to Sage and Felt. The town is bustling now that summer is in full swing. As I push the wooden doors of the shop open, three other groups are picking out hats. Not too bad for a Saturday.

Soft country music plays over the speakers. Rows and rows of hats of every style, color and size line the four walls of the small shop, leather couches and cowhide rugs sprawled out in the middle. It's a bit overwhelming.

"Hey, new girl!" Codie says from behind the small counter at the front of the store.

"Hi," I smile, walking over to her. "It's so beautiful in here."

"Thanks! We try to keep it high end and all that." She clicks her tongue, pointing a finger at me. "I have a book for you."

Codie reaches into a cabinet on her side of the wooden pedestal, taking out the Willa Gray book she had when I first met her at the Alpine Rose. She hands it over to me, with a leather bookmark on top.

"Enjoy! I put my number on a little paper inside the cover, you *have* to text me when you finish it. I need someone to talk to about it with and all of my friends are slow readers. It's killing me. And, the bookmark is yours to keep. I make them in my spare time with the extra materials we have laying around here," she says.

"Thanks so much!" I beam, running my hand along the cover of the book. "I'm so excited. I'll definitely text you when I'm done."

"Alright," she claps. "Let's get you a hat, shall we?"

Codie leads me around the store to a wall towards the back. Hats of all shapes and colors decorate the wood slats, bronze hooks about a foot apart holding them up.

"These are our best selling women's hats, the Olivia and the Sadie. The Olivia has a teardrop crown, while the Sadie has a round crown." She hands me the hat she called the Olivia. It's the bent brim hat, with the teardrop shaped top. It's gorgeous, but I'm not sure about the brim.

I place the hat on my head, looking into the mirror on the wall. Codie tells me a little bit more about the beaver fur the hats are made of, and the different weights for different purposes. A heavier hat for working outdoors, a lighter weight for dressier occasions and casual wear.

"I think I like the teardrop, but I like a flat brim better." I hand the hats back to Codie. "Do you have any others like that?"

"Of course! I'll go grab some real quick. Feel free to have a seat."

She points to a bench behind me, made out of a wool blanket with a turquoise pattern. I'd love to use a lot of the furniture they have here for the rental cabin, but I have a feeling it's probably quite a bit out of my price range.

Codie grabs a metal pole to get some hats down from the top rows closest to the ceiling, hooking each one under the brim. She pulls down three more hats, one a lavender color, one black, and one light tan. Her fringe jacket sways behind her as she walks over to where I'm still perched on the bench.

"So are you staying out on Lone Pine while you work?" Codie asks as I try on the hats, one by one.

"Yes, I'm staying in their guest cabin, actually. The cabin I'm renovating isn't exactly live-in ready yet."

"Is Miles still out there? I haven't talked to him in so long. Probably since him and Alex came river rafting with us last. That had to be at least a few years ago." Alex? Must have been a ranch hand at Lone Pine. I can hardly imagine New Miles river rafting. Must have been Old Miles.

"Yep, he's there alright," I laugh. Placing the tan hat on my head, I turn to look back in the mirror. That's it, I've fallen in love with a hat. Didn't think it was possible.

"Oh wow," Codie says so softly it's almost a whisper. "Tan is totally your color."

My fingers run along the firm, flat brim of the hat. The top is shaped like a teardrop, pinched in at the front. It stands out against my coppery auburn hair, fitting on my head like a glove. The brim isn't too short or too long. The top doesn't stand up too far off of my head.

"I think this is the one," I beam, doing a little twirl with one hand on my hat.

Codie leads me over to a table towards the back where dozens of hat bands and accessories are laid out. My eyes are immediately drawn to the examples of burned in designs and brands.

"I personally love the floral designs if you are wanting it branded. We have a few flowers we can do on the brim." Codie points to a binder full of photos of burn designs.

I look through the book carefully until I find myself attached to one of the photos. It's a large poppy design that takes up the front right side of the brim. Poppies have always been one of my favorite flowers.

I pick out a skinny red beaded band and twirl it around in my hands as Codie applies the brand to my new hat. The beaver pelt smokes a bit as the poppy design etches itself into the hat. It's such a cool process to watch. I can see why Codie loves to work here.

Codie places the hat on my head once it's all done, and my stomach flips a bit with excitement. It's perfect.

"That hat is the Amelia, by the way," Codie says as she checks me out at the front of the store.

That catches my attention, bringing me back down to earth. "Did you say Amelia?"

"Yep, the Amelia," she repeats with a smile. "We have pretty limited quantities of that one, it's lucky we had your size right off the bat."

"Amelia is my Aunt's name," I explain. "She raised me. What a coincidence."

"My mom always says nothing is a coincidence," Codie shrugs. "It must have been meant to be."

My heart warms as I reach up and touch the hat on my head. This whole place feels meant to be.

"So, listen," Codie starts. "If you ever feel like going on a hike in the park with a couple of us local gals, we'd love to have you out sometime. We go once a week, usually around Jenny Lake. Kind of a girls day out."

"I'd love to." My heart speeds up. I haven't been so excited to go on a hike in a while.

"We are heading up to Hidden Falls next week if you want to come. It's a super easy hike, but really gorgeous. Big waterfall, great view of the valley. Just text me and I'll tell you what time." Codie says as we head towards the door.

"Sounds great! I'll be there."

"Alright," Codie claps her hands together. "Are you ready to head out? I thought we'd do lunch at the barbeque place next door. Their pulled pork is the best in town."

I grab my brand new hat box off of the counter with a smile. "Sounds perfect."

Codie moans so loudly after her first bite of food, two other tables look our way. I don't blame her. She was right, this place is amazing. Sunlight shines in through the windows, giving the wood floors a glowing red hue. We settled on a sandwich each and a basket of garlic parmesan fries to share.

"Yeah, I'm going to have to come back here just for these fries," I say.

Codie nods, grabbing a fry and popping it into her mouth. "I eat here way too much on the days I work at Sage. It's far too convenient. Plus, my parents hate barbeque, so I'm making up for never having it as a kid."

I laugh, "That's blasphemy!"

"They're both immigrants," Codie shrugs. "They just couldn't get into it I guess. I can't relate."

"Where are they from?"

"My dad is originally from Finland, and my mom is originally from Vietnam. She's lived in America since she was a kid, my dad came over a little later," she explains.

"That's cool! How did they meet?"

Codie smiles, as if she can see it playing out in her head. "When my dad first came to Jackson Hole, he had only lived in America for a few years. My mom owns an apothecary shop called Elevated Earth downtown, things like crystals, essential oils, herbal treatments. One day, he broke his arm skiing. Instead of driving himself to the hospital, he went right to my mother's shop thinking it was a doctor's office." Codie laughs. "She freaked out. She explained to him all she had in her shop was holistic remedies for colds and such, and drove him straight to the ER. They were inseparable after that day."

"That's so sweet," I say dreamily.

Codie nods. "That's what I want one day. Instant attraction. They were married four months later and never looked back."

I finish off my brisket sandwich. "Wow, that's pretty quick."

"When you know, you know." Codie and I pay the tab, taking a last swig of our lemonades before leaving. "They're the most compatible people I've ever seen. They were made for each other. When I was a teenager, they'd constantly be embarrassing me with PDA."

"I literally cannot imagine that," I say. "My parents barely interact."

"That's so sad."

I shrug, "It's all I've ever known with them."

Codie gives me a sad smile. The kind I usually hate because they make me feel small. But for some reason, it feels different with her. Not so much pity, but empathy. "I'm so sorry."

There's a tug in my chest as we walk along the sidewalk. I had Hazel in Juniper Ridge. And Aunt Millie. And sometimes even Wade. But I've never had a group of friends. I've always been a best friend sort of girl. It was Hazel and I all of the time, or just me.

But, I've always secretly wanted a friend group. Maybe this could be my opportunity. Even if it's just for the summer. If Codie's friends are as cool as she is, I'm sure I'll have a blast at the hike.

"How long do you have left on the cabin renovation?" She asks, kicking a pebble across the sidewalk in front of us.

"Probably over a month still. We've got most of the big things done, but it always takes a lot longer to put back together than it did to break it apart," I laugh.

"And after? Will you go back to Juniper Ridge, or is there another cabin out there waiting for the magical Katie MacPherson touch?" Codie asks with a smile. I can't help but giggle.

"Yep, back to Idaho it is."

"Wow, don't sound too excited."

"It's not that I'm not excited to go home, it's just–" I sigh. Boring? Lonely? Back to real life, where I had nothing permanent going for me? "I'm just not sure it's what I want anymore. But that's really intimidating, you know?"

"Sure," she nods.

"I don't want to just hop around from project to project either. I'd love to settle down somewhere. Eventually build a place of my own. Make friends and all that shit. And I love Juniper Ridge, don't get me wrong. I guess I'm just thinking more about those things lately."

"That makes sense," Codie says. "I love Jackson Hole, but I'm not opposed to leaving one day if the need strikes."

"I've been gone for a while, so it's probably just that." It's like a dam has broken inside of me. I've never thought about leaving seriously, much less talked to a near-stranger about it. It's not like I can talk to Hazel about moving away, she'd be heartbroken. "Maybe I'll follow my Aunt Millie to New Mexico. She seems to like it."

Codie laughs, linking her arm through mine as we turn a corner in the square. "I feel like I would thrive there. Creepy alien abductions, desert for miles, turquoise jewelry."

"I wouldn't be surprised if Millie moved there for those *exact* reasons."

I can't help but smile as I pull into the guest cabin a bit later, my tires coming to a stop on the dirt road right in front of the porch I've decorated with a couple of flowers and a welcome mat I found at the local grocery store.

Even if it's just for a little while, this place is starting to feel like mine.

Chapter 12

Muscle Memory

SWEAT BEADS ON MY forehead as I lay in the quiet darkness of the middle of the night. My heart is racing, my lungs trying to suck in as much air as they can get.

It felt so real.

I roll out of bed and over to the window, opening it as much as I can to let in the cool night air at the ranch. The last thing I remember before waking up was the heat of Miles's touch on my skin. He runs so goddamn hot all of the time.

I've never had such a vivid dream in my life. When I first woke up, disappointment hollowed in my chest. All I wanted to do was tug on that fleeting memory of it until I fell back asleep and back into the illusion.

Then, my brain woke up enough to realize what it was I was trying to get back to.

Miles.

Whispering things into my ear, fingers skating ever so slightly across my back, looking at me with those deep brown eyes. I can still remember his eyelashes, the flecks of gold glowing in the dark. A shiver breaks out across my shoulders as I remember it, the ghost of Miles's face skating across my vision. A feeling I can only describe as yearning. For a version of him I'll never have again. Not in this life.

He'd whisper he was waiting for me all along into my hair as he held me close. We'd ride off into the sunset, spending our days together wandering in the mountains and our nights snuggled up together by the fireplace. We wouldn't have to worry about things like distance because we'd always be together.

With a sigh, I fall back into the soft, mussed covers on my bed. A crisp mountain breeze rolls in, cooling me down a bit more. My gaze stalls on the wood planks of the ceiling as I replay the vivid dream over and over again in my head. I think it's safe to say I won't be getting much sleep tonight.

I let out a frustrated groan and hop up out of bed again, pulling on a pair of running leggings. Maybe going for a night run will tire me out a bit. Let off some pent-up energy.

The night air is cold on my cheeks as I step out of the cabin. The stars are out in full force tonight, a full moon lighting up the fields surrounding me. Wooden fence posts pass by as I run down the gravel road, tension melting off with every step I take.

It's been months since I've been with anyone, in any capacity. I'm pretty sure the last human contact I had besides the cowboy at the bar was a drunken kiss on New Year's Eve at Cisco's bar in Juniper Ridge. What was his name? Jason?

Being around Miles is a bad idea. I don't trust myself. Isolated up here in this small town, working in close quarters with no one else around. If I don't get it together, we're bound to make a mistake.

The other day, I caught a glimpse of him taking his long sleeve shirt off to switch to a t-shirt, and I almost lost it right there. If he had looked over at me, he would have probably seen me practically drooling. His tan abs like a washboard make me itch to run my hands up and down them. I can see him standing there when I close my eyes, sunlight outlining his large frame, black hair smattering across his chest.

A flush creeps back up into my cheeks. I've got to stop thinking about him. My calves ache as I push harder, running faster down the road. The faster I run, the easier it is to clear my head. Soon, all I can hear is my breathing and the sound of my runners hitting the dirt.

I've run halfway to the main ranch house when I feel calm enough to turn back towards my guest cabin. My breathing is shaky by the time I get back.

Good.

Maybe now I'll be tired enough to get some more sleep. Uninterrupted, dreamless sleep. The flush that covered my entire body when I woke up is gone, and I'm only thinking about the relief of falling back into my soft bed.

The next thing I know, I'm curling back up into bed, Miles a distant memory.

"Love the hat, Katie." Parker reaches out and taps the front of my hat brim enough it falls into my eyes just a bit.

"Thanks, it's new," I laugh, taking the beer he's offering from his hand and pushing my hat back up onto my forehead. When I arrived at the ranch house for Sunday dinner, I was rushed into the great room at Isabella's instructions, to 'keep those boys in check.' Although, I suspect she just wants me out of the way as she cooks.

Parker and I are the only ones here so far, but judging by the uneasy feeling in my gut, I'm sure Miles is near.

"Oh yeah? Where'd you get it?" Parker asks.

I tell him about the shop in town and Codie helping me pick it out. "I figured I should do at least one touristy thing while I'm here. I'm glad I did, it was fun. Plus, Codie invited me on a hike with her friends this week in the park."

Parker grins, about to say something else, when the door to the back deck opens and Walter walks in. Not far behind him is Miles, nodding along to something Walter is telling him about cattle.

He takes up all of the air in the room when he enters. Jesus Christ, he's wearing another black t-shirt that looks like it's two sizes too small. For my own sanity, I should sneak into his closet and replace everything with one size up. I'm not sure how his biceps haven't torn the sleeves yet.

Heat creeps up my neck, and I'm right back to where I was last night. Yearning.

My pulse races as Parker says something that my head can't process. I can't tear my eyes away from Miles. Visions of my dream play on a loop behind my eyes. Miles's arms circling my waist. Miles's breath skating across my neck. The feel of his skin, as hot as the sun on my face on a warm summer day.

As if he can feel me staring, Miles's eyes snap up right at me. Like he can always sense exactly where I am. A current of electricity passes between us as he stares back. I wonder if it's all in my head, or if it's bothering him too. This energy between us.

"Mac," he grumbles, joining Parker and I.

"Autry," I smile back. It's just a greeting, but it feels oddly intimate this time. I clear my throat, fixing my hat again as I remember Parker is standing right next to us.

"Seems Katie here got a new hat in town. At the place Codie Raisanan works at." Parker hands Miles the beer in his other hand, nudging him in the arm. A lump forms in my throat as the veins on his hands bulge around the glass. Hopefully, he doesn't notice my pulse hammering in my neck.

"Suits you." Without another glance my way, he heads over to the couch. My heart doesn't know whether to be giddy or offended. But, that's nothing new. I always seem to be confused around Miles.

Miles hasn't uttered another word by the time we sit down at the dining room table with Walter and Isabella. Walter leans his cane against the table, slowly lowering himself into the chair. I get the feeling he's the type of man who wouldn't appreciate people fawning all over him to help, so I hold my tongue.

"Where are you going hiking with Codie?" Parker passes the bowl of mashed potatoes to me across the table.

"I can't remember the name. She said somewhere near Jenny Lake. Somewhere I've never been. Apparently they go hiking once a week," I shrug, scooping a generous helping of potatoes onto my plate. Potatoes have always been my favorite food. You can eat them in so many ways. Baked, cut into fries, mashed, in bread. What other food can do that?

"I'm sure it'll be a good one, her ex-husband is a park ranger so she probably knows all of the good spots."

"Ex-husband? I didn't know she was married." Married *and* divorced? She can't have been that much older than me, if at all. Parker shrugs casually, as if I should have already known this. "But, she's so young."

"They got married right out of high school. It wasn't dramatic or anything when they split up. They still have the same friends and everything. Pretty sure they were always just better as friends," Parker says.

"Well, that's good at least," I nod. "I couldn't imagine getting married so young."

"There's nothing wrong with getting married young." Miles's stern growl from beside me startles me enough, I almost drop my water glass.

The fire in his eyes burns a little brighter when I look over to him. His scowl, a little harder than before. Words die in my throat.

I don't know whether to be pissed off at him or turned on. Damn dream, messing with my head. As if I needed *more* confusion between us.

Isabella changes the subject easily, going back and forth with Parker about her favorite places in the National Park. But even as dinner plates are rinsed and wine glasses are being refilled, I can still feel heat waves coming off of Miles. I'm not listening to anything being said at the table, he's too distracting.

Right when I thought we were cool, the Grinch is back to hating me. I can't keep up with the rollercoaster of emotions that is Miles Autry.

Good thing I only have to for a couple more months.

Miles leans up against a wood pillar in the living room, staring at a blood orange sunset framing the dark blue outline of the mountains. His jaw ticks and I can almost see the thoughts racing through his mind. He may be a man of few words, but I can tell his mind is never quiet.

What is he thinking about? How quickly he can leave and go back to his solitude without being impolite? If he can get away with offing me and hiding my body on the ranch? Who would win in a grump-off, him or Ebenezer Scrooge?

His eyes slide over to mine and I'm lost in a golden brown whirlpool. My body immediately reacts to his gaze, as if it's communicating back to him. My chest rises and falls rapidly, pulse speeding up. My core turns molten, goosebumps covering my arms.

Muscle memory. That's the only explanation for this. There's no other reason I should be so affected by him, especially when I know he's angry with me for even being here. He probably can't stand that I'm in his home, much less staring at him like this.

My eyes fall to the bobbing of his throat, snapping back up when I remember he's looking at me and can see where my gaze falls. I might be imagining it, but I swear for just a second his cheeks are slightly redder behind his dark beard.

When I met Miles, he didn't have a beard. I really wish he didn't have one now. I had no idea bearded men are my type until I set foot on this ranch.

I need to be more careful around him. I'm really not used to this. This wanting. Usually it's the other way around, I meet a guy always when I'm never really looking, they pursue me, and I go with it until the heat dies down and things start to get mundane.

Then, I feel trapped going down a path I don't want to be on. Right into my parents' life. A marriage full of disappointment, kids who resent me, nothing ever being enough. So I run back to where I'm comfortable.

Alone.

When I'm around Miles, that pattern goes out the window. *I* want to chase *him.* I want to convince him to want me back. I want to go on a hundred dates with him and never get bored or unsatisfied.

I don't want to have to wake up in the middle of the night yearning for something I can't have. I want the dream to never end.

But that's not sustainable. One of us will inevitably end up hurting the other. And, I'm not willing for that to be the case for either of us. It's best just to ignore the burning in my heart.

It takes more effort than I'll admit to myself to pull away from his gaze and turn around. That's probably why I sneak to the front door in the shadows like a spy retreating from a mission.

Chapter 13

For The Memories

T HE STONE WALL WARMS the palms of my hands as I lean against it. It's the perfect day for a hike in Grand Teton National Park. I was instructed to meet Codie and her group of hiking friends at Jenny Lake, near the ferry dock. A tan stone wall borders the sidewalk overlooking the lake and the gray mountains jutting out of it at sharp angles.

The tops of the peaks are covered in a blanket of snow even in June. The contrast between the field I drove through to get here and the tall mountains is so jarring, it's hard to believe a place like this even exists.

In Idaho, our mountains are more gradual. Crawling out of the ground slowly enough that people build homes on the benches. Green and filled with grass and trees.

Here, they're so severe I can't imagine what event occurred in Earth's history to cause such an abrupt change. The gray rock shutting out any hope for grass and plants to grow on the steep cliff faces. These mountains are drastically newer, not yet shaped by millenia of weather rounding them out.

Jenny Lake doesn't look big enough to have a ferry to cross it, but a water taxi heads towards the dock in front of me with a white wake trailing behind. It's really just a big silver pontoon boat gliding across the water, with rows and rows of forest green faux leather chairs to transport hikers to the start of the trailhead.

It's a crowded day in the park. When I got to the parking lot, it was already filling up even at seven in the morning. I'm glad we got an early start today. The water taxi is only about half full, and the line waiting to board to cross the lake isn't very long.

"Katie!" Codie runs towards me, arms outstretched, pulling me into a hug. "I'm so glad you came!"

"Thanks for inviting me! It's such a perfect day, I'm so excited," I exclaim.

Codie introduces me to her three other friends hiking with us, Erin, Morgan and Nicole. They all live in the Jackson Hole area and are around our age or a little older. Codie tells them I'm here for the summer renovating the old barn on Lone Pine Ranch. All of them seem to know exactly what she's talking about.

"We've all been to a few gatherings out on the ranch, especially back in the day. Those ranch hands know how to throw a good Branding Night. And don't get me started on their Fourth of July fireworks," Erin says, her blue eyes crinkling at the sides. "Plus, Morgan has a huge crush on one of the cowboys there."

"Hey, that was a million years ago," Morgan shoots back, her brown curls bouncing as she talks. "I haven't seen Parker in so long."

"You have a crush on *Parker*?" The words come tumbling out of my mouth before I have a chance to stop them.

"Yeah, have you met him?"

"Actually, yes. A few times. The Autry's invite me over for dinner every Sunday and he's usually there."

"You have dinner with the Autry's?" Nicole, who hasn't spoken more than a quick 'hello' since she arrived, gasps, eyes wide.

"Yeah, every Sunday. I'm staying in their guest cabin. It's been pretty fun." I shrug. I didn't realize how small of a town this is. Everyone seems to know Miles's family.

"I can't believe you get to have dinner with Miles *and* Parker every week, at that mansion of a place they call a ranch house. You're so lucky," Erin says, eyes wide. They all know Miles too. Great.

"Wait, you actually see Miles? I haven't seen him in... probably years. That guy has become such a hermit lately," Morgan chides.

"Honestly, I wish I saw Oscar the Grouch a little less," I reply. That earns a laugh from the girls.

"Come on girls, let's get down to the boat," Codie says, waving the giggling group towards the dock where the boat has come to a stop. Hikers file off of the boat, and we hop in line to get on board. We take up two rows of seating in the middle.

The boat ride over to the trailhead is pretty short, but it's the prettiest one I've ever been on. And I've spent a lot of time at beautiful lakes.

Nothing compares to this.

The blue of the water and white of the wake trailing behind us. Full panoramic views of the Tetons jutting out from all around us. Pine trees climbing up the mountain and lining the lake, their scent surrounding us. The cool mountain air whipping my curls around my neck.

I take out my phone and snap a few photos of the mountains, and a selfie of our hiking group. I want to remember this day.

We are ushered off of the water taxi when it docks at the trailhead. The dock on this side of the lake is much smaller, and there's a lot less of a line. The trail starts immediately afterwards, a dirt trail heading up into the tall lodgepole pines.

"Okay ladies," Codie claps her hands, standing in front of us. "We are hiking to Hidden Falls today, and then up a bit further to the Inspiration Point. We'll have a great view of Jenny Lake from there."

"Lead the way!" Morgan shouts.

Our hiking boots crunch on the dirt trail as we head up the hill into the pine trees. A mix of green and blue fills my vision. I've spent my life exploring the mountains, hiking up to peaks, riding horses on rocky trails. But this is different somehow. More majestic.

I listen to them update each other on their jobs and their lives, and more than a few dating horror stories from Morgan. Erin reminds me a lot of Hazel. She's got the same grit, a determination that flows off of her naturally.

For the first time since I got to Wyoming, I really miss my friends. I love being independent, but I miss having Hazel a short drive away. I wish she were here on this hike with us. She'd love it. I would love to bring her here someday.

The trees sway in a cool mountain breeze as we hike up and up, through switchbacks and over rocks solidified into the trail. The scent of pine fills my lungs. Truly fresh air. Before we've even reached a waterfall of overlook, I already love this trail.

Morgan and I fall into conversation about her many jobs around Jackson Hole over the years.

"I'm a bit of a wanderer, as my parents say," she smiles, looking down at the dirt trail below us. "I love doing all kinds of things. So I do. And I love Wyoming. I couldn't imagine living in a big city."

"I get that," I reply. "That's why I like my job so much. It's always different every day. Sometimes I'm turning over the properties, sometimes I'm helping guests plan their vacations, sometimes I'm renovating houses and decorating rooms."

"Sounds like you love it."

"I do. And I love that I get to learn different places while I'm at it. Be a resident of a different town every once in a while." I reach back, clipping my hair up onto my head as the breeze turns from cool to warm.

"Do you think you'll stay in Idaho forever?" Morgan asks.

I've never planned on staying in Idaho *forever*. In fact, I've always thought I'd move away eventually. Probably a few times. Explore new places. Open up new areas for MacPherson. Like what I'm doing here, but on a bigger scale.

But now? I'm not so sure. I could see myself wanting to find a home and stay somewhere. Traveling is fun, but it would be nice to have a place I can call my own.

I never really had that growing up. I've always pretty much been able to live out of a suitcase ever since my parents shipped me off to Juniper Ridge. Even with all of my Aunt's efforts to make me feel at home and welcome there, it still wasn't ever *mine*. Not in the way that it's Hazel's. I still feel like somewhat of a guest there. A transplant.

"I'm not sure. I think I want somewhere to call home, but I don't know if I've found it yet."

Morgan considers my words for a minute before replying. "I could see you here, you know. You fit in pretty well. Plus, we could really use another hiking buddy. We even have a book club in the winter when we're all stuck inside."

My heart swells a bit in my chest at her offer. I haven't let myself consider it, but I do feel like I could stay here. I love it already. What if I could live in Jackson Hole? I know I've only been here for a short time, but maybe.

No, that'd be crazy.

I don't even know what I'd do here. We just have the one cabin to run, that wouldn't be enough to justify me hanging around.

Codie stops in her tracks in front of me so abruptly I almost trip onto the dirt. When I glance up at her, she's staring ahead through the clearing of trees at a beautiful waterfall. The water had been rushing past us in a small creek for the entire hike, I must not have heard the waterfall as we snuck closer to it.

Hidden Falls isn't the tallest waterfall I've seen, but it's by far the prettiest. White water rushes down dark gray rocks between the pine trees, with the jagged mountains raising up impossibly tall in the background.

The creek after the waterfall rushes past a viewing point a few people take photos at, around a bend and down the mountain towards Jenny Lake. The water shines a light turquoise color as it flows past us.

"It's beautiful," I murmur to no one in particular.

"I thought you might like it." Codie nudges my arm with a laugh.

We stay and take a group photo in front of the waterfall with Erin's phone. Codie insists on taking one of just me 'for the memories.'

The next half of the hike is a lot faster. Or, rather, it just feels that way. We laugh and talk the entire way up the mountain. I'm not sure if I could remember anyone else that passed by, how loud we were, or anything outside of the fun we were creating.

Seemingly out of nowhere, we stumble upon another clearing. This time, on top of a rocky mountain face.

"Come on, let's sit on the edge," Morgan yells from behind me, rushing past me with surer footing than I could hope to have.

We all make it over to the edge of the rock, taking in the view at the lookout. In front of us, Jenny Lake stretches out from the mountain we stand on, its dark blue water sparkling in the sunlight.

Past the lake, rows and rows of lodgepole pines lead to open fields of light green grass, just starting to turn golden in the summer heat. I can see all the way to the cabins on the other side of the clearing, built in the early days of ranching in Jackson Hole.

The sun warms my cheeks and I take a moment to take it all in. The summer breeze blowing past. The calm of the mountains in the middle of the day. The songs of the birds flying by, making nests in the trees nearby. The feeling of the rocks, sturdy below my hiking boots. The comradery of hiking up this mountain with new friends.

It's been a while since I've slowed down to evaluate how I'm feeling in the life I've built. I'm proud of the work I do. I'm not sure where I'll end up, or what's next for me in the grand scheme of life. But, here, in this moment, I'm happy.

I know after this hike, I'll return to renovating the cabin, and eventually, back to real life and the shuffle of everyday tasks.

But just for now, I breathe a sigh of relief and take in the moment. Give myself time to stay in the feeling of being content.

I look over to the other women surrounding me and think about how grateful I am to have this experience with them. It's nice to not be alone. It's nice to have friends.

The Hole

THE WEEK GOES ABOUT as well as it can during a renovation of an extremely old cabin. There's a bit of mold in the bathrooms that has been removed, wood boards replaced. The walls have turned into more of an open concept, the hard wood floors refinished and carpet replaced in the bedrooms.

Except for one floor board in the kitchen my foot went through earlier this week, the interior is in great shape. I'll have to wait for a couple of weeks until my crew is back from another job to get that fixed, though. The hole remains.

Outside, the rich brown of the cabin exterior has been re-stained and is more vibrant than ever. The flowers I planted in the backyard are slowly but surely blooming, a vibrant display of red, yellow, orange, and purple.

It's starting to look like a cabin I'd want to spend a few days at. Sitting on the back porch taking in the view of the Teton Range, reading a book in the sunshine.

Right now, as I look out the window, there's an obstruction to the view. Although, I can't complain.

Miles works on the last bit of the fence, wiping the sweat from his brow under his baseball cap with his forearm. His t-shirt is riding up his arm just a bit further than usual, and I can see higher up his tattoo sleeve than I usually can. The bottom half below his elbow is a winding road crawling up into the mountains, surrounded by fields.

What I've never seen before are the pine trees, all different shades and sizes, wrapping around his bicep. Even this far away, the detail of the trees is clear, sharp points poking out of the mountains.

It's unfair how much of an effect he has on me, even still. Why couldn't he have been repulsive?

That'd make it much easier to convince myself it's not a good idea. Even though it's tempting to run over there as fast as I can and pick up where we left off four years ago, I have to remember he's not the same Miles as before. New Miles doesn't want to be around me at all, much less in that capacity.

I pull my gaze away from the back window, heading back to my laptop. I thought my other properties would be neglected during my time in Jackson, but it hasn't been too bad. The cleaners we have worked with for years are great at turning over rentals, the guests have been relatively low maintenance, and no one at MacPherson Enterprises has come running to me asking for help with anything.

At this rate, I'll be able to go on another hike with Codie and the girls again soon without the guilt of taking a step away from work eating at me from the inside out.

It takes me a few hours to update the books and check the rental calendar one last time to make sure reservations are all good to go. Then, I'm up again, painting the cabinets. The monotonous back and forth of the paintbrush darkening the pine wood relaxing my brain. This is why I love hands-on renovations.

Would I want to paint cabinets for a living? No.

Do I want to break up my usual work with some cabinet painting every couple of months? Absolutely.

I'm not sure how much time has gone by when the warm breeze returns, but it's been about two cabinets worth. I freeze in my tracks, surveying the room.

A smudge of black catches my eye in the corner of the cabinet, where I haven't quite reached yet. Another brand, burned into the wood. I squint my eyes, moving closer to see the shape, but all I can make out is it looks a little bit like a playing card—

"Oof," I grunt quietly as my head runs right into the top of the cabinet. I back out a bit, checking to make sure I didn't knock over my paint can in the process. It's still standing upright, intact.

Glancing back to where the brand was in the cabinet, my breath catches in my throat. It's gone. No matter how far I lean into the opening, I can't see it anymore. Grabbing my phone from my pocket, I shine the flashlight in the cabinet.

There's not a trace of anything besides wood, and the paint I've been using.

I breathe out a shaky breath. The paint fumes must be going to my head. This whole cabin is going to my head.

As soon as I lift the paintbrush in my hand to start again, Miles bursts through the back door and into the kitchen. His eyes are wide, looking around frantically. His broad chest rises and falls quickly.

"What?" I say, startled.

"Are you okay?" Miles demands, his tone a little panicked.

"I'm fine, Autry. What's wrong?"

"I heard you yelling. Is everything okay?" Miles runs a hand through his already mussed hair, replacing his ball cap.

"I wasn't yelling," I squint my eyes in confusion. He heard yelling? I haven't heard anything but the silence of the mountains in hours. I wasn't even listening to any music like usual.

"Yes, you were. I heard your voice. You were yelling my name." Miles stands with his hands on his hips, looking just as confused as I feel.

"I swear I was not yelling. Seriously. I didn't hear anything. Are you sure you're not just getting senile?" I stand from where I was crouched on the floor, brushing off my overalls. Miles's eyes track over my body, until he remembers I'm here and snaps his gaze back up to my face.

"Yeah, I get it, I'm old," he deadpans. "I'm not messing around. I heard yelling."

"Okay, well, I didn't. I'm not sure what you heard, but it wasn't me. And last time I checked," I spin my arms around, gesturing to the empty room, "there's no one near here."

He sighs, rubbing his hand down his beard, a little longer than the last time I saw it up close. Now that I think about it, he does look a little run ragged. The slightest dark circles darken his eyes, and he just seems tired.

"Well, I'm sorry then. I really thought I heard you yelling."

"That's okay." I shift on my feet, suddenly aware we are the only ones in the house. It's like I forgot how to talk to him. I never have this problem with anyone else. "Are you okay? You look really tired." I lift my arm to comfort him on instinct, but catch myself.

He huffs a laugh without a smile. "It's been a week."

"It's only Wednesday."

"I know."

Miles pulls a chair out from the tiny table I use as my desk and sits. His large frame looks ridiculous in the tiny chair I barely even fit in. I'm pretty sure it was some sort of kids table the crew picked up on the side of the road just so I had *some-thing* to work at until we get actual furniture in here. I don't mind.

He leans over, elbows on his knees, head in his hands.

I walk over to the fridge, pulling out a half-drank six pack left over from the crew.

"Here," I hold out a beer towards him. "You look like you could use this."

"Thanks." He lifts his head and takes the beer, a small smile on his face. His finger brushes mine as he takes the bottle, and a literal spark passes between us. We both jump back a bit.

A beat of silence passes between us as we take swigs of beer. We're sitting closer than I thought. So close I can feel the warmth radiating off of his arms. His brow furrows as he stares down at the table in front of him.

It's the first time I've looked at him long enough to notice the toll the years have taken on him. He may be four years older since we first met, but I get the feeling they were rough years.

"I don't know if he told you," Miles starts, his rough voice interrupting my thoughts. "But, my dad is sick. Terminally sick. He has been for a few years. It's getting worse, and he's had a really bad week. I shouldn't be complaining about anything while Walt is laid up in bed."

"Oh." *Shit.* A sinking feeling fills my gut. No one should have to go through something so awful. "No, I had no idea. I'm so sorry. Is everything okay? Can I do anything?"

He doesn't so much as look up from his hands as he fidgets with the glass bottle. My heart squeezes in my chest for him. If I wasn't positive he wouldn't want it, I'd have already pulled him into a hug.

"It's okay." A dry laugh escapes his throat. "Actually, it's not okay. But you know what I mean. It's just... I never thought I'd have to take care of him like this. He's always been such an unbreakable force. And now, he's a shell of that man. It's depressing to watch. There's nothing I can do, nothing my mom can do." He runs a hand down his face again, taking a deep breath.

"Sorry, I shouldn't be telling you all this," he waves a hand, as if that will take it all back. "It's just been a really hard day for him and I can't fix it, no matter what I do."

"That's okay, Miles," I reach over and place a hand on his arm, unable to resist the pull to try and help him feel a little bit better. To my surprise, he doesn't shake me off. Instead, his expression softens a little bit. "I can't imagine how hard that is. I'm so sorry you have to go through that. You can talk to me about it anytime."

"Thanks," he grumbles. I can tell he doesn't want to talk about it anymore, so I don't push any further.

"My parents sent me to live with my Aunt when I was young. I couldn't imagine what I'd do if anything happened to her. I'd be sick with worry. I already worry about her, and she's totally fine. A little wild, but fine." Another weight lifts off of my shoulders. Who knew telling someone besides Hazel about my parents would feel so nice.

"Your parents just sent you away? Why?"

I shrug. "They're not exactly the most family-oriented people. I was a high energy kid that needed attention. We didn't mix."

Miles looks at me like I've grown three heads, "Didn't mix? You can't just send your kid away because they're being a kid. There's not a return policy."

"No, but there is a send-to-sister policy, apparently." A dry laugh escapes me. Miles's expression softens so much that I can't read it. Not pity, but something else.

"That's shitty, I'm sorry Mac. No one deserves that."

"Thanks."

Our gazes catch as I look up, and linger for a beat too long. He clears his throat, sitting up. We finish our beers without another word, in a limbo we haven't been in before. I don't share details about my family with almost anyone, and judging by his demeanor, neither does Miles.

But, this isn't the Miles I've gotten used to. This is a much softer version than the hard edges in his usual demeanor with me. Not Old Miles either, with his laughter and lightness about him. A different version altogether.

One I thought I'd never see.

"The good news is, the fence is done. I just finished the last section before I came in. Hopefully that'll hold a lot better than the one before."

"Oh. That's great. Awesome." My stomach drops a bit. I didn't realize he was so close to being finished with the entire fence. I guess I won't be seeing him around the cabin anymore.

"Yeah," he says so quietly it's almost a whisper. "I guess I better leave you to it. Sorry for rushing in here."

"No worries," I wave him off. "Just a weird day all around."

"I guess so." The corners of his mouth turning upwards just enough a regular person wouldn't think it's a smile. I know better.

He tucks in the chair and walks around the inside of the kitchen instead of straight towards the door. Right by the–

"Oh, watch out there's a–" I try to warn Miles, but I'm interrupted by a grunt as his foot falls directly in the floor hole I haven't been able to repair. "Hole," I finish, too late.

"What the hell?" Miles turns to look at me, half in the floor. "What happened here?"

I try not to laugh, but a smile escapes onto my mouth. "Earlier this week, I sort of fell through the floor. It's okay, though, the crew will be back to fix it in a couple of weeks."

"You *sort of* fell through the floor?" He gapes, staring at me in shock. "A couple of *weeks*?"

"Yeah, it's really not that big of a deal, we expect this with old homes. Probably just rotted in a spot, or termites. Hopefully not termites," I shrug.

"*Termites?*" Miles repeats.

He pulls his foot out of the floor, stepping carefully around the hole. His left boot and pant leg are covered in splinters of wood.

"You can't just work here with the floors crumbling beneath your feet," Miles says decisively.

"I don't really have a choice. My crew is at another job for two weeks, and I don't feel comfortable fixing hardwood floors and doing a good job. I've never done it before. Things have to get done, I'm on a deadline. I'll step around the hole."

"What if another hole appears? What if you break your leg?" He demands, arms crossed. The Miles I'm used to is back. Grumpy and worked up about something that isn't a big deal.

"I'm not going to break a leg. Really, Autry, I'm all good. Sorry you fell into the floor." I throw my bag over my shoulder, heading towards the back door to lock up. Miles follows close behind, annoyance radiating off of him like heat.

"You can't be serious. If you don't have anyone to fix the floors, I'm coming over to start on it tomorrow. It's unacceptable to work somewhere that is rotting out from under you."

His eyes pin mine in place, fire burning in his gaze.

"Like hell you are. You can't just keep fixing shit around here, you have a real job. I bought this cabin as is." My voice raises. He's so stubborn, it kills me.

"I've put new flooring in my parents house and the bunk house at the barn. It's easy. You clearly should have had an inspector before you bought the cabin, these things would have already been fixed." He stands, immovable, just inside the door. If I don't agree to this insanity, he might never leave.

"We bought the cabin knowing we wanted to fix it up. It comes with the territory."

"Just let me fix the floors. It'll make me feel better about my dad selling you a half broken cabin. Please." The look in his eyes is so sincere. I haven't seen that from him in a long time. I can't even remember if I've ever heard him say the word please.

"Okay. Whatever. You can fix my floor," I concede.

"Good," his gaze remains hard and unrelenting, keeping me in place.

"Sure," I whisper.

Miles pushes past me, heading out towards his truck on the side of the house. By the time I lock the back door and walk around to the driveway, he's heading down the road.

A smile creeps onto my face as I stare out into the twilight sky. I have to admit, I was a little sad when he finished the fence. As annoying as he can be, it's fun to spar with him every once in a while. And now, I won't be completely alone for the next two weeks.

Oh shit. Miles and I are going to be in the house *alone* for the next two weeks.

I didn't think about that when I agreed to this. This could go down in burning flames, for better or for worse.

My mind wanders to the pain in his eyes tonight. Another crack in his shield, this one bigger than any before. One step closer to... I'm not sure. Being friends?

I laugh to myself. I couldn't really see ever calling Miles my friend. But, who knows? Maybe we could be a little closer to that. Better than just civil.

Maybe it won't be so bad after all.

Chapter 15

Only One

THE REFLECTION OF MY fifth attempt at an outfit to wear to dinner at the Autry's stares back at me in the mirror, somehow looking worse by the second. I'm not sure why it's so hard to choose today, but my brain feels like mush and I look like either a hippie or a potato sack in every single outfit I own.

Usually, I love clothes. Picking out an outfit has always been a fun part of my day. It's like a grown-up game of dress-up. What do I want to look like today? What shoes go with my bright pink shirt? What colors can I coordinate to create the exact vibe I want?

Not today.

With a groan, I fall face first onto the bed in my cabin. If I give up now, I won't have to pick a stupid outfit. Or see stupid, confusing Miles. Or come up with stupid conversations at a dinner table. I could just lay here all night, pretending I lost track of time.

I breathe out a sigh, taking my phone out of my pocket. Dinner starts in twenty minutes, and I have literally nothing else to do. Nowhere to go. No escape.

You're being overdramatic, I tell myself. *Stop it. You're not get-ting too close to him, you just had one conversation that didn't end in a fight. Pull yourself together.*

My cabin looks like a war zone. Clothes are strewn every-where. My curling iron and straightener are both plugged in, unused. The corner of the rug is overturned, revealing the orig-inal stain of the floor, a deep, rich mahogany.

I refuse to have my personal life reflect the mess that is my cabin. I decide on a head-to-toe denim jumpsuit partly because it's cute and I wear it more often than anything else I own, and partly because that way I don't have to pick a shirt *and* pants.

Throwing my hair up into a clip and my all pink cowgirl boots on my feet, I head out the door before I lose the nerve.

You wouldn't think that I, confirmed Social Sally, would ever have days filled with social anxiety. But, I do. Not often, but enough I've had to force myself out of my house enough times. I'm pretty good at it now.

Usually, days like these can be tied back to boys, and end in some sort of break up around the second or third date. This is a rare occasion that has nothing to do with my dating life at all, and everything to do with my grumpy neighbor.

I take another deep breath as I start my car, blasting a 90's country station with the windows down as I roll towards the main house on the gravel road. Overstimulating my senses with noise strangely calms me down a bit.

Once I get to the door, smoothing my jumpsuit a bit with my hands, I'm thirty percent less jittery. Almost there.

This time, my knuckles don't even meet the surface of the door before I'm pulled in and whisked into the living room again by Isabella, coming face to face with Miles. I brace for the stomach flips, the spike of anxiousness that usually comes on days like these. But nothing happens.

Well, something happens. He says, "Mac," in that deep voice of his that vibrates low in his chest, nodding in greeting, giving me his full attention. And, my anxiety melts away like a popsicle on a summer day.

Okay, then.

"Autry," I reply, sounding a little more breathless than I'd like. My racing heart calms down as I walk over to the small table in the back of the room and grab a can of soda.

"Parker couldn't make it today so it's just us." Miles sounds a lot better today than last time I saw him. More himself.

"Next time, let me know if Parker's not coming, I'll make sure to stay home," I wink at him and I swear I almost catch a smile in his eyes.

He scoffs. "We're grilling tonight. And by we, I mean me." He cocks his head towards the back porch.

I've always wanted to see the view from their porch, its sprawling fields filled with cattle, mountains glowing above it all with the sun just behind their peaks. I follow Miles out back, and it's even better than what I could see from indoors.

Although we were on the main level of the house, it's built into a hill so while you walk into the main floor from the front door thinking it's the ground floor, out back you're two stories up. Looking down at the sagebrush and golden grass fields.

I can imagine how green they'd be at the beginning of spring. Now, in mid-June, the tall grass has started to turn gold in the summer heat. My feet carry me to the edge of the balcony as I take in one of the most beautiful views I've ever laid eyes on.

"Nice, isn't it?" Miles's voice from behind startles me out of my daydreaming.

His attention is focused on me, the slightest smile on just one side of his lips. "Better than nice. This is amazing. I can't believe you grew up with all of *this*." I gesture to the majestic display behind me.

"It's kind of cheating to show it to you right now," he shrugs. "The ranch is by far the best looking at sunset. In the midday heat of July, I'm not sure you'd feel the same."

"I don't believe you," I tease. "This looks amazing at any time of day, I just know it. Don't worry, I won't get too used to it. I'll leave you alone once the cabin is done." I meant it as a joke, but something passes over Miles's face that looks a little like anger.

Desperate to bring back Slightly-Less-Grumpy Miles, I change the subject. "Do you guys do anything special for the Fourth of July out here?"

It's one of my favorite holidays back in Juniper Ridge. The whole town fills up with vacationers from all over, spending their days out on the lake and nights at all of the local shake shops. We have a parade in the morning, folk singers all day, and a barn dance at night.

"There's lots going on in Jackson Hole. Out here the guys usually light off some fireworks in one of the less-dry fields. Walt isn't a huge fan of fireworks after they set the field on fire once," he laughs. "It didn't spread, but it was threat enough for him to ban fireworks ever since. Not that it has ever stopped them."

"Sounds like chaos. And very dangerous." I smile.

"Let's just say it's not my idea of a good time. But if you can't beat 'em, join 'em or however the saying goes. If I'm there to encourage better decisions, there's less trouble in the end."

"It's nice they have such a good grandpa like you to protect them."

Miles's laugh fills the evening air, igniting sparks of happiness in my blood. It's been quite a while since I made him laugh. It feels good.

"Yeah, yeah, we get it, I'm old. You're the one who's into older men, if I recall correctly." His flirting catches me off guard. My cheeks start to heat. Two can play at that game.

"Only one," I chide. "A really long time ago. Kind of ruined me for any others."

He chokes on his beer, turning beet red. Mission accomplished.

As much as I don't want to admit it to myself, Miles ruined me on a few counts for other men. I certainly haven't been with anyone that much older than me since. They could never live up to him. Miles is in his own category.

Not that I'd *ever* admit that much to him for real. His ego would have a field day.

Just as Miles regains his composure, Isabella pops her head outside and calls his name. They chat about when dinner will be done and a few other ranch related subjects, and when he returns to the grill at my side, his mask of seriousness is locked back on.

"Are you busy tomorrow?" He asks. My heart stutters as I find his gaze. Brown eyes aflame.

"No, why?"

"I was thinking of heading up to Ember Meadow. Give Claro a bit of exercise. Walter's horse needs it too, and you mentioned before that you ride," he avoids my gaze, suddenly intent on checking on the steaks sizzling on the rack of the grill.

"Are you asking me to go on a ride with you tomorrow?"

He sighs, finally looking up at me. There's hesitancy in his gaze. "Yes, Mac. Parker is gone and I need someone to ride with me so both horses can get a walk in. Are you in or not?"

Right. Parker would normally go with him, I'm just the back up. My chest deflates a bit. Maybe this will be good. I haven't been on a horse since I was at Hazel's dude ranch. It'll be relaxing to let my mind wander a bit. No to-do list tempting me.

"I'm in," I nod. Hopefully I won't regret it.

It feels good to be back in the saddle.

Literally.

Riding horses is muscle memory for me at this point. I grew up riding with Hazel and Wade at her dude ranch, and it's one of my favorite things to do. The feeling of freedom that comes with it is unmatched.

I'm not sure how much riding Miles thought I had done, but it seemed to surprise him when I didn't need his help mounting or keeping up with him. The upward twitch of his eyebrows was all he let on.

Walter's horse, Sundance, is gentle and pretty old. He's a great horse for a beginner. Even though I ride horses with Hazel back home often, I still appreciate not having to worry about a just-broken horse. I pat Sundance on the neck, feeling his mane under my fingers.

We've been riding for about an hour now, in complete silence. It's not an awkward silence, though. I can tell Miles is just lost in his thoughts and prefers to stay that way. I'm sure he has a lot on his mind between his dad's sickness and running the ranch pretty much on his own.

Most of my thoughts are centering around not staring at his ass in his saddle, however. So far, it's not working very well.

His wavy hair bobs up and down as I follow him on horseback through the mix of aspen and pine trees that cover the back section of the ranch. His hair is longer than when I arrived at the cabin at the beginning of summer, just peeking out of the bottom of his cowboy hat.

It still feels like I just got here, even though it's been more than a month already. With less than a couple of weeks until July, my summer project is already halfway over. My heart sinks at the realization that I'll have to leave soon.

I've come to really like this place during my time here. The cabin is starting to look really beautiful, and I'm proud of our work so far.

I rush Sundance up a bit to ride side by side with Miles and Claro. I've had enough silence for one ride.

"Hey," I say, matching my pace to his.

"Is there something you need, Mac?" Miles's words don't match his tone. He can pretend to be annoyed with me all he wants, but I can hear past that. Behind the tough exterior is a softness I saw through the cracks the other day, and I'm determined to see it again.

"Some human company would be nice. Do you have any of those here, or is it all just robots like yourself?"

He rolls his eyes, looking over at me with a scowl. A sarcastic smile paints my lips.

"Ha-ha. That bit isn't getting old at all."

"Well, you would know," I say. "Get it? Because you're old."

"I've heard the best jokes are the ones you have to explain."

"I think I heard that somewhere too."

Miles laughs a real, actual laugh and I almost fall off my horse in shock. If I make a big deal about it I'll probably never get to hear it again, so I laugh with him.

"My Aunt Millie is a much better jokester than me. Sometimes she'd say something and I wouldn't get the joke until hours later," I smile, missing her again.

"Are you still close with your aunt?" Miles asks. There's no judgment to his tone, no prying question. Just curiosity.

"Yeah, she raised me for most of my childhood. At least, the formative years. We talk more in a week than I ever have with my parents." I look down the path in front of us, concentrating on the wheatgrass swaying along the sides.

"I still can't believe your parents just shipped you off. That should be illegal."

"It was better that way, I think. After I got over the whole 'leaving my friends and family thing' I loved living in Juniper Ridge with my aunt. She's so much fun. Stern at the right times, but my best friend when I needed it. I'm lucky to have her in my life." I can't help but grin. Miles is looking at me with a lightness in his eyes that wasn't there before, setting off nervous sparks in me.

He clears his throat, looking ahead. "Do you still live with her in Idaho?"

"No, she moved to New Mexico a couple of years ago. It hasn't been the same since she left."

He nods, still focused on the path ahead. We are starting to come out into a clearing, the sun almost set behind the mountain. It'll probably only be another twenty or so minutes.

"Where are we heading, anyway? Won't it be too dark to ride?" I ask. Miles picked me up at the Old Cabin in his truck, driving me up to the barn by the main house where the horses were. We left from there and while I could tell we were heading in the direction of the Old Cabin at first, I've lost track of where we are completely.

"You'll see," is all Miles says before taking off again, leaving me in the dust.

I kick my heels in, and Sundance runs after him through the last of the aspen trees. My hair whips in the wind behind my back. When I catch up to Miles, he's slowing down in the middle of a golden field of grass. It's untouched by cattle tracks, standing tall except for the skinny path taken by our horses.

He stops in the middle of the field, dismounting. I follow suit, my boots hitting the ground with a quiet thud.

"Mac," he calls from the other side of the horses. "Come here."

I follow his voice until I see him standing in the middle of the field right as the sun hits the valley between two mountain peaks in front of us. And then, the most magical thing I've ever seen in my life starts right before my eyes.

The field starts to glow in the light.

The sun hits it at just the right angle that the golden grass illuminates, shining around us. Gold turns into a burnt orange as the sun creeps lower behind the mountain. The grass around us is ablaze. I've never seen anything like it. I spin around, taking in the entire field.

Miles stands in front of me, hands on his hips and a smile on his face. "This is Ember Meadow," he explains. "We call it that because every night at sunset, the light makes it look like it's set on fire. My great grandpa used to come out here with my grandpa every week to see it, and on down the line until me. I haven't been out here with my dad in a few years, but sometimes I come out here on my own. I'm not sure how it works, right place at the right time I suppose."

"It's breathtaking," I whisper, running my hands across the tops of the grass. Miles adjusts his hat, stepping into my space. His warmth reaches out to me, pulling me closer.

"It is," he says, but his gaze never leaves mine. I'm lost in his deep brown eyes sparkling in the golden light.

The grass comes up to my waist at least, taller in some spots. It feels like we are in the middle of a flame, light dancing all around us.

"I don't know how you aren't out here every single night."

"I used to be," Miles laughs, his fingertips brushing against mine as we stand shoulder to shoulder in the middle of a field on fire.

I turn to face him, and he does the same. As if there's an invisible pull between us. He picks a single blade of wheatgrass, bringing it up to my face and delicately brushing the end of it across my nose.

My eyes flutter shut, and when they open back up, he's smiling back at me, bigger than I've seen him smile in years. I echo it with a smile of my own. Then, we're both laughing. I feel like I'm floating into the sun.

Miles's hand brushes against mine, holding my fingers so lightly I almost can't feel him. If it weren't for the warmth he always seems to be radiating, he might be an illusion. I take a step closer and place my other hand on his chest.

His eyes widen, smile faltering just a bit. I don't let him overthink what's happening before pushing on his chest until he falls over into the grass with a thud.

"What the hell, Mac?" He laughs from the ground, wheatgrass outlining him in a shine of sunlight like a halo around the contrast of his dark waves. I laugh, turning to run away, but I'm not quick enough. Miles reaches up and grabs my calf, pulling me down with him.

I topple down next to him, the golden grass framing the pink cotton candy clouds of the sunset in the sky above us. We lay next to each other, catching our breaths, faces sore from smiling. Neither of us willing to say anything and pop this bubble.

The glow gets brighter and brighter until the sun finally dips mostly behind the gray mountain and it goes back to the usual muted yellow of golden grass. As soon as it goes away, I miss it. I have to come back and see it again.

Once the sky turns from a fiery yellow to twilight blue, Miles stands up, reaching a hand out to me to help me to my feet. I dust myself off the best I can but I'm sure I still have a fair amount of wheatgrass in my hair.

"We're just a stone's throw from the cabin. So you don't have to ride back in the dark. I can take both horses back from here—"

I cut Miles off with a hug neither of us are expecting. He stands as stiff as a ruler for a few seconds, then eventually gives in just a little bit, one arm wrapping around my waist.

"Thanks for taking me here," I whisper into his chest. We are so close. Closer than we have been in four years. Dangerous territory. And he's not exactly hugging me back. His other arm sits firmly at his side, back stiffer than a board.

Great, I've made him uncomfortable. I pull away quickly, trying to hide the pink tinge of my cheeks.

I don't get far enough to see his face before he pulls me right back in. My heart races as I'm enveloped with Miles's signature cedar smell. He pulls me into his chest, which is a lot harder than I remember, his beard scratching into my hair.

He's holding me close, like if he lets go even a little bit, I'll slip right out of his arms. I get the feeling Miles isn't a big hugger. The last thing I want to do is spook him. I don't dare move a muscle. I hug him back, as tight as I possibly can while I have the chance.

And then, something utterly terrifying happens. As I stand in Miles Autry's arms, in the middle of a field in Wyoming, so far out of my comfort zone I can't even see it from here, my heart sighs and the wind whispers the word *home.*

Chapter 16

I'll Marry You

I'VE ALWAYS BEEN AN extrovert. That's probably part of the reason I got along so well with Hazel. We're like yin and yang. I do the talking when her social battery is depleted, or pull her out of her comfort zone when she needs it. She talks through things with me when I need her logical, overthinking brain to help me figure things out instead of going off like a bomb every time I'm upset.

I can't count how many times I've dragged her out of her house, away from her stress-inducing spreadsheets, and into some random dive bar when she's getting overwhelmed. One of my favorite things to watch is Hazel starting to come back to life under the glow of some neon lights, french fries on her plate and not a care in the world.

The only thing is, I'm always the one to extend the invite to go out. I don't mind it, Hazel is always the one to text when we have a girl's night in at the ranch, or go on a horseback ride. But when we go out? That's all me.

They say how you recharge shows if you're an extrovert or an introvert. I recharge when I'm around people. Talking to my friends takes a weight off of my chest. Checking in with Aunt

Millie resets my mood. Being alone just makes me sad at best, anxious at worst.

So when I open my phone to a text from Parker, I'm pleasantly surprised.

PARKER

Coffee?

I shoot back a quick yes, opening my closet with a giggle of glee. A hike with the girls and now coffee with my favorite cowpoke on the ranch? How did I get so lucky?

Ten minutes later I've got on a black denim vest, red cowgirl boots, my favorite pair of flared jeans, my hair thrown up into a ponytail tied with a bandana and I'm out the door. And, to think, Hazel tried telling me I wouldn't need half of my wardrobe for one summer of renovating a cabin in Wyoming.

It's mid-morning when I sit down at a high top table at my new favorite coffee shop in Jackson Hole. Parker saunters into the warm glow of the cafe's low hanging lights just after I take my first sip of caramel latte. The first sip of coffee and the happiness it brings should be studied. He gives me a quick wave before placing his order at the counter.

Parker slides into the wooden barstool across the table from me, depositing his cowboy hat on the wall hook next to us. Western towns. They always have a place to hang your hat and tie up your horse, like it's 1855.

"Hey there, Idaho."

"Hi, cowboy."

Parker's smile grows that much more as he gives me a wink, combing through his light brown hair with his fingers. I'm certain he's always smiling. His cheek muscles must be jacked.

"I'm loving the whole Canadian tuxedo look," he gestures to my outfit. I give him a little hair flip, which makes him laugh. "We should have coordinated outfits, I'm halfway there."

Parker's blue jeans are significantly less dusty today. It must be his day off at the ranch or something. Instead of a plaid, pearl snap button shirt like usual, he's got on a plain white t-shirt and a tan corduroy jacket. Definitely not ranching attire.

"Next time," I chuckle.

A petite, blonde barista stops at our table, handing Parker his coffee in a clay mug with an antler stamped on the side. He thanks her with a smile, and I swear she almost faints on site. I roll my eyes at him once she's out of sight.

"Seriously?" I cross my arms.

Parker laughs, lifting his mug to his lips and taking a sip of what looks like plain, black coffee. Not what I would have guessed for him. "What can I say, the ladies love me."

"Yeah, because you're Wyoming's biggest flirt."

"I can't help if I've got a flirty personality, Katie. It's like I always say, women value humor first, looks second. Which works out really well for me since I'm not much to look at." I roll my eyes for the second time in five minutes. He definitely has humor *and* looks going for him, but for some reason, I get the feeling he'll argue with me if I try to tell him that.

"So why are you still single, you clearly have plenty of options," I ask, taking another sip of my coffee. I got mine in a to-go cup just in case, but now I'm a little jealous of Parker's mug. I make a mental note to get that next time.

"None of the options I want." He sighs, looking down at his cup as if it's going to give him the answer. "I'm not a casual dater, and it seems like that's all anyone wants these days. One or two nights and then move on to something more exciting. Flirting is one thing, but taking it any further is another."

I nod, trying to ignore the pit settling in my stomach. I know I shouldn't feel guilty for being a casual dater like Parker says, but it's hard not to sometimes. *It's better for the general population if someone like you isn't in long term relationships anyway,* I tell myself.

"What about you?" He asks.

I shrug, taking another sip of coffee. "I'm not the relationship type. Kind of hard to be with parents like mine." He looks at me silently, urging me to continue. I sigh and take a deep breath. "I've just never felt like I should be in a relationship, you know? I'm more like my Aunt Millie. She's been a strong, independent woman her whole life. She doesn't spend time crying over men, or worrying about what someone else thinks of her. She just... thrives. I love that about her."

He nods, taking in everything I've said before responding. I like that about Parker. He's a thinker like Hazel, not hotheaded and quick to a comeback like me. "I think you could be in a relationship some day. I think you'd be great at it, you just don't know it quite yet. Or you could be completely a completely independent badass like you are now. But, I wouldn't worry about it too much. I've got a feeling you're going to be okay. We both are."

Suddenly, I have the urge to rub my chest right over my heart. Who knew Parker of all people could pull emotions out of me so easily? "Thanks, Parker," I say.

"And if you're not married by the time you're 40, I'll marry you," he shrugs, taking another sip from his mug, casual as can be.

"Fine, but if you're going to make a marriage pact with me, you'd better mean it. I take these things very seriously," I say.

Parker's eyes shine with glee. He holds a hand out for me to shake, "It's a deal."

"Deal," I shake his hand, laughing at his determination.

"Only fifteen years until our wedding, we'd better book a venue now," he says.

"They do book up pretty far in advance. Should we send out save the dates?"

"I don't see why not."

"Me either. I'm sure it won't be awkward for all of your future girlfriends to see your wedding invite hanging on your fridge."

Parker leans back in his stool, against the metal bars shaped like a lasso. "Obviously they'll have to be okay with it, the pact comes first."

"Obviously," I laugh. It feels great to laugh with a friend in a coffee shop. I hadn't realized how much I missed Hazel and our outings.

"Well, Katie," Parker stands from his seat, placing his hat back on his head and extending his arm. "Shall we go buy rings?"

I tuck my hand into the crook of his elbow as we walk out into the morning sun. "Actually, I was thinking tattoos of each other's names on our ring fingers instead."

Parker's head tips back as he laughs into the morning air.

"I had to park a million miles away. It was a lot busier on the street earlier, I swear," I say to Parker as we get closer to his truck just down the street from the coffee shop. He slung his arm around my shoulders when we started walking, and left it there. It reminds me of what my friend back in Juniper Ridge, Wade, used to do when we were young, since he was so much taller than me.

"Do you want a ride to your car?" Parker offers.

"Sure, that'd be great."

We round the corner of the brick building and almost run into someone. Parker pulls me closer with the arm that's around my shoulders, mumbling a quick sorry before we both recognize the someone.

We are standing face to face with Miles.

Angry Miles. My least favorite version.

"Hey man, good to see ya," Parker immediately lights up at the sight of his best friend, but still doesn't step away from me. Miles's eyes settle right on his arm that's around me for a beat too long. Then, as if remembering himself, he clears his throat.

"What are you two doing here?" Miles's voice comes out a little shaky, as if it's the first time he's said anything today.

"Just a morning coffee date," Parker replies. Either he's not picking up on the vibe Miles is sending out, or he's purposely ignoring it. "I didn't know you were gonna be in town, you could have come with us."

"Off day," Miles grumbles. "Gotta go to the bank."

"Right on. Well, we won't keep you. Come on fiancee," Parker says, finally taking his arm off of my shoulders only to grab my hand instead, pulling me towards his truck.

Miles spins around on a dime after we walk past him. "What?" He spits out.

"Have fun at the bank, Autry," I wink at him. His nostrils flare as he opens his mouth to say something else, but Parker is already opening my door and I'm hopping into his truck like we do this every day.

Parker slides into the driver's seat still laughing. "That was fun. Do you think he's gonna pop a blood vessel?"

I smack him on the arm. "You're evil. Isn't he supposed to be your best friend?"

Parker shrugs, pulling his truck onto the road. "Sometimes people need a little push to know what's good for them, Katie.

Plus, I might be his closest friend, but I'll never be his peace. Gotta keep him on his toes."

"Next time we should kiss a little, really sell it." I can just imagine his face.

"Now you're thinking," Parker smirks as we drive away, Miles shrinking in the rear view mirror, still standing in the same spot we left him in.

Chapter 17

Decorating Duty

CRACK.

Boom.

Boom.

I clutch my keys in a fist as I slowly creep through the hallway of the Old Cabin towards the ear-splitting noise coming from the kitchen. Today is Saturday. The crew isn't here, there are no cars parked outside, and I refuse to let myself think it's some sort of ghost burglar.

It's a raccoon. It has to be. I must have left a window open overnight or something, and a wild animal got in to rummage through my garbage can.

Would a raccoon make such loud noises? No, it must be a bear. No need to freak out, I'll just take a quick look, see what it is, then sneak back out and call animal control–

My breath catches as I round the corner. I'm met with the sight of Miles's bare back as he kneels on the floor of the kitchen with a huge metal mallet in his hands. The toned muscles in his shoulder blades are more defined as he swings the hammer onto the floor, breaking the brittle boards with a loud *crack*.

Calm down, Katie, you've seen Miles shirtless plenty of times.

But not like this. Not for a long time. Back then, he wasn't covered in tattoos like stamps on a postcard of his life. I'm dying to ask about them. What they all mean, if they mean anything at all. When he got them. If he has any others. It seems like every time I see him, I notice a new one. Like the small sparrow on his shoulder blade I'm staring way too intently at right now.

"What the fuck are you doing, Autry?" I fold my arms over my chest.

He halts immediately, mallet raised up in the air. Our gazes lock as he looks over his shoulder at me. His expression goes from startled, to confused, to warm and I almost melt into the broken floor on the spot.

"What do you mean?" He turns around, setting the mallet gently on the already crushed floorboards.

I gesture to the gaping hole in the floor in front of him. "I mean what are you doing here on a Saturday crushing my floor to bits?" He laughs, brushing off his hands. He's still only wearing jeans, boots and a baseball cap turned backwards on his head. "And put a shirt on, would you?"

"Why," he smirks, "Is this bothering you?"

I roll my eyes as he grabs a red t-shirt from the countertop, shaking out sawdust from the material before he pulls it over his head. Air fills my lungs with relief now that I can focus.

"I'm here on a Saturday," he starts, walking over to the doorway I'm standing in, "because I told you I'd fix your floor and I have a cattle ranch to run on the weekdays. The floorboards are more rotted than I thought they were, so I figured I'd have to demo this part of the floor. That's a whole-day job."

"And *I* told *you* that you didn't have to fix the goddamn floor," I counter.

"The goddamn floor needs fixing, Mac. If you want to help, grab a crowbar and start pulling."

He turns around, grabbing the mallet again. Help? I guess I could help him. I'm wearing construction clothes anyway, since I was heading over here to paint baseboards in the first place.

"Fine, I'll demo the floors with you. Just please, keep your clothes on this time."

"I won't make any promises," he smiles, handing me some earplugs and safety glasses. The yellow-tinted ones we keep around for the crew.

It takes most of the day to knock out all of the brittle, rotting floorboards in the kitchen. Miles was right, they are in bad shape. We get into a good rhythm– me pulling up the nails and Miles knocking them out. Whoever built this floor in the first place did it well, some of the boards are pretty stubborn.

The very last ones are the hardest. They're tucked underneath the cabinets just enough we can't use Miles's big mallet to knock them out of place.

"Hang on," he says, running back to his tool box. When he returns, there's a smaller rubber mallet in his hands, bright orange and filled with some sort of bead that sounds a little like a rain stick when it moves.

"Hold onto the board here, and I'll tap it up from the other end," he says.

I nod, taking a hold of the wood board with my gloved hands. Miles carefully taps on the underside of the board. It lifts up a bit more each time he hits it.

"It's working!" I say. The board comes loose with a small thud against the cabinet above it.

We gather the tools, brush most of the dirt and sawdust off ourselves, then collapse on the porch swing cushions. My chest heaves, sweat plastering my hair to my shoulders and neck.

"I don't think I've worked that hard on a demo in years," I say.

Miles laughs with a nod. He's not nearly as tired as I am. All that ranch work sure comes in handy I suppose.

"I'll grab us some drinks," he offers, standing up. "What do you want?"

"Water is fine."

My phone buzzes with a notification in my pocket. I groan, moving to the side just enough to pluck it out. The screen lights up with a news notification, pulling another groan from my chest.

This can't be good.

I have notifications on for any time either of my parents' names are mentioned, as well as MacPherson Enterprises. Usually it's a press release of some sort for the company, but this time my mother's name stares back at me in a headline.

Florence MacPherson Announces New Project in Wyoming

I skim through the article enough to get the gist. She's been interviewed by a local paper about *her* new project *she* has worked so hard on. They ask her about the construction, her plans for the area, and how she came up with the idea to expand to Jackson Hole.

Her answers drip with entitlement and power. Each one carefully crafted by her team. My name isn't mentioned once.

"There wasn't any ice, but it's probably cold enough from the fridge– hey, what's wrong?" Miles returns with two of the mason jars we have been using at the cabin filled with water. His brows furrow with concern as he searches my face.

I force a smile and take the glass from his outstretched hand. "Nothing, just work stuff. It's not a big deal."

"What is it?" He asks again, sitting on the porch swing next to me.

"It's just my mom," I say. I pause, taking a long drink of water as he waits for me to continue. "She was interviewed for a newspaper and she basically took credit for this whole renovation, including the idea to come up here to Jackson in the first place."

"You're kidding."

"Nope." A dry, humorless laugh escapes my throat. I trace my fingers over the sparrow design sewn into the cushion of the swing. "It's nothing new, I just have to get used to it."

"That's bullshit." I glance up at Miles, but he's already looking at me with a wild look in his eyes. "You've worked your ass off on this place, and for what? Someone who hasn't stepped foot in it the entire time to take credit for it? No way."

"There's not much I can do about it, it's already done." I sigh, slinking back into the swing.

"You've got to get that article taken down," he says.

"Even if I could do that, she'd just do another interview with a different paper. It's useless. My team knows the work I put in, that's all that matters. It's always been like this with them."

A flicker of something softer lights up his gaze. "Always?"

I nod. "When I was younger, after they sent me away, they'd bring me back once a year for their Christmas party to show off for their friends. All of their rich friends who look for reasons to bring each other down. I'd have to pretend I was off at a boarding school all year, and that I was happy to be back to visit them for the holidays. They'd dress me up in some dress I hated and cart me around the party until I got too tired, or said something sarcastic, then they'd send me away again upstairs where I'd sit and wish I could go back to my Aunt Millie faster."

Miles sighs, raking a hand through his hair under his hat. "That's fucked up."

"Yep," I pop the "p" and take another sip of water. "It only took me three years of that to realize it wasn't going to change.

They weren't happy the first year I didn't show up, but at least I didn't have to hear about it from them in person."

"I can't imagine not wanting to be around my parents for the holidays. That must have been so lonely," he says.

I wave him off, "I had Aunt Millie. And Hazel. It sucked, but I'm better off now. Now when they do this type of thing, I'm less and less upset every time."

"Still..." he mutters under his breath.

"What are the holidays like on a cattle ranch? Snowy, I assume?" I ask.

"Yeah, definitely cold," he chuckles. "My mom goes crazy for Christmas. We cut a Christmas tree from the back acres of the ranch every year for the living room, and she has artificial trees for every other room of the house. It takes about a week to set up. But it's worth it. Ever since my dad had his stroke, winters have been harder. Luckily, we have Parker now as foreman so it's a bit off my back. I try to help her decorate when I can, now that she spends a good amount of time taking care of Walt."

"Have they always loved Christmas?"

Miles smiles as if he can see happy memories playing on a loop in front of us. "Yeah, pretty much. My mom is from Colombia. She moved to the US as a teenager to work for the national park and spent her first winter in Jackson Hole working in a tourist shop that was dedicated to just Christmas. Ornaments, trees, lights, you name it. She must have bought half of the shop."

"Sounds like a fun place, is it still around?" I ask. My knee bumps into his. Somehow we've inched closer without me noticing. The deep brown of his eyes almost sparkles as he catches my gaze on him.

"No, they went out of business years ago. Probably when my mom had too many Christmas decorations to buy any more," he says.

"That's too bad," I shrug. "I was thinking of a year-round Christmas theme for the Old Cabin."

"Shut up, Mac," he nudges my shoulder with a laugh. I can't help but smile back. I love his laugh. On the rare occasion it slips out.

"If you need decorating help this year, let me know. I'll drive up here through the snow if it means Isabella gets what she wants," I say.

"Oh yeah?" Miles raises his eyebrows. Even sitting down, he towers over me as he looks down. An electric charge sparks between us. I wonder if he can feel that too.

"Yeah," is all I can say.

He's the first to break eye contact as he leans back onto the cushion at his back. "Alright, I'll pencil you in for decorating duty."

Red numbers flash in front of my eyes, changing from 5:13 to 5:14. When I started staring at the alarm clock beside my bed, the numbers said 4:27.

Close to an hour of laying here trying to sleep again. Probably more than an hour, but I didn't bother to look at the clock when I first woke up in the middle of the night. Between this and having trouble sleeping in the first place, I've probably gotten three hours of sleep total.

Even then, I was dreaming fitfully. Pine trees on fire all around me. Running through the mountains in Idaho until I tumble into the big lake Juniper Ridge is built on the shores of. Being pulled under by waves as big as they are in the ocean. Waking up gasping for air.

It's time I admit defeat and just get started on my day. Might as well be productive if I'm going to be awake anyway.

Rolling out of bed, I find my footing and walk over to the window facing the dirt road that leads up to the ranch. A blanket of stars paints the night sky, which has just slightly started to light up with the hint of the morning sun. The outline of the mountains behind the ranch set a stark contrast of black against the morning sky.

By the time the door clicks shut as I head out for my morning run to the Old Cabin, the sky is a deep purple, stars disappearing in the morning light. The dirt road is hard against my running shoes. My legs ache already, even though the day hasn't started for me yet. It's going to be a long one.

The ranch is beautiful this morning. Tall grass fields wave gently on either side of the road, a group of cattle feeding a few hundred feet out. The gray mountains jut out of the earth to my left, bright green trees mixing with dark green pines until about halfway up. The smell of morning dew on the wind, birds singing their songs as Wyoming wakes up.

I breathe a sigh of relief as I walk up the driveway to the cabin. I'm the only one here. For now. My heart rate kicks up as I imagine Miles walking through the front door. For once, I'm not dreading his arrival. I'm looking forward to it.

For the first time in a long time, I have a full on crush. I debated texting him last night so many times I had to charge my phone in the bathroom so I couldn't reach it. I Google'd the guy, for God's sake. He's living in his own little corner of my brain every second of the day.

I'm not being careful enough with him. I let myself get way too wrapped up in that field. Miles is so not a possibility for me. No long term relationship is. And that's exactly what he is.

Long term.

Miles Autry isn't a guy I can be with once and leave. It didn't work out well the last time, and I refuse to make that mistake again. He's boyfriend material. The one thing I can't handle.

Not to mention, he's not exactly interested in me either. I represent everything he hates. I'm loud, I'm flighty, I work for a big corporate empire that bought part of his family ranch.

I've got to get a grip. I breathe in and out until all of the air has left my lungs before stepping up the last of the porch steps.

The wood cabin door creaks as I open it and step inside. I flick on the lights and a warm glow fills the entryway. My boots click against the wood floors as I walk back to the temporary desk and set up my laptop for the day.

I open up a scheduling spreadsheet and stare at the screen for five minutes. My mind wanders in every possible direction except work. I open my phone only to grimace at a text from my mother, reminding me on no uncertain terms they'll *be checking in with my supervisor on my progress at the cabin.*

I roll my eyes, exiting out of the message thread. More work has gotten done at this cabin in the short amount of time I've been up here than any other property I've worked on. But, none of that matters to them. None of it will ever be good enough.

If I didn't love this job so much, I would probably cut them off for good. I don't think either of them would have a big problem with that, either. It's not like my mother checks in on my personal life.

The sky outside of the large windows on the back of the cabin turns from a deep purple to hot pink. It's a perfect view of the sunrise from where I'm sitting, as if this spot in the house was built specifically to watch the sun come up.

My head whips to the side as a creaking sound rings out from the great room.

"Hello?" I call out. No response.

I walk into the hallway as quietly as I can, towards the sound. Silence rings in my ears. As soon as I get to the great room, an ember floating out of the unlit fireplace catches my eye. I follow it with my gaze, watching as it glides across the room, landing on the floor in the opposite corner.

Swallowing my unease, I pad over to the spot the ember landed. In its place, the corner of a photograph pokes out of the floorboards, as if it was trying to wedge its way out of the floor on its own.

I kneel down, unable to contain my curiosity, squinting at the small photograph until I can see it better. It's a photograph of a young couple standing in front of the fireplace, looking into each other's eyes.

The paper is old and wrinkled, as if it's been sitting here for years. It could be a photo of anyone. I reach out to pull the tiny paper out all the way to get a better look.

The instant my fingertips touch the photo, I'm pulled through a grey, wispy haze until I'm sitting in the same spot in a very different looking cabin. A worn leather sofa sits next to me, covered in throw blankets. Tables sit comfortably in the room with books stacked on top and loose papers.

The shape of the living room is the same. It's like someone completely rearranged the living room in the Old Cabin and added some furniture. The only thing that remains the same is the fireplace.

Voices cut through the air as a man and woman enter the room talking and laughing. I can hear them, but it's almost as if I'm underwater. As if I'm in a memory, not quite as clear as the original moment.

The woman turns towards the fireplace, her raven hair shining in the sunlight. The man trails behind her, beaming as if she's the sun.

It's the couple from the photo.

But, that's not the only reason they look familiar. I just can't quite put my finger on it. They stop in front of the fireplace as the man takes the woman's hands in his. Although I can't hear his words, his lips say "I love you."

Right when he says the words, the fireplace jumps to life. A fire burns so brightly, it's almost like someone flipped a switch. Wood crackles and sparks fly upwards into the chimney. The couple doesn't seem to notice, caught up in each other.

The woman jumps up, wrapping her arms around the man's neck. I study the man's face as he lifts her off of the ground. I know him. I just can't place it.

Before I can look any longer, the hazy, grey fog surrounds me again. The cabin melts away into nothing, before reappearing exactly how I left it this morning. Empty, dark, dusty.

The photograph in my hand has changed. Gone is the couple standing by the fireplace, the exact scene I just witnessed. In its place is a picture of the Autry family from years ago, standing next to the Old Cabin.

Walter wears a tan cowboy hat and blue button up, looking like the picture of health in his youth. His hair is light colored and a lot longer than it is now, poking out the sides of his hat. Isabella looks similar to how she does today, long black hair and a comforting smile.

It's Miles who looks drastically different. I'd guess he's about 8 years old in this photo. A toothy grin spreads across his face as his parents hold onto each of his arms like he's their pride and joy. A ratty old baseball cap sits on his head, his brown eyes just as dark as they are today.

The corners of my mouth lift as I stare at little Miles. He looks so... happy. Like he did the day I met him. Carefree and full of wonder.

The cabin looks much better in the photograph than it did when I got here, but it still isn't what it had to have been when it was new. Seeing it like this, with the Autry's standing outside, sets a dagger into my heart.

I feel a twinge of sadness for Miles. Until I saw this, I didn't really understand why he'd be so upset about MacPherson purchasing the cabin and land. Of course he's upset. He grew up here.

He has good memories at this place. Probably lots of memories with his dad.

It was just another business deal to me. Another vacation rental to fix up for tourists to enjoy. But for him, it's a piece of his home. I can't blame him for being angry.

I don't know what it's like to have a family like his. Close. Loving. But if I did, I'm sure I'd be the same way if we lost something important to a corporation. Even if they did decide to sell of their own free will, obviously Walter and Isabella didn't tell Miles about it.

If his dad is as sick as it seems from talking to Miles, it may feel like things are being torn away from him one piece at a time.

I remember when my entire life was torn away from me in an instant, dropping me in Juniper Ridge where I didn't know anyone. I couldn't pack all of my things, had no way to stay in contact with any of my old friends. Not even my parents visited me for a good long while. I wouldn't wish that upon anyone.

Standing up, I brush my jeans off and take another look at the photograph. Now that I think about it, Walter and Isabella look a lot like the couple I saw by the fireplace. Take off a few years of age from this family photo and...

Holy shit. That was them.

That was Walter and Isabella before they were married, in this exact cabin.

I look around for the glowing ember that flew around the room, but it's nowhere to be found. The fireplace is cold and perfectly clean, no evidence of a fire being lit in the hearth.

What is going on in this place? First the postcard, now this photo. It can't be a coincidence.

I take the photo over to my folio and tuck it in next to the postcard I found before. I'll take these over to Walter when I go up to the house next. And, maybe I'll ask him about the photograph I saw before this one.

Chapter 18

Inside of an Oven

B Y THE TIME FRIDAY afternoon rolls around I'm ready to be done for the week. It's been a busy week without the crew here to absorb some of the work, and I'm desperate to stay on the timeline.

I shut my laptop so hard it makes Miles jump from where he's sitting on the floor in the kitchen. We've spent the entire week working in the same room and not one of us has died yet. In fact, we've become sort of... friends.

A true miracle.

In fact, it's been kind of nice. I'm a pretty social person, so I wasn't exactly loving working all by myself in the cabin while the crew is gone. And even though he's a man of few words, Miles has listened to my chatter and stories without complaining. He's even talked back. I've found myself leaning back in my folding chair laughing more than once.

I'm pretty sure he could recite my high school experience in Juniper Ridge from memory, and rattle off all of the names of Hazel's horses. He told me a bit about the ranch, too.

For instance, his dad snuck him on a horse years before his mom said it was okay for him to be riding. When she finally let him 'try it out,' he was so comfortable in the saddle she immediately knew he'd been riding a while already.

Then, there was the time he and Parker snuck a couple of girls over to the cabin in their early twenties and the biggest raccoon to ever exist scared them so badly, he didn't come back to the cabin for over a year. The girls never agreed to go out with them again either.

Everytime Miles talks about his childhood on the ranch, I feel a little pang of sadness in my chest. It must have been so nice to grow up here with such caring parents. I can really tell he loves them by the way he talks about them. There's no loneliness in his memories, no question if he was loved by them.

He doesn't talk about after high school, and the years up until I met him. But I can only imagine it's more of the same joy he had before then. If I could pick anywhere to grow up, it'd be this magical little mountain ranch in Wyoming, with its acres of glowing fields at sunset and warm, close-knit people.

"I'm headed out for the day," I call out to Miles, slinging my bag onto my shoulder. Miles stands up from where he's been working.

I look up at him once I've collected all of my things, and for a split second, his shoulders drop. My instincts tell me to drop everything and stay here to talk to him longer.

I've been spending way too much time not hating Miles Autry.

"Okay. I'm probably going to be gone soon here too. See you next week."

Miles turns his attention back to the floor, prying up another dusty floorboard. His forearms flex as he pushes on the prybar, sending a spark through me. A memory clouds my vision. Miles's strong arms pulling me through the door of my hotel room, both of us already breathless.

I've got to get out of here.

I had big plans to go straight back home to my guest cabin and curl up with a good book, a cup of coffee and some snacks. All of that is put on the back burner now, as I walk my way back to the Old Cabin.

I left my phone at my desk when I packed up. I'm not attached to it, but I can't exactly leave it in the cabin for the night. If something ever happened to Aunt Millie and she needed to get ahold of me, I'd never forgive myself for not answering the call.

I take my key out of my back pocket, opening the front door and making a beeline straight for the desk. Sure enough, there's my phone sitting right on top. No notifications, thank goodness.

I take a sigh of relief, soaking in that nothing bad has happened in the time I didn't have my phone. It has always been hard for me to fully disconnect. Probably something to do with waiting for my parents to call me. Not that they ever did.

When I turn to leave, a spark of light catches my eye by the front door. Great. I'm seeing things again. What is with this cabin? I swear, it has a mind of its own.

A warm breeze throws my messy curls back over my shoulder as I walk towards the front door. Like usual, there's nothing there. Although, the temperature of the cabin is a lot higher over by the door where the spark of light was.

I can't deal with this right now. I'm tired from work, and all I want to do tonight is relax. Take my mind off of renovations. And mysterious indoor breezes in a cabin I'm pretty sure is haunted.

I wonder what Codie is doing tonight. We are halfway through the renovations, after all. I should have the girls over for a little party to celebrate. There are beers in the fridge, and we could order takeout. It might be fun.

Pulling out my phone, I shoot off a text to Codie and the girls in our hiking group text thread. Within five minutes, I've got confirmations from Codie, Erin and Morgan. Nicole is out of town visiting family.

I clap my hands together, turning back around to face the cabin. I'm pretty sure there are some blankets in the cabinet we can put out on the floor. I can play a movie for us on my laptop, or we can just hang out. A smile spreads across my face.

Yep, this is exactly what I need.

An hour later, Erin and Morgan are here and we are all sitting on the blankets two beers in. Well, the girls and Hunter, Erin's boyfriend. He's quiet, letting us all chat and do our thing. Codie texted us she's running late.

"It looks amazing, Katie, really. The fireplace is gorgeous," Erin looks around the cabin.

"Thanks, but I can't take credit for that. It was already here," I shrug.

"Really? I could have sworn it was brand new. It looks like it's never been used," Morgan says, her brown eyes growing wide.

"I thought the same thing when I saw it, but I asked Parker and he said they for sure have used it many times." I tuck a strand of hair behind my ear. "But the rest of the house is pretty new with everything we have done. I'm excited to see the final result."

"Speaking of Parker—" Morgan starts with a smirk.

"Oh my god, you shouldn't have mentioned him, she's obsessed with Parker Bailey," Erin laughs.

"What can I say, he's super hot!" Morgan exclaims, arms flailing.

Erin rolls her eyes and laughs. "She's been saying that about him for years. I swear, he could be an ax murderer for all she knows, but she's smitten anyway."

"You're so lucky you see him all the time, Katie," Morgan says.

I've missed nights like this. Hanging out with friends, not doing anything at all but having fun. As much as I'd like to be productive every second of the day, I need this.

A bead of sweat collects on my forehead. "Is it getting hot in here or is it just me?" I ask. I swear it's at least eighty degrees in this cabin. The air conditioning was installed a few weeks ago, I wonder if it broke or something.

"I think it's just you," Morgan giggles, taking another sip of beer.

I pad over to the thermostat to check it out just in case, but it says sixty-eight degrees. Perfectly cool. Why am I sweating if the air conditioning is on?

I walk back to the living room through the dark, narrow hallway, but as soon as I take a step, I'm dizzy. As clear as day, a memory flashes in my mind of the night I met Miles. So vivid I could reach out and touch it, if I weren't so afraid it'd vanish into dust.

Miles pulls me along the sidewalk of the busy street in downtown Salt Lake City. It's dark out, but when I look up at the sky expecting thousands of stars like back home, I'm disappointed. Another reason I could never live in the city. The sound of car horns, sirens and people laughing surround us. The skyscrapers spin before my eyes as I look straight up at them, still tipsy from the whiskey sours we shared at the bar.

"One more block, Mac," Miles says, his low voice rumbling all the way to my gut. I detect the smallest slur in his words.

I look down, right into his chocolate brown eyes. "You're so handsome."

He chuckles, pulling me closer as we walk towards my hotel. I couldn't care less where we are. I just want to be near him. Soaking in his energy, staring at his smile, feeling his arms wrap around me.

His hand grips mine as we walk, and I find myself fixated on it. We fit together so perfectly, it's almost like it's meant to be.

No, we can't be meant to be. I don't do meant-to-be. I need to get a grip on myself. I like him way too much. This isn't good.

But, as soon as he looks back at me, wavy hair falling in his face, five o'clock shadow just starting to show, joy sparking in his eyes like a burning flame, I know I'm a goner.

The memory clears, and I'm left standing in the hallway again. I mentally tally the amount of beers I've had so far. Three, I think. Am I so exhausted I'm starting to have hallucinations? Did I eat something bad?

My worries are interrupted the second the doorbell rings. Closing the rest of the distance in the hallway, I open the door to a smiling Codie and Parker on the other side. Parker is wearing a long sleeve plaid shirt, even though it's approximately eight hundred degrees outside.

"Sorry I'm late! I stopped by the store to grab some snacks and drinks. Look who I found in town on my way over here," Codie says with a grin the size of Texas, nodding towards Parker. "Not sure what you have, but I brought Tequila." She shakes a bottle of Tequila in his hand, with two shot glasses balancing on the top.

"Well in that case, come on in," I reply, stepping out of their way. "Guys, Codie brought us shots!"

A few hollers come from the living room as Codie walks in, Parker trailing behind her laughing. I'm sure Morgan will be thrilled. I could use something stronger too. Something to get Miles off my mind for the rest of the night. I deserve one night without thinking about him and his stupidly frustrating effect on me.

Since we are halfway through renovating this cabin, there aren't any glasses anywhere, so we drink shots out of our empty beer cans while we play a card game I don't know the name of. It involves a lot of fast movements to grab cards, which none of us are in the state to do right now. It's the most fun I've had in a long time.

"Were you waiting for me? You guys clearly were not drunk enough when I got here," Codie winks.

"You fixed us," I slur. A bead of sweat falls down my face. I'm burning up in here. It feels like a sauna. "You guys really aren't too hot? I feel so hot right now. It feels like I'm inside of an oven. And ovens are notoriously hot."

"No, but if you want we can open some windows," Erin offers with a shrug.

"Yeah. Yeah maybe we can get a breeze in here," I nod. This sounds like a great plan. I am on board with this plan.

Parker and Hunter stand from our picnic blanket on the floor to open the windows in the living room. A cool draft blows in, which helps a tiny bit, but not enough. I reach down and touch my skin. It's pretty red. White marks stay for a few seconds after my fingertips leave my skin.

"Are you okay, Katie?" Codie says, putting her hand on my forehead. "You're burning up. Do you have a fever?"

"No, I don't think so. I feel fine. It's just so hot in here." I take the hair tie I always keep in my front pocket up, twisting my hair into a high ponytail on top of my head.

"Here, drink some of my water. You could be dehydrated," Erin offers.

That must be it. Erin is a genius. I take a few swigs of the water and wait for it to kick in. I'm not sure if that's something water does, but I'm willing to try.

"I'm going to go splash some cold water on my face." I stand up, a little wobbly, and head to the bathroom.

The cold water feels great. I dry off my face and stare at my reflection for a couple of minutes, trying to cool myself down. So far it's working. Until my vision goes fuzzy again, and I'm right back in Salt Lake City.

Miles stares back at me from the opposite end of the elevator, going up to the twenty-first floor of my hotel. We told each other we were coming back here because it was too loud at the bar. We wanted to talk. To watch a movie. To eat the snacks I've stockpiled in my room for this trip. But we both know what's going to happen the second we get alone.

His eyes travel up my body, leaving shivers in their wake. How is it possible he can elicit such a reaction from me without even touching me? I want to reach out and grab him but I can't move from where I stand, leaning up against the cold steel wall.

Miles moves towards me slowly. I brace myself for his touch, to be wrapped up in his arms again. I'm a flame burning with a bright glow every time he touches me. My skin feels hot, like I could combust at any second.

My breath catches as he reaches out to touch my cheeks. But right before he can, the elevator dings, startling us both. Miles stops dead in his tracks before looking at the floor. I grab his hand before he can second guess anything and pull him through the door into the dimly lit hotel hallway.

The sound of loud laughter pulls me out of the memory. I may have been cooling down before, but remembering the night we met hasn't helped at all. If anything, I'm redder than before. I splash water in my face once more for good measure, towel it off, and head back to the living room.

I thought this would take my mind off of Miles. I thought I could have one fun night without being reminded of the amazing night we had four years ago. Without being reminded that we aren't like that now. Miles has changed. So have I, but not as much as him.

I miss his smile, his laugh, his casual affection. I had him for such a short time. Just a few hours. But he stuck with me all these years. I left the next morning in a panic because I *knew* I was in trouble.

That I liked him way too much.

He's dangerous. The way he makes me feel is dangerous. But at least I always remembered him the way he was that night. Happy. Now, I know he's not. I've seen his sadness, his anger, mostly directed at me. Even worse, I've seen his struggle watching his dad slowly get sicker and sicker.

Now that I know those sides of him, I'm more likely to wander too close to the fire and get burned.

I sit back down on the blanket with my new friends as they argue about who won the last round of their card game. I'm not as drunk as I could be. Between that memory and the water, I've sobered up a bit. Enough to feel a gnawing feeling in my gut, pulling me to Miles like a magnet. And he's not even here.

"Codie, give me that bottle," I say, reaching for the Tequila. One more shot will do it. I've only had a few anyway, it's not like I've never gotten drunk off Tequila before. I'll pay in the morning, but if it gets my mind off of Miles, so be it.

I take a swig right from the bottle, eliciting a few cheers from my friends. Codie shoves a lime into my mouth as a chaser, the sourness burning my lips.

As they turn back to their card game, as if some magical force is laughing at me for trying to keep the memories away, I fall into another daydream.

I fumble with the key card to my room as Miles stands so close behind me I can feel the heat radiating off of him. The door finally clicks open, but before I can finish stepping inside to reach for the light switch, he's turning me around by my shoulders, lips crashing into mine.

Yes.

It's all I can think, over and over again. Yes.

His hands travel through my hair and I arch into his touch. I'm vaguely aware of Miles closing the door behind us and spinning us around. Cold metal once again digging into my back. Then, it's my turn to explore him with my hands. I play with the hem of his shirt as he lets a muffled groan out into my neck.

It's the invitation I need to rip his shirt off completely. Even in the dark, I can see his eyes boring into mine, so much heat in his gaze I can practically see flames. Then, he's kissing me again and I'm dissolving into his touch.

Right, right, right, *my brain says on repeat. It feels so right. Miles is right for me. I don't know him very well, but my soul is reaching out for him like we've known each other for years.*

I've got to get out of here. Get some air. Anything to keep these memories from playing on a constant reel in my head. Stumbling a little, I make my way down the hallway.

My hand freezes on the door knob as I catch something out of the corner of my eye. There, on the railing heading upstairs, is another brand. Etched deep into the wood in black, as if it's been there all along. Even though I know for a fact it hasn't, because I just finished sanding that exact banister.

Pine trees wrap around the banister, all different heights and shades. They're drawn so intricately that I can see the needles even from a few steps away.

A bead of sweat trails down my temple. I must still be seeing things.

Miles's weight settles on my hips, his knees nudging mine apart. A shiver races through me as he runs the back of his hand along my cheek. Those warm brown eyes bore deep into mine, not just looking at me, but seeing me.

"Are you sure about this?" His hand moves to my chin, tipping it up so our lips almost touch. His warm breath skates across my

cheek. He dips down and presses a soft kiss to the corner of my mouth.

"I'm sure," I nod. My hands roam of their own accord, tracing the indents in his back. I reach down, pulling his hips into mine until there's no space between us.

He groans into my mouth as his tongue pushes past my lips. I let him in, deepening our kiss until we are a tangle of teeth and tongues. I can't tell where I end and Miles begins. There's no softness anymore, only urgency and need.

His hand slides down my body, leaving goosebumps in its wake. He stops just shy of where I want him, dipping just slightly under the waistband of my panties. A frustrated growl erupts from my throat as he draws little teasing circles on my skin.

"Miles," I plead. Burning hunger rushes through me like a flame, bursting from my core.

He chuckles, shaking his head. "So impatient. I'm getting there, Mac."

Flipping him onto his back, I reach down and fumble with his belt until it comes loose. As soon as I wrangle his jeans off his hips, I cup him through his boxers giving him just enough pressure to make him groan.

"So impatient," I tease back at him with a grin. He smiles onto my lips.

My breath hitches as his arms wrap around my waist, flipping me onto my back again.

Miles peppers soft kisses down my neck, making his way down my stomach. Breath is hot against my skin. A molten hot ache fills my core. I reach for his shoulders, trying to get enough of a grip to pull him back up to me.

"Miles, please. I want you."

His gaze meets mine, eyes dark and steely. "I want to take my time with you, Katie. Memorize every curve, every freckle, every fucking inch of you. You're perfect."

I blink away the memories, flinging the door open. Wholly unprepared for what I see when I open the door. All of those old feelings come flooding back to me so intensely I falter, almost falling down on the floor. The only thing holding me up is sheer will. I'm pulling on the door knob so hard I'm sure it'll break off.

Black hair falling over his forehead. Eyes burning with a flame I can't explain. One strong arm lifted as if he was about to knock. The only difference is the beard and the scowl on his face.

Miles.

A Group Gathering with Shots

Brushing away a stray piece of auburn hair that fell straight onto my face when I opened the door, I try my very hardest to collect myself. Although, it's not working very well so far. The alcohol is causing my vision to sway and I feel like I'm standing on the surface of the sun. Maybe if I focus really hard, I won't look like I feel.

Miles looks a little disheveled too. I step back and take him in. Sexy gray sweatpants cling to his hips, shoved awkwardly into a pair of dusty cowboy boots. It's an effort not to look at his ass. He looks like he threw on the closest wrinkled black t-shirt he could find. His hair is mussed, like he rolled out of bed and ran his hands through it a couple of times.

His lips are moving and I realize I haven't been listening at all. "What?" I say, squinting at him as if it'll help me think better.

"Jesus Christ," he sighs, rubbing his temple with his hands. "I said, are you okay? I saw a big flash of light coming from the cabin, so I came running over here as fast as I could. I thought someone was breaking in and setting it on fire or something."

Flash of light? "I'm not sure what you saw, but we are all fine here," I say, suddenly remembering there are other people here. Other people like his best friend. Maybe he won't notice?

"*We?*" Busted.

"Yeah, I'm halfway done with the construction thingies so I invited my brand new friends over to celebrate so that's what we are doing. And you can't be mad at me because it's my cabin. I bought it. It's not yours." I hear my words slurring but I can't stop them from tumbling out of my mouth.

"Who's at the door?" Parker yells from the living room. I ignore him, keeping my eyes on Miles and a tight smile on my lips.

"Oh yeah, and Codie found Parker on the streets and brought him too. They brought Tequila and card games," I say.

Miles's face falls as he looks down at the ground. For a second there, he almost looks sad. But as soon as his gaze lifts back to mine, there's only anger there.

"Mac, are you drunk?" He asks.

"No."

"Yes, you are."

"No, I'm not."

"I can tell that you are."

"Are *you* drunk, Autry?"

"No I'm not–" Miles sighs, hands on his hips. "Nevermind. I was just coming over to make sure no one was setting the cabin on fire. I'll let you get back to your little drinking party with Parker."

That's all it takes to set me off. "Excuse me? It's not a party, I'm not eighteen years old. And it's not just with Parker, he just came later on because one of my friends has a crush on him, not me by the way. I told you it was with my friends, but Erin brought her boyfriend so now there's five of us. Five people isn't a party, it's a group gathering. With shots."

I know I'm not making any sense, but now I'm too pissed off to care. Who does this guy think he is, waltzing over to my fun night to crash it and judge me?

"Fine, I'll let you get back to your group gathering with shots. My mistake," Miles's tone hardens with each word. What reason does he have to be mad at me?

"Yeah, it is your mistake. You can't just come over here and ruin my night with your judgment and your ass-hugging sweatpants. The whole point of this was so I didn't have to think about you any more and now you're here, in real life. Cowboys aren't even my type. It's not fair."

Oh crap, did I say that outloud? Maybe he didn't hear me.

"What?" Miles freezes with his arms crossed. He definitely heard.

"Nothing. I didn't say anything," I deadpan.

Miles and I face off in the doorway, neither of us uttering a word. But it feels like an entire conversation passes between our gazes. I can feel the heat radiating off of him. Or maybe it's coming from me.

I've always been pulled to him like a magnet. A moth to the flame. I can feel it as I stand here right in front of him. A pull so strong I have to physically resist taking him in my arms. It's a bad idea. We have a history, and even though it's been better lately, I know he's not my biggest fan.

There are some other reasons too, but I'm having a hard time remembering them right now.

"You know, I remember when you were all smiley and kind and funny. What happened to that Miles?" I take another step closer to him until we are almost touching.

"That was a long time ago." Butterflies flutter in my stomach at the low rasp of his voice.

"Not that long ago," I counter. I reach up and run my fingers through his hair, unable to hold back any longer. I'm not sober enough to stop myself around him.

Miles sighs and leans just slightly into my touch. "Katie…" he starts, closing his eyes.

"Yeah?" I breathe. He doesn't respond. Words fall out of my mouth like a firehose, filling the heavy silence.

"You're just so tiring. I just want you to like me back. We could be really good friends, or we could be friends that kiss a little. I think I'd prefer that. You're a really good kisser. The best probably. But you're always mad at me, and it's not fair." The alcohol rushes straight to my head as I lean onto him, wrapping my arms around his neck. "Don't you want to kiss me?"

His fingertips brush against the waistband of my jean shorts at my hips so lightly I barely feel it, causing goosebumps to pop up all over me. His eyes look so different close up. Lighter, almost. I can pick out a few gold specks I could never see from afar.

His expression wholly darkens as he looks at me. Having his full attention on me is intimidating, but I love it. It's like a drug. His gaze drops to my lips, and I instinctively brush my tongue across my bottom lip. He tracks the movement, throat bobbing as his eyes dart back up to mine.

I'm sure my entire face is flushed. It doesn't take much. But I can't find it in me to be embarrassed about it. I want him to know how he makes me feel.

"You're drunk," he whispers. The heat in his gaze diminishes, like a coal turning to ash. "You should go back inside."

"I don't want to go back inside. I'm fine right here," I say, taking another step closer so we are chest to chest. My skin ignites at the contact, but now that he's here the heat isn't uncomfortable. It's addicting.

"I'm not having this conversation with you when you've been drinking tequila like it's water. You need to sober up."

The air leaves my lungs. His scolding tone is like a bucket of ice water dumped all over me. I step back, creating as much distance between us as I can. This was a mistake. I never should have opened the door in the first place. He doesn't want me.

"Don't tell me what I *need* to do, Miles. I work hard, I deserve to have fun every once in a while. *You're* the one who crashed this anyway. If you don't want to be here, just go," I snap.

"Katie, wait, that's not what I–" Miles starts, but it's too late, I'm already back inside the cabin with a hand on the door.

"Just stop, okay? I get it," I interrupt.

"Katie, who's at the door?" Morgan hollers from the living room.

"It's Miles," I holler back. "Don't worry, he was just leaving, he doesn't want to hang around. He hates me." The words feel poisonous as they roll off my lips, but I don't take them back. Miles rears back a step as if I've hit him.

"Miles, hey man," Parker shows up at my side, leaning into the door frame. "Want us to deal you in?" He nods towards the living room.

"No, Mac is right. I was just leaving," Miles says, voice rough. He never takes his eyes off of mine, not even a sideways glance at Parker. He turns around and walks back down the driveway, leaving me standing at the door frozen in place.

I watch until he's back in his truck, tail lights disappearing into the black night.

Chapter 20

Laying on a Ranch Alone

"I**T'S LOOKING AMAZING, KATIE.** I mean it. You've really been able to breathe life back into this cabin. Never thought I'd see the day." Walter stands next to me in front of the fireplace in the Old Cabin. He stopped by today on his way into town to see the progress after I let him know we are about halfway done.

"Thanks, Walter," I smile. "It means a lot to me that you approve. I know how special this place is."

"You have no idea," he chuckles.

I still feel bad for canceling on Walter yesterday for Sunday dinner, but between my hangover and whatever happened with Miles I wasn't in the mood to get out of bed at all. Much less spend a couple of hours over at the Autry family ranch house pretending like everything is okay.

I still haven't seen Miles since that night. I'm avoiding him, and I'm sure he's avoiding me right back. The Tequila fog was fuzzy at first, but once I sat in my guest cabin and recapped the night to myself, I could have crawled into any hole on the ranch where no one could ever find me.

Even the pine tree drawing I saw branded into the banister wasn't there the next day.

It's hard to tell what parts of it I exaggerated to myself due to the booze and the crazy overheating and flashbacks I was having all night. When he showed up, I thought maybe he was ready to give in to whatever is between us. I'm sick of fighting it. But instead, I drunkenly climbed all over him and he rejected me.

So embarrassing.

And, because I made a complete and total fool of myself, I'm avoiding him for the time being. Which has been pretty easy to do since he hasn't been to the cabin yet. This week is the Fourth of July, so I'm sure he's busy with other things or maybe taking some much needed time off. Maybe I should take some time off. Clear my head.

"Oh Walter, that reminds me," I say, grabbing my bag from the floor. "I found this the other day, and I think it's yours. It was lodged in one of the floorboards by the fireplace."

I fish out the photograph I found of the Autry family when Miles was a kid. I've been meaning to give this to Walter, but it keeps slipping my mind. He takes the photograph from me, eyes sparkling as he gets a good look at it.

"Oh yes, this was quite a while ago," he chuckles, smiling down at the image. "Miles was still a little guy. And I was a spring chicken. This brings back great memories."

"Did you spend a lot of time out here? I noticed the cabin in the background. It looks like it's in great shape in that photo," I ask, my curiosity getting the best of me.

"Yes, we loved taking Miles on horseback rides out here when he was a boy. And he always loved the place. Until a bit ago, I suppose. It's a special place for Isabella and I too. When she came up to Wyoming for the first time to work in the national park, she had arranged with my mother to stay with us for the summer. I'm not sure how they got in contact, something like an exchange student situation I believe. We lived in the cabin back then. As soon as I laid eyes on her that summer, I couldn't stay away."

"That's so sweet."

"She was something, I'll tell you that," he laughs. "She sure didn't make it easy on me. It was all meant to be in the end, nothing either of us could do about it. But this cabin had a lot to do with it. Isabella used to say there's some sort of old magic in the very bones of this place. It'll lead you where you need to go, whether you want it or not."

His words rattle around in my brain as I soak them in. I'm not one to believe in anything like that, but I also wouldn't ever discount it just in case it is true. Not to mention, I've thought before that this cabin has a mind of its own.

"Anyway, I'm glad someone like you came along to bring it back to life. As much as I'd like to keep it forever, it was time to pass it along to continue its adventures with someone else." Walter pockets the photo, stepping towards the front door. "I'll get out of your hair. Thanks for letting me come check up on the place."

"Anytime," I smile, walking him out the door. A pang of jealousy echoes in my chest knowing that Miles gets to have Walter as a father. He's such a good man, cares so much about his family and everyone else he knows. He's only known me for two months, yet in that time he's been kinder to me than my own parents ever have. I've never felt so welcome in a place.

"I hope we'll see you next Sunday for dinner," he calls out as he walks back to his old rusty pickup truck in the driveway.

"I'll be there. I just wasn't feeling very good yesterday." Technically true.

"Yeah, it seems Miles wasn't feeling good either. Maybe you had the same bug," he says with a wink. My cheeks heat as guilt settles in my gut like a rock.

I wave goodbye as Walter pulls out of the driveway and heads back up to the ranch house. The sun is just about to reach its golden hour. I've been at the cabin far longer than I should have today, but time gets away from you when you're reliving one single night over and over again in your head.

I can't remember the last time I was that drunk. Never, probably. And of course, it had to happen around Miles of all people.

Sighing for the hundredth time today, I turn around and collect my things before walking back up the dirt road towards the guest cabin. I don't have it in me to run today, and I'm in no hurry to get anywhere.

The sky is a wild array of pinks, reds, oranges and yellows when I finally get back home. I set my things inside then go back out to the small front lawn and lay out on the grass staring up at the sky.

There's not a more beautiful place in the world to be laying on a ranch alone.

Chapter 21

Fire

THE FOURTH OF JULY on a ranch in Wyoming is just different. Even back in Idaho, where I thought we had pretty fun celebrations, it was never this much. All of Jackson Hole is transformed for the week.

I went all the way into town yesterday morning to get a coffee drink that's mostly milk and sugar because I've missed it, and was unprepared for the level of festivity this town has.

American flags everywhere, red white and blue ribbons hanging from the shops, fireworks painted in every color on wooden signs. And tourists. So many tourists. Codie assured me it's like this every holiday, for said tourists. Either way, I'm soaking it all up.

Parker texted me about the fireworks show the ranch hands put on up at the barn every year. I spent the morning of Fourth of July in Jackson Hole with Codie and Morgan at the parade, catching candy thrown from the rodeo horses like we were kids. We even walked to The Dust Jacket afterwards and picked out a new book for each other.

It's been a perfect day.

My boots hit the gravel of the road leading to the barn as the sun is just starting to dip behind the tall, gray peaks. I decided to lean into the festivities with a navy blue tank top sundress, my brown cowgirl boots with the white flowers embroidered all up and down the sides, and red and white ribbons tying up my two braids cascading down my shoulders.

I make my way over to the group of Lone Pine Ranch cowboys, all suspiciously standing over a big wooden crate. There are a couple of other girls here, girlfriends of the ranch hands I assume, Parker, Reed and the others. But Miles is nowhere to be seen. Yet.

"I told y'all, it'll be fine. I promise. I got the extra long flares this time, and Miles cleared the tall grass last week. We've got about a dozen hoses ready at a moment's notice, and I already wet down the grass all day with the big rotating sprinkler. Safety first," Parker is saying as I join the group.

"Alright, I just don't want to get in trouble with the boss man again is all I'm saying," a cowboy I don't recognize says, his brows furrowed with concern. I peer over the edge of the crate and immediately understand the sentiment. Parker has ordered some of the biggest fireworks I've ever seen in my life.

Parker laughs, closing the lid of the crate. "Miles isn't that scary, trust me. He just acts like it so you'll think he's always watching."

"I *am* always watching." A familiar low voice rumbles through my bones as he walks up from behind Parker. His eyes flit over to me for a second, lingering just long enough to cause heat to rise up to my cheeks.

"There you are, buddy. Great timing. I was just telling the fellas here they have nothing to worry about. Everything's super safe this year. Right, guys?" Parker looks expectantly at the group of cowboys, his megawatt smile shining on his face.

There's a chorus of grumbled yeses from the guys. Miles and Parker share a look that I'm sure communicates a thousand words before Miles reaches up and scratches his beard. He's trimmed it again, shorter each time. It's no more than a bit of scruff now.

"Alright, Reed, Wes, you go with Parker to take the crate out to the field. There are markers where it's safe to set the fireworks off from. Please pay attention to those. Everyone else, you know what to do," Miles instructs before heading back into the barn.

Parker, Reed and the concerned cowboy from earlier who I assume is Wes tie up the crate to two horses waiting in the corral next to us. I catch up to the rest of the group, walking towards the back of the big red barn.

"Hey Katie, glad you could make it," Raife drawls. I met him on Branding Night, one of the many ranch hands at Lone Pine. He's one of the younger cowboys at the ranch, just barely twenty-one. I remember thinking he's probably quite the lady killer with his tan skin, bright blue eyes and dark brown curls.

"I had to see this for myself. I heard it's been quite a dramatic event the past few years," I chuckle.

"Yeah, you could say that." Raife's hands slip into his pockets as we approach the back patio of the barn. The two girls that were out front before are stringing lights across posts covering the patio, while the rest of the cowboys move over some tables from inside the barn. "Miles wasn't super excited about trying it again this year, but Parker can be pretty convincing. I guess we'll see how it goes."

Wow, I guess all of the guys are a little worried. I'd be worried too if Miles was my boss.

"Miles doesn't seem like a big fireworks guy," I laugh.

"Actually, Parker tells us stories all the time about how when they were younger, it was Miles's idea to do fireworks on the ranch. Apparently he used to plan out an elaborate show each year all by himself, and piss off Walt in the process," Raife says.

"I can't imagine that, he's so serious now." But I can imagine it. I've seen it with my own eyes, four years ago. That fun, spontaneous side of Miles that doesn't come out any more.

Someone calls Raife's name from inside the barn. He flashes me a swoon worthy smile then heads inside to help the guys setup.

I look around, taking in the view from behind the barn. The barn is on a tall grass hill overlooking a big section of the ranch. I can see almost where Ember Meadow is from here, already glowing from the rays of the setting sun.

The Grand Tetons in the distance tower over the ranch, creating a feeling of protection. Almost like nothing can harm this beautiful place with the watchful eye of the jagged, gray peaks. The smell of sage fills my lungs in the light summer breeze.

My gaze travels across the ranch, past a small group of cattle, nothing more than a few black dots in a golden field. I can see the guest cabin, just a bit further into the field from the main road. Behind it, the Old Cabin, so far it's almost to the horizon.

Is that a light on in the Old Cabin? I squint, trying to make it out from here. There's definitely a light on upstairs.

Shit.

I must have left it on when I stopped by last night to grab some papers from my desk. That means it's been on all day long.

"Hey Raife," I call out. "I'll be right back, I left one of the lights on at the Old Cabin."

"Alright, we'll save you a sparkler," he says from the patio behind me.

Walking back to my car, I glance one more time into the barn windows. Still no Miles. I was hoping to clear the air with him a bit since we haven't talked since I threw myself at him the other night in a drunken haze. Maybe I'll catch him later.

I throw the car in drive and head back down the dirt road to the Old Cabin. I almost trip running out of the car once I pull up to the front porch. I'll just be quick. In and out. Then back up to the ranch. It's already starting to get darker outside, and I don't want to miss the fireworks.

My heart rate picks up as I make my way upstairs to the room I saw the light on in. But when I get there, it's dark. No lights on at all, not even a lamp. The window is open, however.

How odd. I never open the upstairs windows. I'm never up here to use them in the first place. I wonder if maybe someone did the other night when I had my friends over. Or maybe it's been open since the crew was working up here.

I rush over to the old wooden window frame and shut it carefully, double checking the room for any lights on before I head back downstairs. A familiar black brand is burned into the wooden window sill, one I've seen multiple times around the house but still haven't gotten used to. This time, it's a much more intricate design.

In the corner of the window sill, a rectangle shape of swirls and lines makes up a sort of tribal looking symbol. Every other brand I've seen on the cabin has been western-themed, but this one is completely different. The design is etched into the wood darker than the others, as if it's new. Maybe it'll stick around longer.

This cabin is freaky. I *swear* I saw a light on from the cabin, and now another symbol stamped into the wood. I just wish I could find some sort of pattern, a reason these things keep happening.

I shrug, heading back down the spiral staircase. At least I checked, I suppose. No harm in making sure the lights are off.

Locking the front door behind me, I turn towards the road when I hear the familiar sound of hoofbeats. I can just make out the silhouette of a man riding towards the cabin driveway.

As the horse gets closer, I can make out the unmistakable backwards baseball cap, the broad shoulders, the sparks igniting in my heart every time he's around.

Miles is riding towards the cabin on horseback.

Why is Miles here? And why does he ride a horse everywhere he goes? I know he lives on a ranch, but does the man ever just drive anywhere?

He dismounts Claro easily, throwing the reins around the fence post without even looking. His eyes remain on me the entire time. It's intimidating enough it shouldn't be hot, but somehow it is.

"What are you doing here?" I blurt out. He stalks towards me, stopping just a few steps shy of where I stand on the wide oak porch. Now that he's closer, I can see the fire in his deep brown eyes in the blue glow of the twilight.

He adjusts his cowboy hat as he walks towards me, giving me a flash of his hair poking out of the back. His gaze meets mine again as he stops a few feet away and I already feel light-headed under the weight of his full attention. Unable to hold his gaze, my eyes fall down to where his t shirt sleeves tighten against his tanned biceps. The butterflies instantly return.

Oh my god, is there nowhere I can look without sending myself into a spiral?

"I saw you leave, and I wanted to make sure you weren't going to miss the fireworks. The guys almost have them ready to go. Are you okay? Is something wrong?" His concern surprises me. I thought he'd want nothing to do with me after the other night. He certainly didn't then.

"I'm fine. I thought I saw a light on in the cabin, but it turns out it was nothing. My eyes playing tricks on me or something. I was just heading back up to the barn," I say.

His chest sags with a sigh of relief, his hands propped up on his hips. Miles's usual conversation stance. It's almost as if he has to brace himself to interact with anyone. "Okay, good. You left in such a hurry I thought maybe something was wrong."

"No, I'm good," I assure him, fidgeting with the hem of my dress.

"Good. That's good."

"Okay well–" I start.

"I just wanted to–" he says at the same time.

An awkward, dry laugh bubbles up my throat. "You go," I gesture for him to continue.

"Alright. I just wanted to talk about the other night..." He says, trailing off. A spark of something flits across his face. Shyness? It can't be.

"Look, I'm sorry if I made you uncomfortable. I wasn't really thinking straight," I rush out. The last thing I need is another rejection from Miles. The other night was more than enough. I'd rather give him an easy out and just skip this conversation altogether.

A boom rattles the air from behind us, then a flash of red light. The fireworks have started. Hopefully the guys have enough so we don't miss the entire show. It sure looked like they did in that crate.

The red light illuminates the right side of his face, casting him in a slight glow. Dark stubble already coats his jaw. My fingers itch with the need to reach out and touch it.

"Yeah you were pretty drunk. I didn't realize you were still such a party girl," Miles says. I grimace at his harsh words.

Boom. Boom. More fireworks go off in flashes of blue and green.

"What's that supposed to mean? *Still?* You don't know what kind of person I am, Autry. Just because we hooked up one night four years ago doesn't mean you get to judge me," I snap. Red rushes to my cheeks as the anger spills over.

Boom.

This man has a power over my emotions I desperately wish he didn't have. I shouldn't care what he thinks of me. It doesn't matter if he thinks I'm some party girl. But for some reason, it hurts more than it should. I'm used to people thinking that of me. I like to have fun, I'm pretty spontaneous, I go on a lot of dates.

But I'm not dumb. I work hard, and I'm good at my job. I'm a great friend. I'm sick of having to defend myself to people in my life, especially my own family, when I want to let loose and have fun every once in a while.

It seems like no matter how much work I do, how many nights I stay in reading a book or starting a new project, people only remember all of the other stuff. I'll forever be a one night stand type of girl to Miles, and he will always think that's a bad thing.

"I'm not judging you, that's not what I meant–" he starts in a fluster, his dark eyes wild.

Boom.

"I don't care what you meant. I get that you hate me, okay? You've made that abundantly clear. No one is forcing you to be around me. I'll be out of your hair soon enough, you're not obligated to be around me. I thought we could be friends, but clearly I was wrong. That'll never happen." My hands are shaking with either anger, embarrassment, disappointment or a mix of all three.

Boom. Boom. Boom. Miles's face lights up red and orange in the light of the fireworks.

I shouldn't be this worked up, but he really hurt me the other night. Even if I was a little out of my mind. The last thing I need is Miles coming over here and making me feel worse than I already do.

"Stop saying I hate you, Katie," Miles yells, catching me off guard. I jump a few inches in the air. "Shit, I'm sorry. I didn't mean to yell. I just– I can't stand when you say that." He moves closer to me, closing the distance between us. My heart rate speeds up at his close proximity, my hands itching to reach out and grab him. I hold them crossed to my chest as tight as I can.

Miles stares at me for what feels like an eternity, but is probably only thirty seconds, and shakes his head. "God, you're so infuriating," he says softly. I can barely hear him over the sound of the fireworks.

"Excuse me?" My hand comes up over my chest as I step back. He follows immediately, as if pulled by an invisible force. His jaw hardens as he holds my gaze, crowding over me. I lean into him slightly, pulled by that same force.

"Oh, don't act like you don't know what you do to me," he grumbles. "You make it your goal to push my limits. You have to know you are *constantly* in my head. No matter what I do, or where I am, you're like a tapeworm in my brain or something. It's *infuriating.* Right when I get you out of my head, you show back up here to torture my mind again saying I hate you. As if I could ever hate you. And then, I get around you and I say the wrong things, and it's not what I mean. It's like my brain doesn't function properly or something."

My chest rises and falls, my breathing picking up speed. I'm torn between hating him for everything he just said and taunting him some more to see if he'll push me up against the wall at my back. I can't remember the last time I was this turned on. Brimming with red-hot need.

Maybe four years ago, in a bar in Utah.

Stupid, stupid, stupid.

"Did you just compare me to a tapeworm?" I say dryly. "So much for becoming friends."

Boom. Boom. Bright, purple light covers the ranch.

"I don't want to be your friend," he growls.

"Great. Thanks for saying that. I didn't really need confirmation, but what's another hit while I'm down, I guess," I start to step around him, eager to get to my car and get out of here before I start to cry. "I don't really feel like watching fireworks tonight, I'm going back to my cabin–"

"Katie, stop." Miles grabs my arm as I try to squeeze around him. His hand is warm on my skin, sending shivers up my spine. Where I expect to see anger and annoyance on his face, there's something softer.

His eyes dart down to my lips and linger there, sending a warm feeling straight to my gut. It's so hard to stay mad at him when he looks at me like that. Like he wants me as much as I want him. A low sound comes from the back of his throat, like he's physically restraining himself from me.

"What do you want, Miles?" I watch as the final thread of his control snaps.

"What do I want?" He laughs, but there's no humor in his eyes. "What I want is to be able to control myself when I'm around you." He sighs, resting his forehead on mine. My eyes fall shut. "I would light the world on fire just to keep you warm, Katie. And, I'm not sure what to do with that."

Before I can even begin to process his admission, Miles leans in, crashing his lips into mine.

For a split second, I'm so surprised I don't know what to do. He looks just as shocked as I am, his brown eyes wide as he realizes what he just did. He starts to pull away from me, but I grab his shirt in my fist, pulling him back in to me.

I'm not letting him go this time.

He kisses me back, his tongue sweeping past my lips, setting off sparks. The fireworks behind us go off every couple of seconds lighting up the sky. He groans over the loud booms as he wraps his arms around my waist, pulling me in. Rough calluses brush through my thin dress, scraping along my hip bones.

He tastes like longing and cedar wood and *mine.*

He's not my anything, I remind myself. I'm losing my mind.

I feel something hard at my back as he pushes me backward. The cabin. It's freeing, being under his control. Letting him tower over me, pin me against the wall, his weight pushing up against me. For once, I'm not in charge of anything.

And I love it.

My palms press against his chest, finally set free to touch him. It feels like all summer has been leading to this. Every memory of four years ago, every heated glance, every argument. We fit together so well. Fighting it feels wrong, but this feels so right. His hips push up against mine, setting off an involuntary hum from my throat.

Sparks ignite in my heart, just like the fireworks going off all around us. Saying Miles is the best kisser I've ever had is an under exaggeration. I forgot how mind-blowing kissing him is. His lips claim mine like he knows me. Like we've been doing this forever. We melt into each other as I frantically grab at his collar, like I can't get close enough to him.

We are explosive.

My hands find his beard scruff as he kisses my jaw, then my neck, then right below my ear. I'm burning up, my entire body warming at his touch. The air feels twenty degrees warmer than when we started talking. I feel like a living flame.

Fire.

The word repeats on a loop in my head as his lips return to mine, claiming me in a rough kiss.

Fire.

Fire.

Fire?

Fire!

My eyes fly open at a bright light coming from the field Parker is lighting the fireworks off from. It takes me a second to register what I'm looking at, my heart still in a haze from the Miles effect.

"Fire," I choke out, pulling away.

"What?" he grumbles, scrambling to not let me go.

"Miles. Fire!" I step out of his arms, pointing towards the field. He spins around, hair mussed and lips swollen. All I want is to tackle him to the ground. My chest heaves as I try to catch my breath.

"Fuck," he spits out, straightening out his black t-shirt and running a hand through his hair. He starts down the porch steps, then abruptly turns back to me, grabbing my wrist.

He pulls me in for another hurried kiss before whispering in my ear, "Do not think this is finished."

I'm only able to nod as he runs over to Claro, swinging a leg up, and riding back to the barn as fast as he can. Leaving me on the porch burning up brighter than the flame in the field.

Chapter 22

Brick By Brick

"**O**H, KATE, I'M SO sorry," Hazel says over the phone. I swear she sounds like she's on the verge of tears for me.

"There's no reason to be sorry. It's just how it is. I'm used to this," I say, matter-of-factly.

"It doesn't have to be," she counters.

I sigh, not wanting to argue with my best friend about my love life. Or lack of love life, I should say.

It's been three days since Miles and I kissed, and I haven't heard from him at all. No calls, no visits to the cabin to work on the floors, not a single glimpse of him and Claro riding around the ranch.

Radio silence.

Do not think this is finished.

Yeah, right. So much for Miles being different. It turns out that this time, I'm the fool still attached to him after the best kiss of my entire life, and he's the one acting like nothing ever happened.

I spent the next day at the cabin after the insanity that was the fireworks show pacing the floor, waiting for him to walk in.

Wondering what I would say to him. Trying to figure out if I should even talk at all, or just kiss him again.

It's all I crave now that I've reminded myself what it's like to be wrapped up in Miles. And apparently, it was a huge mistake. Because he never showed up.

"It doesn't matter, Hazel. He clearly does not want to talk to me. He could call, text, come by, send a carrier pigeon. But he hasn't. I got way too attached, and now it's biting me in the ass. This is why I don't date long-term. It's just setting myself up to be hurt." I twist a section of my hair in my fingers.

"I just really thought he was different," Hazel says, her voice quiet.

"Me too," I manage to choke out. Nope, I'm not crying over a man. Not even this one. "I'm just upset because I really thought we were getting somewhere. I don't expect him to drop everything and spend every waking second with me, but I thought we were getting sort of close."

This is exactly why I don't do relationships. Every time I get involved with someone, I get hurt. Even my own parents couldn't stand to be around me. It's better when I just don't get attached in the first place.

"Listen, I've got to go. Walter and Isabella are expecting me for dinner," I cut Hazel off before she can say anything else. If I don't, she'll say something sweet that'll make me cry and I don't have time for that right now.

Autry family dinners have become a rock for me while I've been here. After more than two months of weekly dinners, I've come to look forward to them. It feels weird missing one. And, if I'm being honest, I'm hoping I'll see Miles there and he'll be forced to talk to me.

Him saying anything at this point would be better than the silent treatment I've gotten all week. I know it's counterproductive to want to see him when I'm trying to move on and forget that he ever happened to me. But, I can't help the tiny spark of hope I feel when I think of seeing him at dinner.

The possibility of seeing Miles is definitely not why I pick a brand new red ruffled dress out of my closet before heading up to the ranch house. I've just been wanting to wear it. It just happens to be short enough to accentuate my legs, with long, sheer sleeves that make me feel like I could take on the world.

Of course I have to wear the matching heels I brought with me just in case I decided to go to a nice restaurant during my time here. This type of dress isn't meant for my cowgirl boots.

I throw half of my barrel curls up into an updo, the others cascading over my shoulders as I check myself in the mirror one last time.

If Miles isn't at dinner tonight, he'll be missing out.

Miles isn't at dinner tonight.

It's a good thing I was going to wear this outfit anyway. Parker is here, however. He whistled at me when I walked in the door, followed by a very loud *damn, girl, you look hot.* So I guess it wasn't a total wash.

This time, instead of being kicked out of the kitchen right as I cross the threshold, I ask Isabella if I can help. "I'm not taking no for an answer. I haven't done hardly any cooking since I got to Wyoming, and I miss it."

Isabella smiles, her eyes crinkling at the sides. "If you insist, I suppose there's nothing I can do to stop you. Rinse the beans, then we'll put everything into the pot to cook."

I nod and reach for the pot of beans on the stove. "What are you making tonight?"

"Bandeja Paisa. Have you had it before?"

"No," I shake my head. "What is it?"

Isabella starts to dice what I think is a plantain. It looks slightly like a banana, but different enough I know it's not. I think I've seen them at the store, but I've never tried one.

"Bandeja Paisa is the National dish of Colombia. I ate it so often there that when I moved to the US, I couldn't stomach it for a few years. But when we had Miles, I wanted more of my culture to be a part of his life. So now, I make it once a month. He used to complain as a kid, but now he likes it. Or at least, he tells me he likes it and that's all that matters," she laughs, shrugging as she reaches for another plantain.

"I wish he were like that around me," I chuckle. "He's definitely not afraid to tell me when I'm bothering him."

Isabella stops chopping, turning towards me. I meant it as a joke, but she's not laughing. The smile falls from my face.

"That's because he's himself around you, Katie. I've seen it plenty of times. Walter is the same. Miles doesn't want to disappoint me. He wants me to be helpful, not cause any problems to me, especially since his father had a stroke. He thinks I do not see it, but I do. I see him hide all of his feelings behind a smile for me. I see him working too much when he tells me he's resting." She takes my hand in hers, and only then do I realize it's shaking. "And, I see how he is around you. He's real. He doesn't hide anything to save your feelings. I'm so glad he finally has let someone in. What Miles has been through already, it's too much to shoulder alone."

Isabella smiles so brightly at me, I feel my heart crack. "Thank you, Isabella. I hope you're right."

"I'm always right. Now you shred the carrots, then you leave my kitchen. You're a guest, not a chef here," she swats me away from the pressure cooker all of the ingredients have been dumped into so far.

After dinner, Parker and I sit out on the deck watching the sun fall behind the mountains, casting a beautiful orange glow over the entire valley. I swirl the wine in my glass absentmindedly as I take in the view. I'm really going to miss the beauty of this place.

"I can't believe you guys get to see this view every single day. I thought Idaho mountains were pretty, but this is another level," I say to Parker in the chair next to mine.

"You could stay, you know. Then you can see this every day. Move into the bunkhouse with us, I'm sure we can find some room somewhere," he jokes, eyes lighting up in the sunset.

"Yeah, I'm sure Miles would love that. Me hanging around every day to annoy him. I think I've done enough emotional damage to him by renovating that cabin." I laugh, but there's a sad tilt to it. Hopefully Parker isn't paying too much attention.

"Nah, Miles likes you. I can tell. I think the only problem he'd have is you living in the bunkhouse with all of us rowdy cowboys," he winks at me, taking a sip of water.

"Yeah, right," I scoff.

Parker doesn't push it though, just laughs and turns back to the sunset as it finally disappears behind the mountain.

I can see why Parker is so popular with the ladies around here. He's got a natural flirtation going on pretty much all the time. He's probably the easiest person on this ranch to talk to. It's no wonder Miles is always with him, he's social enough for the both of them.

The sad part is in the time I've been up here, I haven't just gotten attached to Miles. I'm attached to everyone on this ranch. Parker, Walter and Isabella, Codie and her girl group. It was all so easy to fall into. I'm just not sure how I'm going to leave it all behind without looking back.

Usually, when I do jobs like this, I talk to my crew and occasionally some guy at a bar for a little while. There aren't any feelings involved. There definitely aren't friend group hikes, weekly family dinners that show me what I missed growing up, and conversations with friends out on a deck while the sun sets. And there definitely isn't Miles Autry.

My heart sinks when I think of leaving this place. I've gotten way too used to life here. Way too comfortable. I'm already in too deep for this not to hurt at all. The best I can do from here on out is to slowly build back up my walls that have mysteriously disappeared.

Brick by brick. Until the hurt is so far behind them I can pretend it's not there.

Why Not?

THE POINTED TOE OF my pink cowgirl boot taps against the hardwood of the Alpine Rose in time with the beat of an old country song. I plaster a smile I hope looks real onto my face as Codie makes her way through the shoulder-to-shoulder crowd to the tall table I'm standing next to.

It's a miracle we even got in tonight. If we'd been ten minutes later, we would be stuck in the line that is now starting to snake around the block past the coffee shop next door. Despite there being a whole town to explore, it seems I've been stuck to this block during my time here. There's a bar, a coffee shop, and a bookstore all within feet of each other.

What else does a girl need?

"Damn, this place is hopping tonight," Codie says on a laugh. She sets down a beer for her and a whiskey sour for me onto the table. Clinking our glasses together in a quick 'cheers,' we turn to survey the crowd.

"Especially for a Tuesday night," I nod. A whiff of honey catches my nose, putting another smile on my face. This time for real.

I didn't want to go out tonight. But when Codie offered to pick me up from the ranch, I couldn't exactly say no. It's not like I have any excuses not to. But now that I'm here, I'm glad I came.

I've gotten comfortable in this place, as much as I don't want to admit it. It feels homey. I've fallen into a routine with work, morning runs, the coffee maker in my cabin, texting Codie about the books we're reading. Even this little cowboy bar in town.

"How's your big project coming along? Any new developments since we were there?" Codie asks. Her fringe suede jacket brushes up against the table as she reaches for a toothpick from a little red cowboy boot in the center.

"Just doing the finish work. I should be done with door trim and window sills in the next two weeks, then the crew will be back to help out with the rest. It's starting to look like a B and B." I tuck a strand of hair behind my ear. "I'm not sure what I'm going to do about the floor, though. Miles was working on it, but he hasn't been back all week. I'll have to talk to the crew. It might take some extra time."

Codie's jade eyes sparkle as she takes another swig of her beer. She has always been so easy to talk to, since that first day we met. Something about the way her eyes crinkle at the sides when she smiles makes you feel like you've known her for years. "Well, I'd say I'm sorry, but I'm pretty stoked you'll be trapped with us for a little while longer."

"I'm not mad about it, I really like this place," I laugh.

"What happened with Miles? I thought you guys were getting along pretty well," she asks.

"We were. Or at least, I thought we were. We spent a lot of time together while he was at the cabin fixing the floors. On the Fourth of July, we ended up at the cabin during the fireworks, and we kind of... kissed." I duck my head down, hoping she doesn't see me blush.

"What? You've been holding out on me! You *kissed* Miles Autry? Oh my god! Was it good? I've always thought he's gotta be a good kisser." She nudges me in the arm, eyes wide and a huge grin on her face.

"It was great. That's the problem. I'm not really a stick-around type of gal. I'm getting too attached."

"It must have been some kiss if you're already attached to him, hot damn," Codie laughs.

"Well it wasn't exactly our first kiss," I mutter.

"You kissed him before? When?" Her jaw hangs open.

"Four years ago." I launch into an abridged version of the story of our one night stand. Meeting Miles at the bar in Utah, taking him back to my room, the best sex of my life, leaving in the morning and him never calling. Then, seeing him again at Lone Pine Ranch. Miles immediately hating me, bickering with me over every little thing. How much he's changed over the years.

She listens the entire time, not interrupting except for a few gasps and chuckles. She's just as good a listener as Hazel. My heart squeezes when I think about how much I miss her, how I wish she was here to meet Codie.

"I'm kind of glad he left right after we kissed. He must have realized it was a bad idea. Honestly, it's just what I needed to feel better about leaving. I was getting too attached to him and this place," I lie.

"Yeah, I guess so..." Codie trails off, looking at me like I just kicked a puppy.

"What's that face for?" I ask.

"Well, it's just..." she pauses, her face scrunched in thought. "It just seems like it's meant to be, you know? You find this guy after four years, and you have a chance to fall in love all over again. And he's into you too. I guess I'm just a hopeless romantic."

"My best friend Hazel is a hopeless romantic too," I giggle. "I'm more of a realist. I'm going to have to leave at the end of the summer. He knows that, I know that. There's no reason to get involved in something that can never happen."

"Why?" Codie's eyes go wide in wonder.

"Why, what?"

"Why do you have to leave at the end of the summer?"

"Because I live in Idaho. I can't just move to Wyoming," I say.

"Why not? You said yourself that Idaho doesn't feel like your permanent home. Your only family there moved away, and you can work from home. Plus, it's only like, three hours away," she shrugs. Presenting me with an option to move away like it's not life-changing.

I don't want to admit it, but what she's saying *does* make a lot of sense. After Aunt Millie moved away, there's really not a lot left for me in Juniper Ridge. Hazel is busier now than ever with her family's dude ranch, and I don't really have anyone else. I can visit her whenever I want to, we don't have to be neighbors. We'll always be best friends.

I've been thinking about moving somewhere new. Starting fresh. I'm just not sure where I'd go. It'd have to be somewhere I could still do my job. I'm not willing to let that go. But I always thought it'd be a place MacPherson Enterprises sent me to live in, or somewhere I've always wanted to go.

I'd never move back east near my family. That ship sailed far, far away when they sent me away. I love the west way too much now.

Even so, staying here after one job in Wyoming seems like too much of a leap. I don't even know the first thing about living here. Bed and breakfast laws? I've got those down. The history of Jackson Hole? I could write a book. What to do for tourists in every season? I can give a hundred suggestions based on my research. But staying? Living in Wyoming? It seems too far-fetched.

"I can't move here," I laugh.

"I think you can," she sing-songs. "And I know a cowboy that could keep you company."

"Stop it," I laugh, nudging her shoulder. "Cowboys aren't my type. Besides, I'm not a relationship girl. Never will be."

"I'm just saying, I think it's worth a shot. What do you have to lose?"

My dignity if it doesn't work out here. My confidence in moving anywhere else. Juniper Ridge, the only place I've ever felt even a little bit comfortable.

Miles presents a whole other set of problems. He can never be more than a crush. We had our one night together. It can never be more than that. I'm not built for relationships. Not with my upbringing. We'd both get hurt, and my living here would only make that infinitely more complicated.

"Either way, I don't think you should let Miles push you away. From what I've observed, he's the type to retreat. I think you should go for it. The worst that could happen is you go back to being grumpy towards each other again," Codie raises her eyebrows at me, driving her point home.

"I don't have any extra time to invest in figuring out the jig-saw puzzle that is Miles Autry," I scoff. I lift the cold glass to my lips, tossing back the rest of my drink before taking Codie's hand and pulling her towards the dartboards in the back corner of the bar. The light is lower back here, glowing orange from an old stained glass pendant light that's probably older than I am. "Come on, I want to kick your ass in darts."

"Good luck," she laughs.

Chapter 24

Summer Storms

THE BUZZ FROM MY one drink tonight has worn off halfway through our second game of darts. But after my drunken performance at the cabin, I'm sticking to one drink only. I gulp down a glass of ice water while Codie's dart flies right to the number nine on the board, exactly the number she was aiming for.

"I'm on eight," she cheers, turning towards me with a mocking smile. "What are you still shooting for, twelve?" I won our first round of Around The World, but just barely. This time we are counting down from twenty, and it's not going as well for me.

"Might I remind you, I did *win* our last round. So technically, I'm just defending my title as the current darts champion," I tease.

"What are we playing ladies," a low, flirtatious voice drawls from behind Codie and I. Strong arms wrap around each of our shoulders, as I turn to see Parker's jean jacket pushed up against me.

"Oh shit, the party's here," I holler snaking my arm around his side giving him a squeeze before pulling away. "You can join our game if you want, but you'll be a bit behind."

"I'll hop on the next round if it's alright with y'all." Parker flashes a grin our way, sitting at the stool I've been leaning against in between turns. "Codie," he nods, tipping his hat to her.

"Always a pleasure to see you, Parker," she laughs.

"Did you know Codie once knocked books out of my hands at the bookstore like a bully from a really bad teen movie?" Parker winks at Codie from behind his drink.

"Oh, shut up, you're making it sound like it was my fault," Codie scoffs. She turns towards me and crosses her arms. "What he neglects to mention is the gigantic wolf spider crawling around on his books I saved him from. Yes, they were knocked down in the process, but it could have been much worse had I not intervened."

Parker laughs, "Oh right, there was that little detail. All I knew is my books were knocked right onto the ground by Codie Raisanan, of all people. Prom queen of western Wyoming."

I gasp, "You were prom queen?"

Codie waves me off, throwing her last dart at the board. It lands perfectly even though she's barely looking. "It was one year. It's not exactly impressive when your high school class is 80 people."

"Well, I'm impressed," I say.

At this rate, Codie is going to win this round any second now and Parker will be joining us sooner than we thought. If I wasn't so competitive I might not care, but I really am bummed I'm not dominating in darts right now. That's the best part of going to the one bar in town back in Juniper Ridge with Hazel and Wade. I always win.

"What brings you in here tonight, Parker?" I ask, turning back to the dartboard to take another shot at the number twelve. Another miss. This time, my dart bounces off the wall next to the board, which is thankfully already covered in holes from similar shots.

"Just early to meet some of the guys from the ranch for a drink. Miles has been gone all week so I'm in charge of the hooligans we call cowboys. You don't happen to know where he is, do you?"

I swallow, trying not to read into the fact that not even his best friend knows where he is. "No, I haven't heard from him either."

Parker must not notice my shaky voice. He chuckles, "I hope he's somewhere relaxing for once. The guy deserves a vacation every once in a while, instead of moping around the ranch taking his frustrations out on us. Just because he's divorced doesn't mean he's dead."

My stomach drops the rest of the way to the floor, every bit of my buzz from earlier gone in an instant. "What did you just say?" I whirl back around to see Parker's eyes go wide and panicked at the look on my face, which I'm sure is pure shock.

"I didn't say anything," he says, looking over to Codie for a save.

I follow his glance, over to a very awkward looking Codie. Unless she's the best actress in the entire world, she doesn't seem surprised. Not at all.

"What did he say?" I ask her.

"I'm sorry, Kate, I thought you knew he was married," Parker apologizes, jumping up from his stool and wrapping a hand around my shoulder. But it's too late, I'm already two steps away, my feet feeling like they're going to slip out from under me.

Married.

Miles was married. At least it's past-tense, I guess. How could he not tell me this? This is a huge, important thing. A thing everyone knew but me. Do I know him at all? I thought I did. We shared stories from our childhoods, about our families, I told him about my bad dates, my worst times with my parents.

Now that I think about it, he didn't tell me anything about his adult life after high school. There's about a ten year gap he avoided completely, right up until I met him. I thought he'd just been working at the ranch, spending time with Parker and the ranch hands, dealing with his dad's illness.

But he was married. To a person. His friends knew her. My new friends knew her.

He probably *proposed* to her. Probably stood up in front of their families and recited vows. His parents knew her. She was their daughter-in-law.

"When?" I croak out, surprised I'm still upright. My knees have started to shake despite my efforts to stay steady.

"What?" Codie says from my other side.

I look up into her eyes, now full of worry. I must look like an absolute wreck. "When was he married?"

"I think you should talk to him about it, hon." Codie leads me over to a stool, a hand on my shoulder. "It's not our story to tell. I didn't mean to hide it from you, I just figured he already told you. You've known each other a while now."

"Well, he didn't," I say. Tears cloud my vision. "I'm sorry, I just need to go. I can't be here. I know it's not your fault, thanks for everything." I throw my purse over my shoulder, checking my pockets for my phone.

"Aw, Katie, please don't leave, I'm really sorry. It's none of my business. I shouldn't have said anything." Parker rushes to my side as I walk towards the front of the bar, his voice shaky.

I turn towards him, offering him a watery smile. "It's fine, really. I'm not mad, just a little confused. You didn't do anything wrong. I'll see you soon." I pat his arm, leaving him rooted in his spot. His usual sunny smile turned upside down.

Blood rushes in my ears as I walk to my car outside of the bar as fast as I can. I suppose I never thought I knew everything about Miles. He keeps things pretty close to the vest when it comes to his personal life. It's not like we're together.

But maybe I don't know him at all. First he leaves for days without a word, and now I find out he's been withholding this? It's all too much.

Rain drops sting my face as I walk down the narrow sidewalk of the crowded street. The open sky has changed from a light gray overcast to dark thunderstorm clouds while I've been inside the Alpine Rose. I rush to my car, slamming the door behind me once I'm inside.

A boom of thunder that sounds like it's right above me echoes through the mountain-surrounded valley, startling me at least an inch out of my seat.

The ignition fires up and I don't hesitate to immediately pull out onto the road towards Lone Pine Ranch. The rain has picked up, washing down my windshield and pooling up on the road. People rush into buildings along the streets to find cover.

By the time I make it to the dirt road to the ranch, my mind is no longer on Miles. I'm strictly thinking about survival. The wind has picked up, pine trees swaying violently outside of the blurry windshield.

No matter how high I turn my windshield wipers on, I'm having trouble seeing out of my car at all in this storm. The sky is growing darker. As I come up to the turn off for the Old Cabin, it's gotten so bad I'm not sure I can make it the rest of the way to my guest cabin.

I'll have to wait out the storm at the cabin, probably in my car, then I can drive the rest of the way once this passes. I've never been a big fan of thunderstorms. In Juniper Ridge, a storm disrupts the entire valley. Boats have been tipped over and sunk, buildings and trees regularly hit with lightning. Summer storms are nothing to mess around with in the mountains.

The roar of the rain and blasts of thunder are all I can hear as I pull up to the Old Cabin. I almost don't hit my brakes fast enough to see the pickup truck in front of me, parked in the gravel drive.

Miles is back.

Chapter 25

Am I Okay?

MY HEART SKIPS A beat, sending a rush of excitement through me before I remember I'm mad at him.

Miles kissed me and then ghosted me. Miles was an ass to me when I got here, and for a while after. Miles was *married* and didn't tell me.

The soft glow of light shines through the windows on the front of the house. I debate going in or not. If I go in, I'll be soaked and risk getting hit by lightning or something ridiculous. If I go in, I'll have to see Miles. I'm not sure I'm ready for that.

Movement at the front door catches my eye. Miles is standing in the door frame, looking serious as always in his signature outfit of a black t-shirt and jeans. He yells something that looks like my name and steps towards the porch steps.

The rain soaks his hair and shoulders as he runs out to my car. He shields his eyes from the downpour. He opens my door and I slip out of the car quickly. Icy rain drops sting my skin as Miles puts an arm around me, guiding me to the covered porch. His body shields me from the rain a bit, warming my side.

We run towards the direction of the porch, my boots covered in mud by the time I get there. It's not until I'm up the steps and out of the rain that I look up, right into Miles's golden brown eyes.

About two inches from my face.

"Are you okay?" He says, searching my face. Am I okay? Not when he's looking at me like this.

His black waves fall over his forehead a bit. I'm not used to seeing him without a backwards baseball cap or cowboy hat. I immediately melt inside in his presence, like ice cream on a hot day. We are breathing the same air and it feels a little too intimate for how confused I am about him right now. Too close proximity.

I step back a step, putting some distance between us. Disappointment flickers on his face as he fights the urge to step back towards me. He stays rooted in his spot, shoving his hands into his pockets as if he's restraining himself.

"I'm fine," I start, "I couldn't make it back to my cabin with the rain, so I stopped here until it passes." He nods, sagging with relief. "What are *you* doing here?"

Miles is here, at the cabin at night. With absolutely no reason to be here. In the middle of a thunderstorm.

He pauses for a minute, looking down at his boots. "I was looking for you. When you weren't here, I started on the floors again."

His gaze finds me again. I nod, pressing my lips into a thin line. A flashback of the last time we were on this porch passes through my mind. His lips on mine, my hands bunched up in his shirt. I wish I could go back to that moment. Before he left without a word. Blissfully unaware of anything he was hiding from me.

I wish I could just grab him by the shirt right now and pull him towards me. Feel his short beard brush my cheeks, run my fingers through his hair. It'd be so easy.

I stare down at my feet, hoping he can't somehow read my mind. My hair is plastered to my head. I brush a couple of wet strands off of my face, more dark brown than red in the rain. Miles clears his throat, his eyes darting over to the door, and I feel like I've given myself away.

"Well, I'm here now. What can I do for you?" I ask.

"I was hoping we could talk."

"Now you want to talk to me? Okay, let's start with why I haven't heard from you in a week." I cross my arms, looking at him expectantly. He shifts on his feet a bit.

"I'm sorry for not calling." His gaze fixates on me as he reaches for my hand. The pressure of his fingers on my palm is a calming presence.

I pull my hand out of his grip, not ready to move on from my frustration quite yet. It's bubbling to the surface after brewing deep down all week long. "I thought you were different. For some reason, I thought maybe this time it didn't have to be a physical attraction. I actually *liked* you. Can you believe it? I can't." Miles's eyes widen, his jaw going slack. "But you saved me a lot of time, actually, so I should be thanking you. This was a great reminder why I don't do relationships."

"I know you don't do relationships, Katie. I know that. And I *only* do relationships. That guy you met in Utah? That wasn't me. That's the only one night stand I've ever had in my life, and I hated that I couldn't see you after. It was like a knife twisting in my gut for weeks. So trust me when I say I'm truly sorry for doing the same thing to you." The pain in his eyes is so real, I reel back a bit. His cheeks warm slightly, as if he didn't mean to say that but couldn't hold it in.

"You could have seen me after, I left you my phone number," I say softly.

"No, you didn't. You left me a note, but there was no number on it. I would know, I looked everywhere on that thing and it wasn't there."

Holy shit. This whole time I just thought he didn't call because he didn't want to see me again.

"Oh," I say as he steps closer to me. Always chasing each other absentmindedly like magnets, attracted without thinking about it. If I take a step, he follows. If he takes a step, I crash into him.

"I didn't see you after the Fourth of July because I had to go take care of something. But I'm back now, and I'd really like to see you now," he says, voice so low I can barely hear him over the rain.

"I can't do this." A tear rolls down my cheek, and all I can think is I'm grateful for the rain to blend it in.

"What?" he says, eyes crinkled with confusion.

"I don't really know you, Miles. You don't really know me, either. There's a reason I don't do this. It's too complicated. My entire life is already complicated enough," I breathe.

He crosses his arms, "Of course you know me."

"I didn't know you were married until today."

Miles freezes in his place. He definitely wasn't expecting me to know that. My heart sinks at the confirmation he was hiding it from me.

"Who told you that?" he says, voice rough.

I sigh, "It doesn't matter who told me. *You* didn't. It should have been you. I've told you all about my shitty family, living with my aunt, my dating past for God's sake. And you left out a huge, important detail about yourself. Were you ever going to tell me?"

"Of course I was going to tell you. I just– it's not really something I like to relive," he says carefully. "I haven't talked about it."

"*Ever?*" I ask.

Miles sighs, running a hand down his face. "Look, can we go inside? It's not safe out here. I'll tell you anything you want to know."

I nod as his hand comes instinctively to my lower back to lead me inside the cabin. I'm not sure he even realizes he's doing it. His touch is warm, as always, against my rain-soaked clothes.

We kick our mud-covered boots off outside, and I take off my raincoat once I get in the door. I use the inside as a makeshift towel to ring out my hair a bit. I've never been in a downpour that has instantly soaked me before today, like we were in a movie. Under a hose for dramatic effect. Not even the rain in town was as heavy as it was out by the cabin.

I follow Miles to the fireplace, where a small fire bursts to life. We both jump back slightly at the flames.

"Did you start a fire?" I ask.

Miles turns to me wide-eyed. "No I didn't. Did your crew install a starter or something?"

"No," I reply. "We didn't touch the fireplace. It's the one part of the cabin that didn't need any updating."

I've never seen an actual fire in it before. It's gorgeous, casting a soft glow throughout the entire room. Yellow and orange flames flicker under the chimney, warming the room.

Miles grunts, shaking his head at the fireplace. "This cabin is so weird. I'll see if I can fix that."

He stops at the hearth, sitting on the edge of the rock in front of the fire. I sit on the other side, just a few feet separating us. But it feels like miles.

At first, I'm not sure if he's going to talk at all. He sits with his elbows on his knees, staring at a spot on the floor. A dozen emotions pass through his eyes, although I'm sure he thinks I can't see them. He clears his throat a few times. I'm about to say something just to break the silence when he starts.

"Alex and I met when we were kids. We started dating when we were seventeen years old. My family knew her family. We went to school together. After high school, she stayed in Jackson Hole, and so did I. I thought it was meant to be. We didn't really fight. We argued sometimes, but we were so alike that we got along pretty well most of the time. I proposed to her when we were twenty-one, and we were married by twenty-two. Everyone expected that of us. The whole town knew us as a couple. I thought that was how it was supposed to be. You find someone you can love easily. She was easy to love."

He swallows, looking up into my eyes for the first time since he started speaking. My heart cracks when tears form in his eyes. The gold specs glow in the firelight.

"We were married for four years. Everything was going pretty well. Now that I have spent time looking back and decoding everything, I can see there were signs that we weren't happy. Like I said, we never fought. We didn't care enough to. She was gone a lot, beyond normal things like having friends or work. She'd be gone for weekends at a time and I'd only get a text when she was on her way back.

"I tried so hard. My parents even tried. They gave us this cabin. I don't think you know that. We were going to fix it up together, her and I, and live in it. Start a family. But she was never around, and when she was, there was always something stopping her from wanting to start on it. Then one day, I woke up and she was–" Miles's voice cracks on a word.

I wait, not making a sound, as he takes a deep breath. Afraid that if I say something I'll scare him back into his shell.

"She was gone. She didn't even pack her things. She just left, in the middle of the night, I guess," he laughs dryly. "It all sounds so ridiculous when I say it outloud. I never thought I'd be divorced. But I guess no one does. Anyway, she sent me the divorce papers in the mail six months later and it was final a couple weeks after the year mark of her leaving. I haven't seen her since. I guess I've begun to hate this cabin somewhere along the way. Everything it represented. All of my plans, crushed. Until you came along to bring it back to life."

My heart sinks. "I'm sorry, Miles, I had no idea." I shift towards him enough to be able to put my hand on his knee. Static electricity zaps us at the contact, probably from wearing my socks on the plastic film covering the floors from construction dust.

"I should have told you. I just haven't really told anyone. My parents know, and Parker knows because he was there with me through it all. But we don't really discuss it. I can't stomach the pity looks from anyone who knows she left," he says softly. His gaze shifts to the fire, the flames reflecting in his eyes.

I always thought he had fire in his eyes. But now, I can see it was just pain. No wonder he was mad at me, I left him after one night when he had just been left by his wife. That was probably just about a year after she left, if he was twenty-seven when we met. Right when his divorce was final. My stomach bottoms out at the thought.

"I may not know exactly what you've been through, but I know being left sucks. I'm sorry you never had an explanation," I offer.

"I didn't. Until last week."

Chapter 26

Say Something

HE LOOKS UP AT me, and there's something different in his eyes now, the pain burned away in the fireplace.

Before I can ask, he continues, "That's why I was gone. I went to find her. I had a pretty good idea from the address on the papers, but I wasn't sure she'd still be there. She was."

I suck in a breath, holding it in my lungs. He went to see his ex-wife, who he's probably still in love with. Great. They've gotten back together. He isn't sharing this with me because he wants me to know him, he just wants to let me down easy.

Oh my god, was it because I kissed him? He probably thought it was terrible. Or he missed her so much he couldn't stand to be around me. I'm the reason he went to find her–

"I don't know why I went, now that I look back," Miles's gravelly voice interrupts my thoughts. "After we kissed, I just knew that I needed to close that chapter. I wasn't ready the last time we met, but I want to be ready now. I don't think I can take you leaving again.

"So, I went to see Alex. She lives in southern Colorado now. A man answered her door. Her new husband. I almost lost it, Katie. Seeing her happy was a knife to the gut. Not because I want her back or anything, but because she's happier now than she ever was with me. I couldn't make her smile most days, much less so content that even when her ex-husband shows up at her door out of the blue, she still looks peaceful.

"We talked for a bit and she apologized. There were some things I needed to apologize for too. I think she knows what she did was shitty, but she couldn't figure out how to seek me out and say she was sorry without reopening the wound. Apparently, she met the new husband while we were together. Nothing happened physically, but she liked him enough to wonder if we were really happy. Anyway, I'm not on speaking terms with her or anything, but it was nice to have closure after all these years. I came back with this whole plan of how I was going to come back and take you somewhere special and tell you everything.

"But on my way home, I panicked. If I couldn't make her happy, if she couldn't even try to stay married to me, how can I make anyone happy? Then, I remembered everything you said about how you don't do long-term relationships on that night we met, and how you're just so... free. You're this shining light, flitting from place to place, brightening up the world. And you've been through so much already. I just couldn't add to that. I took way too long getting back to the ranch because I was scared." He runs a hand through his hair, sitting up straight. The fire still flickering to his left.

"Then I got to the ranch house and it was completely silent. And I realized that the only person I wanted to talk to about it was you. But I couldn't, because I didn't let you in enough to know about my failed marriage. So I came out here to find you. I know you're planning on leaving at the end of the summer. I know I messed up. But, Katie, I don't know how I'm supposed to just carry on with my life once you go and pretend like I'm okay."

I can almost hear the sound of my heart cracking.

He's looking at me like his entire life lies in my hands. I suck in a breath of air, trying to ignore the pounding in my chest. I know I'm supposed to be happy about this, but after this terrible week, I can't be.

"Please just say something," he whispers.

"I don't know what to say, Miles. I wish you would have told me all of this a week ago. Or, ideally, before that. I don't know what to do with this now. It's just too little too late." I sigh into my hands, running them across my cheeks and into my hair. "I'm sorry, I'm just feeling a little overwhelmed right now. All week I was convinced you would call me or show up at any time, but you never did. Then I find out you were hiding this huge part of yourself. And now you're asking me to stay."

He doesn't respond, frozen in place like a statue. I look into the fire, trying to find the words to describe the huge black hole that has opened up in my chest.

"I just don't know if I can trust you with my heart, Miles," I whisper.

"You can," he says, voice cracking a bit. I concentrate on the orange glow of the flames.

"I can't go days without hearing from you. That kiss might have been a realization for you, but it was big for me too. I don't do feelings. I don't 'like' guys. I can't remember the last time I've actually wanted to see someone again as much as I wanted to see you. You broke my heart, Miles." A hot tear runs down my cheek. It hits the brick mantle with a small splash, and as if it was a bucket of water, the fire dies on a puff of smoke. I run a hand along his forearm, over his playing card tattoo. The warmth from his arms seeps into my fingertips, urging me to curl up into him as if he were a warm blanket on a rainy day.

"One of my biggest fears is becoming emotionally attached to a guy who's going to realize one day that I'm too much and break my heart. That's why I don't do relationships. It's happened before, and I just... I can't do that with you. I'm already a lot more attached than I should be. It's just not like me, and I can't get hurt by you again."

Miles reaches out, catching a tear rolling down my cheek with his thumb. "Too much? Katie, I can't get *enough* of you. It killed me being away from you this week."

"Yeah, but you did it though. You left, and I was alone. Again."

"Please don't do this, Katie."

It takes all I have to stay where I am even though my heart wants to crash into him and forget all of this ever happened. I wish I could go back to the night we met and live there forever.

Part of me wonders what would have happened if he hadn't left. If he'd come back that night and kissed me again. Would we be in the same place we are right now? Would I even be able to give him the parts of me I've kept closed off for so long?

But he did leave. And he could do it again.

"I think we should just be friends." His chest deflates as soon as the words leave my mouth. "I'm not ready for this. I thought maybe I could be, but it's clear that I'm just not ready for a relationship right now. And maybe you aren't ready either. I'm so glad you finally got closure, but maybe you should just digest it all for a little while. It might not seem like it, but I am so far out of my comfort zone with all of this. Even just talking about it right now is a new thing for me. Whether you meant to or not, you really hurt me. And I'm not ready for that kind of pain."

He nods, his gaze trailing off to the ground. The ache in my chest has gone straight to my stomach. It's silent for what feels like an eternity until Miles stands up. He runs a hand through his rain-soaked hair before finally looking at me.

"I don't want to be your friend, Katie. But if that's what you want, if that's what makes you happy, I'll try." He sighs, crossing his arms across his chest and looking at his boots. I can feel him retreating into himself as if all of the warmth is sucked out of the room. "Can I just ask you a question?"

"Of course," I whisper. He takes my hand in both of his and I pretend I don't feel the electric current.

"Do you feel this too? This thing between us?" His deep brown eyes capture mine as he looks at me with so much hope my heart breaks again. This time into pieces so small I'm not sure I can put them back together.

Do I feel it? The raging fire between us that I can feel even from miles away, over days of distance? The magnetic pull, so hard that even now I want nothing more than to jump into his arms and stay there forever? It started with a spark years ago, but that spark has grown into a flame so large it takes up my entire soul.

"Yes."

He nods, looking back down at his feet as if he's piecing something together in his brain. He drops my hand and my arm falls like deadweight. When he looks back up at me, he's a different Miles altogether. His eyes are hardened, his lips pressed into a thin line.

"I'll see you around then, Mac," he grumbles, pushing past me to the door. I glance out the window long enough to see the rain has stopped, but the dark clouds linger in the sky.

It's not until the familiar rumble of his truck pulling onto the road fills the air that the tears begin to fall.

Chapter 27

Welcome to my Crib

"KATE, YOU SO UNDER-PROMISED and over delivered here. This place is amazing. Why didn't you tell me it's literally surrounded by fields and mountains as far as you can see? I would have visited a lot sooner." My best friend in the entire world looks around the completed cabin like it's Buckingham Palace.

I laugh, breathing my hundredth sigh of relief since Hazel arrived in Wyoming. "I thought it was pretty clear when I told you the cabin is *surrounded on all sides* by the ranch."

"Well, you weren't kidding, I'll give you that." Hazel absent-mindedly twirls her dark brown waves in one hand as she walks down the hallway towards the back of the cabin. "Everything looks just perfect." Her lilac dress swishes as she walks, giving her the illusion of floating, if it weren't for the dirty cowgirl boots poking out the bottom. You can take the girl out of the ranch, but you can't take the ranch out of the girl.

The past two weeks have been a blur of finishing touches on the cabin. With everything that happened with Miles, I've been happy to throw myself into working all day and night anyway. It's definitely a welcome distraction.

Miles must have finished the floors after I left the other night. When I came back the next morning, they were done, cleaned, and all of his tools had disappeared. I suppose it's for the best. I know I'm the one that wants to stay just friends, but I'll admit, it's not going to be easy.

The one and only silver lining of all of this time alone to work is that the cabin is done. Completely finished. Cleaned and decorated and ready for visitors. Codie and I stopped by a flea market in town one day, and I ended up getting quite a few vintage items for the cabin at a bargain. I picked out the larger furniture pieces from a few local stores, which hurt my company credit card quite a bit, but succeeded in helping the place fit into the high end brand MacPherson Enterprises has built.

The living room looks straight out of a western movie. Extra long off-white curtains reach the floor, tied back to let in the natural light. A brand new leather couch made in Wyoming sits in front of the fireplace, atop a brown and white cowhide rug. There are photo frames hanging on the walls and placed on tables with images of the ranch throughout the years courtesy of Walter. He brought those by last week.

The rest of the cabin is similarly decorated, with each room just slightly different. One bedroom focuses on sage green colors, while another has warmer hues. The kitchen was the easiest to put together, since it was already great on its own after installing new warm oak cabinets. I made sure the photographer came at sunset for the perfect glow in the listing photos.

The only detail I just can't quite get right are the flowers in the garden out back. I've been watering them on a regular schedule, but for some reason, these past two weeks they haven't been living their best life. They've all wilted and have lost a lot of their color. The petals on my marigolds are touching the ground. I've tried giving some more water and some less, with no change. I even bought flower food, and added some nutrient-rich soil.

Nothing has worked.

The photographer, luckily, is able to angle them out of most of the shots. I was so proud of my little garden, and now all of a sudden, it's as good as gone.

"Are you ready for tonight?" Hazel smiles, looking out the large windows on the back of the house. For a second I think Miles is out there fixing the fence, but once I blink, he's gone.

I sigh. "I'm ready to be finished with this project."

"I'm sorry it's been so hard lately, Kate. I promise the second we get home I'll take you out for shakes." Hazel's arm wraps around me pulling me into a hug I didn't know I needed.

I told Hazel a short version of what happened between Miles and I. I haven't processed it enough myself to get into it now. Hopefully I'll feel like talking about it when we get back to Idaho.

Tonight, I'm not thinking about it at all. I'm having some of my new friends over for a housewarming party at the cabin. It started small, just Codie and the girls, and Hazel since she's in town helping me with the final details.

Then Codie and Hazel suggested I invite the crew. Then Parker and the ranch hands. Then some of Codie's rodeo friends.

I'm pretty sure they even texted Miles, much to my chagrin.

Hazel squeals as the doorbell rings, a low chime I haven't heard before. I don't even remember this cabin having a doorbell.

"They're here!" she sings, grabbing my hand and pulling me to the front door. As soon as it opens, a real smile bursts out on my face for the first time in weeks.

Codie, Morgan, Erin, and Nicole stand on the porch. "Hey ladies, welcome to my crib," I joke, opening the door further so they can shuffle inside.

"Wow, Katie! This place looks amazing," Codie says, pulling me into a hug.

I introduce Hazel to the girls, and just as I suspected, they hit it off right away. We walk through the cabin on a quick tour, all of them poking their heads into each room and telling me their favorite parts.

"Do you have any openings in November? I know it's close, but my family visits at the beginning of the month and I really think it'd be extra special to stay here. Also, I never want to leave. Like, ever," Morgan says, collapsing onto the oversized leather couch.

"Seeing as I haven't listed it anywhere yet, yes. I have a lot of openings." I'm proud of this place on my own, but seeing other people enjoy it as much as I do really makes me feel accomplished.

"You'd better be booking some dates for yourself, Katie." Codie sits in a chair across from the couch, sloshing a glass of wine from the box they brought over. Giggling friends, boxed wine, a cozy fireplace. There's not much that could make this moment more perfect.

"I'll come visit, but probably not here. I can stay in town while I'm checking up on the cabin." I lean against the couch, plastering a smile on my face. I'd love to come visit and stay here. I stay at the other rentals with Hazel for shits and giggles sometimes.

But this place is different. I didn't do this on my own. Miles was here every step of the way. Fixing things, helping me paint, frustrating the hell out of me, kissing me on the porch. There are too many memories.

The doorbell rings again and Erin gets up to let in whoever else has arrived. I pull myself together, taking a deep breath. Soon, this place will be filled with people wanting to talk about the cabin.

My gaze catches on Hazel across the room. She's already looking at me, with concern in her eyes. I can practically read her thoughts asking me what's wrong. I shoot her another smile and her eyes narrow.

More and more guests arrive, and I'm starting to wonder if all of Jackson Hole is here to see the cabin. Someone put the record player on at some point, the living room filled to the brim with people chatting.

Some of the ranch hands are already chatting up Hazel in the kitchen. I roll my eyes and walk towards the front of the house. I'm not surprised in the slightest, Hazel is drop dead gorgeous. If anyone can handle rowdy cowboys, it's the cowgirl herself.

I make my way to the living room to check up on the supply of wine, beer, and snacks that people brought to share. The hallway is so crowded, I don't even want to know how many people Codie invited. Luckily, no one is straight-up partying or drunk, so the cabin should hopefully stay intact.

A familiar laugh booms throughout the living room over the chorus of voices. I whirl towards the sound, familiar chestnut hair poking up over the crowd next to the fireplace.

Parker.

Pushing my way past shoulders of people I've never met, I hear a group of girls asking each other where the booking link is for this cabin so they can come back. A smile forms on my lips. Codie's plan seems to be working. Convince me to invite a ton of people over and they'll all want to book the cabin for their vacations.

I should probably get this place listed on the vacation rental websites soon.

"Katie!" Parker yells as soon as he can see me.

"Hi, Parker," I smile. He drapes an arm around me when I finally reach him, a cold bottle of beer in the other hand.

"The place looks great. Sure wish I had an excuse to stay here sometime," Parker says.

"I'll miss it, that's for sure," I nod.

"Look, I know you're heading back to Idaho soon, but don't be a stranger. We're all gonna miss you around here. Especially Miles."

I feel him before I see him. A familiar warm breeze sends goosebumps up and down my entire body. There's a prickling feeling on my neck. My eyes dart around the room looking for Miles until a familiar deep voice rumbles on my other side.

"Don't be gettin' all sentimental, Parker. She's not gone yet." Miles's low rasp travels up and down my spine, sending a shiver through me that I'm sure Parker can feel. His arm drops off of my shoulder the second he notices Miles.

Parker laughs. "I'm allowed a little sentimentality, Miles, our girl is leaving for good."

"I live three hours away, don't be so dramatic," I elbow Parker lightly in the ribs.

Parker's short attention span is captured by someone else in his circle. He turns to the side, leaving Miles and I staring awkwardly at each other.

"Hey, Mac." The corners of his lips twitch upward, as if he's resisting a smile.

"Autry," I nod.

"Place looks great."

"We did a good job," I smile.

"*You* did a good job. I just helped fix some things that should have already been done." He takes a drink from a water bottle.

"This place is better than I could have ever imagined, much less done myself. It needed you."

His body heat seeps into mine and I feel myself flush at his words. "Thanks, Miles. That means a lot to me." My voice comes out barely over a whisper, emotion clogging my throat. But he smiles at my words anyway.

"He's right, you know. We're all gonna miss you."

"I know," I nod. I *do* know. I've never felt so accepted by a group of people in my life, besides Hazel and my Aunt Millie. And that includes my own family. "I'll miss everyone too. And this place."

I've never felt like I'm leaving a piece of my heart somewhere like I do now. I get into town, I do my job, and I leave. Hazel is the one that gets attached to people and places, not me. I'm the jokester. The outgoing one. The one that dates around and travels with nothing holding me down.

But would it be so bad to be held down somewhere? Have a place I can call home, with people who love me? I didn't know it was possible until I stepped foot onto Lone Pine Ranch. I hope I can find that again. That feeling of belonging.

I was excited to get back home and away from all of the intense feelings at this place. But now, I'm not so sure. I can't imagine staying in Juniper Ridge anymore. Especially not without having Aunt Millie around. Sure, I want to see Hazel when I can, but we don't need to be right next to each other to be close.

Maybe I'll ask MacPherson for a transfer somewhere. Stop dating all together. Focus on figuring out what I really want in life.

That is, if my parents allow it. It feels so childish to still be under my parents' rule somehow, but they do own the company I work for. If they don't want me to leave Idaho, it'll make it really hard for me to figure out a way to move and keep my job.

I love this job. Even though it's at MacPherson Enterprises, I feel like I make a real difference in the company. I have more creative freedom than I would working for someone else, and I've got a great groove in my role.

Leaving would be tough.

Almost impossible, if I want to still have any sort of relationship with my parents. We may not be best friends right now, but what we have going is still better than no relationship at all.

My relationship with my parents is just another reason I shouldn't be with Miles. I've never been in a committed relationship in my life, and the only examples I have are my dysfunctional parents and my chronically single aunt. Not exactly the best grounds for a stable relationship.

Yes, it's a good thing that everything broke down so quickly between us. It would have happened at some point anyway, better to do it now while it hurts less.

Because if this is how much it hurts before we even gave it a real chance, I can't imagine how much it'd hurt afterwards.

Chapter 28

Quite the View

B Y THE TIME THE sun sets, Hazel, Codie and I have migrated to the front of the wraparound porch, sitting with our legs swinging off the edge. August haze adds an orange hue to the already warm sky. The gray, jagged peaks of the Tetons jut up out of the ground, rays of the setting sun cutting up through the sky around them like a halo.

Everything about the environment surrounding the ranch is all harsh angles and unforgiving terrain. The contrast of the soft alfalfa fields and rolling hills of Lone Pine feel like a hug. A warm blanket in the midst of a cold winter's day.

"So, what's left to do, Kate? When are you heading home?" Hazel asks, taking a sip of her drink.

"I was going to stay until the listing for the cabin is up, but honestly, I'm thinking about just driving home after I drop you at the airport tomorrow." Hazel flew here from an event in Texas she went to for new ideas for her family's dude ranch, so she'll be taking the short flight from Jackson Hole to Salt Lake City to meet up with her parents before heading back to her ranch.

"Are you sure? You can come stay at my place for a few days before you leave if you'd like to," Codie pleads.

"I'm sure," I say. "If I don't leave now I won't ever want to go. I need some time to myself to think."

Hazel hums, looking out towards the mountains. "I can see why you'd have a hard time leaving. You've got quite the view." She nods towards the window into the living room, instead of the picturesque sunset surrounding us. My gaze instinctively snaps around to look inside.

Miles is sitting on the hearth of the fireplace, swirling an amber liquid around in a glass. His forearms flex as he moves the cup around, focusing on the movement of the whiskey. Tiny fireworks go off in my chest at the sight of him. I just want to go over there and tackle him onto the ground. The guys from the ranch all stand around him talking to each other, but he looks lost in thought. And a little sad.

"Ha. Very funny," I deadpan, looking back at Hazel.

She smirks. "All I'm saying is if a big, handsome cowboy was looking that sad over me, I wouldn't be out on the porch with y'all."

Codie and I both descend into a fit of giggles as Hazel bounces her eyebrows up and down. When I look back over at Miles through the window pane, this time he's already staring back at me.

For a second, he looks pained. His eyes scrunched at the sides, lips pursed together. When he realizes I'm looking back at him, his expression softens in the blink of an eye.

Miles nods at me, holding my gaze as he takes a sip of his drink. His eyes don't leave me for a second as he lifts the cold glass to his lips. My eyes dart down to his throat as he swallows the drink.

Slowly, he sets the glass down on the fireplace next to him, resting his elbows on his knees. I can't take my eyes off of him. It's like I'm glued to this spot.

We stare at each other longer than should be comfortable, until Hazel clears her throat, startling me out of my trance.

"Everything okay there?" She teases.

"Peachy." I shoot her a smile over my cup as I take another sip. "I'm going to go check on the drinks, I'll be right back."

I hop off the porch and head up the steps around the front. The cabin isn't as crowded as it was earlier in the night. People started to file out as the sun went down. I have a feeling that the ranch boys will be here a while into the night, though.

The kitchen is empty of people, but full of extra drinks and snacks that people brought. Leave it to Codie to somehow get everyone to bring the party to us, and get some future business for the rental while we're at it. This night couldn't have gone better.

I start to collect some stray plastic cups and throw them into a garbage bag. Cleaning up clears my head. I love having something to do with my hands while I think. Especially when I can be alone with my thoughts.

I'm not alone for very long, though. Boot steps clunk on the hardwood floor until I look up to see a familiar cowboy leaning against the kitchen entryway with one elbow.

Ugh. He even looks sexy leaning on doorways.

"Hey," Miles says.

"Hi," I reply. Apparently our only option for conversation tonight is saying hello back and forth to each other.

"Need any help cleaning up?" He offers.

I shake my head. "No, I just wanted to get away from the chatter for a minute. Nothing needs to be cleaned up right this second."

He nods, considering this, then slowly steps towards me. Grabbing the trash bag from me, he picks up some empty chip bags and cans, then sets the bag down next to the counter.

"Let someone else clean things up. This is your night. If you want to be alone, that's fine. But you shouldn't be the one working," he decides.

"I knew those Lone Pine Ranch cowboys were good for something," I joke.

He laughs, sending a shiver down my spine. "They're pretty good at making the messes in the first place, too."

"Oh I know," I say. "I heard they set a field on fire with fireworks not once, but twice."

"Yeah I think I heard something about that too."

We've migrated towards each other absentmindedly. It's not until now that I notice we are only a foot apart. I can see the twinkle in his eyes up close, the curl of his lips as he smirks at me. I have to tilt my head up just slightly to look at him.

Piano notes ring throughout the kitchen, startling us both. We jump apart slightly, looking to see where the music is coming from. My eyes land on the old record player, sitting on an end table at the opposite end of the room.

A glossy black record spins, playing "Dancing in the Moonlight" loudly enough I can no longer hear the muffled voices through the kitchen door.

No one else is in the room. No one is around to have started the record player. But the needle moves its way towards the center all on its own.

"What just happened," I whisper.

"No idea," Miles follows my gaze until he notices the source of the song.

"I don't even remember plugging that thing in when I put it there. Much less putting a record in it. Someone must have started it."

"Odd," Miles agrees. He holds out a hand towards me. "Would you like to dance with me?"

"You dance?" I feign shock. "They added that to your pro-gramming?"

"Figured it out myself. You can find anything on the inter-net," he winks.

Miles takes my hand, pulling me close to his chest. I sink into him, not meaning to, enveloped by his contact warmth.

"Has anyone ever told you that you always feel like you're running a fever?"

He chuckles, the sound of it vibrating right into my chest. "Just you, Katie."

My heart does a flip when he calls me by my first name. I shouldn't like it so much, but I'm secretly glad he still feels comfortable around me enough to use it. Maybe we can do this whole 'friend' thing.

"You look beautiful tonight."

Or maybe not.

"You can't say stuff like that to me, Miles," I whisper.

"Why?" He says, voice low. His breath skirts right across my ear and into my hair.

"You know why."

We spend the rest of the dance in silence, listening to the music and swaying together. Both guilty of taking as much as we can from this moment while we are in it, knowing we won't get this chance again.

I lean my head against his chest and listen to the steady beat of his heart. I can feel myself getting pulled in. Losing all of my inhibitions to the closeness of Miles. He's like a drug, I can't seem to stop once I've started.

"Katie, I—"

A cheer from the living room interrupts him. I pullout of his grasp, suddenly remembering myself. Right, there are other people here. A lot of them. Including my friends, who I just told every reason why Miles and I can't happen to.

"I should go spend some time with Hazel before she leaves in the morning," I stumble over my words, backing towards the door.

The music switches off, reaching the end of the song. Miles stands in the same spot, arms still outstretched slightly as if I'll come back at any moment. It's too much to take.

The guilt, the wanting, the feeling deep in my gut that I can't have this.

"Of course. I'll see you later on."

I nod, turning around and heading back out to the porch. As I walk down the dark hallway, a couple of tears escape my eyes. I blink rapidly, wiping them off of my cheeks.

I can fall apart later. Right now, it's time to have my last fun night in Wyoming.

"Katherine, where are you?" A voice comes from outside. It's so out of place here, I almost don't recognize it. I stop dead in my tracks as all of my muscles freeze up. It can't be.

"There you are. As a host, you should receive your guests in the entryway so one doesn't have to invite oneself in. Honestly, didn't your aunt teach you anything?" My mother's voice drips with venom as her and my father step into the warm lamplight of the Old Cabin.

They're here. In Jackson Hole.

At my cabin. Well, I guess, technically their cabin. Their money paid for it, their company owns it. I put my blood, sweat and tears into it, but at the end of the day it's not mine.

Florence MacPherson's gaze penetrates into my soul as she stands expectantly in front of me in a deep red silk blouse and matching heels. My father stands at her side, stoic as always, but at least he has the decency to give a small nod and hint of a smile as our gazes lock.

I swallow a lump in my throat, searching for words but none come. This can't be happening. Not with all of my friends here.

Not with half of Jackson Hole celebrating my accomplishment. I can't let them ruin this.

But I can't move. After what feels like a lifetime, a warm chest brushes the back of my arm. "You must be the MacPherson's. Pleasure to meet you. I'm Miles Autry."

My mother doesn't bother to hide her disgust. "Katherine, who is this man?" She says, as if Miles isn't standing right in front of her with his hand outstretched. My father, to his credit, awkwardly takes it and gives Miles half of a handshake.

Miles's presence is enough to melt whatever anxiety has me in a cage of my own making.

"Hello Florence, Callum. This is Miles, his family owns the ranch this cabin was a part of. He's been a big help throughout the renovation," I manage to say without my voice shaking.

Why didn't they tell me they were coming? I could have been a little bit more prepared, at least.

"Help? I hope you're not paying him, Katherine. You were supposed to have this handled, not call in some ranch hand to do all of the work," she huffs, looking Miles up and down as if he's covered in mud.

"She did it all on her own ma'am, Katie's just being humble. All I did was fix a couple of things we should have done before we sold the property in the first place–" Miles interjects.

Florence is quick to interrupt, putting a hand up between her and us. "If you don't mind, I'm speaking to my daughter."

"Please don't speak to him that way, or you won't be talking to either of us," I say firmly. My father's eyes go wide behind her. "As I'm sure the crew can attest, renovations are a huge undertaking and this one was no different. Miles was kind enough to help out with a few problems that started before our purchase of the property. Like every other property I've managed, I handled the project. Now, is there a reason you're here?"

For a split second, she doesn't say a word. But, she quickly recovers, schooling her features back into the cool, calculated confidence I'm used to from my mother.

"We're here to check in on our newest asset in person, of course."

"Well then," I gesture for them to walk further into the cabin. "Don't let me stop you."

My parents shuffle past us, heading into the great room warily. I'm sure they'll find more than a few things that aren't quite to their taste, but at the end of the day, it's my team and I's choice. This place won't hold their interest long enough to actually change any of the details anyway.

"You okay?" Miles whispers from behind my shoulder.

I take a deep breath, turning back around to him with what I hope is a convincing smile. "Fine. I'm fine. Sorry about them, I'd tell you it's not personal, but it probably is."

He laughs, crossing his arms in front of his chest. "Yeah the feeling is mutual. Are you sure you're okay?" Concern furrows his brow as he searches my eyes.

"Yeah, really, I'm good. Just wasn't expecting to see them tonight, that's all."

"They didn't tell you they were coming?"

"No," I shrug. "Usually I get at least a few hours notice. Then I could have... I don't know, mentally prepared myself? I'm sure it would have gone just about the same either way."

Miles nods, looking down at his boots. "Alright, well, I'll be right here if you need anything."

"Thanks, Miles," I say. Turning away, I start towards the great room to hopefully intercept my parents from actually speaking to anyone I know. I get about one step before my mother appears right back in the doorway she disappeared through.

"Katherine, we need to talk about the design of this place. This is unacceptable. What were you thinking? What are all of these knick-knacks?" She holds up a bronze horse statue. One I got from Isabella, in her box of original decor from the Old Cabin.

I reach for it, but Florence snaps it out of my reach.

"Please be careful with that, it's one of the original pieces from the cabin when it was a part of the ranch–" I start.

"This place isn't a part of the ranch anymore. I don't want a bunch of old family *decorations* cluttering up the place. Have it fixed by tomorrow." She scrunches her nose.

My father appears at her side, this time with an older man in a black felt hat. "Florence, there you are. Mr. Osborne is here to speak with you."

The man, *Mr. Osborne*, shakes Florence's hand. "Great to finally meet you Ms. MacPherson. I'm with the Jackson Gazette. This is quite the property you've built."

Florence's demeanor shift is jarring. She's smiling with pride as a loud laugh drips from her lips. "Oh yes, Mr. Osborne, so great to finally meet in person. I'm happy you were able to make it out. It's been quite the endeavor, but we're thrilled to have our newest vacation rental up and running at last."

Always polished, my mother. I look over to Miles, but he's shooting daggers with his eyes her way. My fingers weave through his, an attempt to calm his anger a bit, but it doesn't seem to do much. He grips my hand tightly and keeps staring at the conversation in front of us.

I tune back in just in time to hear Mr. Osborne ask Florence about the time it took to finish the renovation of *this beloved local landmark.*

"Luckily, we were able to finish just before our planned deadline of three months. It's been a lot of work, but I've loved putting this place together. I decided to lean into the local culture with a bit more of a theme than we'd usually do at MacPherson properties, but it's our first Wyoming property so I figured, why not?" She says.

Mr. Osborne nods, writing something in his palm-sized notebook. He gestures to the statue in her hands with his pen, "What is this? A last minute addition?"

"Oh this?" Florence laughs. "I'm so glad you asked. Since this place is so well known in the town, I gathered a few items from the previous owners that originally decorated the cabin when it was first built. Of course, they're a little on the kitschy side, but–"

"That's a lie." Miles interrupts. I whip my head to the side just as he takes a step closer.

"Oh, Miles, I didn't realize you were here. Is your father well?" Mr. Osborne says.

"He's doing okay for now, thanks for asking, Clint." Miles replies steadily.

My jaw snaps open. Of course Miles knows everyone around here. My mother's horrified expression is frozen. I'm sure she's running through every way she can save this in her head.

"As I was saying," Miles continues. "All of that was a lie. This is her first time even seeing the Old Cabin. Katie here did all of the work, all on her own. She put her heart and soul into this place. She worked with my mom to add in the original pieces from the cabin that Florence wanted to throw away about two minutes ago. If you're going to interview anyone, interview her. That's Katie MacPherson, K-A-T-I-E." Miles points to Clint's notebook as he spells my name for him. Clint nods and jumps into action, crossing things out and furiously taking down what Miles just revealed.

"Excuse me, but I'm the owner of this company, not my daughter. If anyone gets credit for this place it's–" Florence flusters.

"Her. It's Katie. Not you, not your company. It may have been funded by you in some roundabout way, but she's worked on this place nonstop for the past three months. Day and night, Katie's been out here. And she did a damn good job, too. It's her vision that made this place what it is now. I'm so fucking proud of what she did with my family's cabin. And I'm proud of who she is, especially knowing she has to deal with you and all of the bullshit you're spinning. If you were a real mother, you'd be proud of her too."

Tears prick my eyes at Miles's words. I can't remember the last time anyone stood up for me. I'm not sure anyone has *ever* fought for me like that. I rub the ache in my chest as I feel Miles's arm around my shoulder.

"Now, if you don't mind, we're having a celebration here of all of the hard work Katie and her crew went through to finish this place," he says, stepping to the side, leaving a clear path out of the open front door.

I've never seen my parents speechless before. Their eyes remain on Miles, wide and disbelieving.

"How about I contact you at a different time, Katie, and we'll see about that interview," Clint says, stuffing his notebook into his pocket.

"Yes, that will be fine. Thank you," I say.

I watch in shock as my parents follow him out of the cabin without a word. My father looks back at me as he steps out onto the porch. For a second I think he might say something to me, but he turns and follows my mother out into the night.

Blood pounds in my ears. What just happened?

I whip around to thank Miles, but he's nowhere to be found. Arms wrap around my shoulders from behind me and Hazel's voice fills the air.

"Holy shit, was that your parents? Are you okay?" She says, a little out of breath.

I search the hallway once more for any sign of Miles, but he's gone. I have a feeling I won't be seeing him for the rest of the night. I don't blame him for wanting to leave after that.

"I'm fine," I reassure Hazel, leaning into her hug.

But, fine is the farthest thing from what I'm feeling right now.

Chapter 29

One Last Time

Cups clatter into the garbage. I tie off another bag of trash from the party, walking out of the great room and towards the front door. The screen door opens with a squeak as Hazel steps inside.

"Just about done here?" She asks.

I nod. "Yep, just got done with the trash. Miles is back in the kitchen cleaning up the floors a bit."

"Oh really? He decided to stick around a bit and *clean up*?" Hazel waggles her brows, a smirk on her lips.

I roll my eyes. "I already told you, it's not like that. That's just Miles, he's always offering to fix things and clean up and all that." If only he could fix us.

"Well, if that's all of it, I'm going to head out and give Wade a call." She smiles at the thought of our best friend back in Idaho. "I missed a call from him earlier, and I know he's been having some troubles getting the shop ready for the Summer's End festival. Can Miles give you a ride back to your cabin?"

"Yeah, that's fine. Go talk to Wade. Thanks for helping tonight, I'm so glad you were able to come out." I give her a quick hug before she heads out the door.

As soon as the front door closes, the air is sucked out of the cabin like a vacuum. With Hazel gone, it's just Miles and I in this cabin. My *friend* Miles.

After tonight, I'm not sure when I'll see him again. I'm planning on heading back to Juniper Ridge tomorrow evening, then I'll only come back once a quarter or so to check on the place. Knowing him, he'll probably avoid me when I come up. I know I'll be avoiding him.

I hate this. Being friends. I know it was my idea, but I'm not sure my heart can take it. It's all or nothing with Miles. And it *has* to be nothing.

I make my way back to the kitchen, sauntering in as Miles stands up from where he was crouched on the new wood floors. They look amazing. Warm wood with plenty of knots, placed in a herringbone style. The entire room looks back to brand new already.

"Hey," I say.

"Hey," he replies on a sigh, smiling softly. His dark eyes twinkle as he looks me over, raking over my entire body. It sends shivers across my skin, as if he were really touching me.

"Thanks for staying and cleaning up. You didn't have to do that."

"It's okay to accept some help once in a while, Mac. If I didn't want to stay and help, I would have left," he gives me a pointed look, crossing his arms across his chest.

"Well, thank you, I appreciate it. The place looks great," I say.

He nods. "I can't believe it's done. Seems like you just got here."

I laugh. "You know, when I first got here and you yelled at me just outside–"

"I did not yell at you."

"–I thought you'd be counting down the days until I left. The hours, even."

Miles chuckles, the sound vibrating through the air between us. "Yeah, well, a few things have changed since then."

I nod. He takes a step closer to me, but doesn't reach out toward me. I wonder if he can feel the pull that I can, the ache to step into his warmth.

"I'm glad they did," I hear myself say. The haze of the night, my parents, prolonged exposure to Miles, and something else threatens to take over. I know I should go, but something is keeping me here. I don't want this night to end.

What if we could have one night? Would that scratch the itch?

The voice deep inside tells me it's not enough, that it never would be. That we shouldn't start something we can't finish. *I* can't finish. But the way he's looking at me is more intoxicating than the glass of wine I had earlier. I want the flames to take over, burning us both to ash.

"I'm heading out for the night, I've got an early morning to-morrow dropping Hazel off at the airport," I say.

"Will I see you before you leave town?" He asks. I can't bring myself to meet his eyes.

"I don't think so."

"So this is goodbye?"

I nod, finally meeting his gaze. Pain is etched into his features as he looks down at me. I close the distance between us, pulling him into a hug. His arms wrap hesitantly around my waist. I bury my face into his chest, taking every liberty I can get away with.

Miles lets out a deep breath, pulling me closer into him. His warmth seeps into me, sending shivers up my spine. I run my hands along the firm muscles of his back as his fingers make their way up onto my neck, then into my hair.

Neither of us pulls away. It takes a couple of minutes of being in his arms longer than we should for me to get the nerve to look up at him.

Miles is already looking down at me, pure need radiating from his gaze. His warm espresso eyes bore into me, snapping my last thread of control.

I close the distance between our lips until they're almost touching. A silent invitation. We hover there, breathing each other in for another moment. On the precipice of a moment that could change everything or nothing.

Miles sighs once, breath skirting across my lips. "Katie," he whispers so low I almost can't hear it. "Are you sure about this?"

"Just once. Please, Miles. One last time."

He nods, bringing a hand to my cheek, slowly stroking with his thumb. I push up on my tip toes, our noses touching.

"I'll have you any way I can," he whispers, so softly it sounds like it's more to himself than to me.

His lips claim mine and we melt into each other. Hands roaming, savoring every second.

This kiss is different than any other time. We're memorizing every detail, taking our time. Miles traces his tongue against the seam of my lips, a silent question. I deepen the kiss, opening to him.

My hips roll involuntarily, eliciting a moan from deep in his chest. He breaks our kiss, trailing his way down my neck. A gasp falls from my lips as he bites my collar bone, licking away the sting right after.

Cold air rushes in as Miles steps back, leaving me panting. "I want to see you," he growls.

My head cocks to the side at his words.

"Strip."

My breath hitches. He looks me up and down, drinking me in. I reach up, pulling the hem of my shirt slowly up my chest and over my head, doing the same with my shorts.

"Fuck, Katie," he mutters. Miles runs a hand over his beard, unable to take his eyes off me.

"What about you, cowboy?" I tease.

He whips his shirt off faster than I thought possible, fumbling a bit with his belt. He kicks his boots and jeans off onto the hardwood.

My bra unclasps with a small click, and I toss it into the floor with the rest. Miles's eyes darken, his breathing becoming labored.

He closes the distance between us, grabbing me by the waist and pulling me against him.

"*Miles*," I breathe. His hands roam up and down my back as he kisses me where my shoulder meets my neck.

"I want to savor this, but I don't know how much I can take," he says.

"Please—" I start.

I'm interrupted by Miles picking me up like I weigh nothing. I wrap my legs around him. He places me on the counter behind us, the cold biting into my skin.

I wrap my arms around his neck, pulling him back into a kiss. His lips move against mine, taking and taking. He reaches between us, and I feel him throw his boxers to the side.

"You just feel so... right," he whispers in my ear.

His hands move down to my hips, pulling me to the edge of the counter. I brace my palms against his chest. Our gazes meet as he reaches between us.

His hand traces my core, finding the spot that makes me overheat. He takes his time seeing what pulls a gasp out of me until I'm practically shaking.

"Miles, please. I need you," I whimper.

He chuckles, not letting up in the slightest until I'm coming apart.

"You're so beautiful. I'm so lucky. God, Katie. I can't get enough." Miles groans into my mouth, wrapping my legs around his waist again.

When he starts to move, I grip his shoulders, tipping my head back. Miles runs his tongue along my throat.

"Oh god," I moan. "*Miles.*" The ember in my chest that has never fully burnt out for him grows. How could I ever think we could have one last time together and be okay after? He's touching me like I'm something to be worshipped, cared for. It's addictive.

Before I came to Jackson Hole, Miles was just a great time to me. Fun, caring, full of life. Now, he's that and so much more. Hardworking, strong enough to take charge but kind enough not to make anyone feel small.

Even the way he's holding me now is a contradiction. He's firm, but also holds me like I might break. He picks up our rhythm, becoming more sporadic as his control slips. Our lips find each other again, frantic and needy.

"Katie, I'm close—" Miles says into my neck.

I pull him closer, my fingers digging into his shoulder blades. "I have an IUD."

His eyes grow wide and he comes apart, clutching onto me like I'm the only thing anchoring him.

We are electric together. I knew it was good last time, but this reminder is almost too much. How am I supposed to love without this again? Without him?

The ache in my chest only grows, the flame erupting into something more.

"Miles," I whisper.

"I know," he says. Our foreheads meet as we breathe, our chests moving together.

The sun hasn't come up over the mountains yet when I feel Miles's lips against my temple. I stir, wrapping my arms around his broad chest. He pulls me in just a little bit closer, letting out a deep breath.

"Good morning," I say.

"Hey pretty girl." His voice is still gravelly with sleep.

I giggle against his chest. For a blissful moment, this feels real. Like I could have this every day. Waking up with Miles next to me, kissing him just because I can.

My heart yearns for it, but my head knows it can never be that way. Eventually, something would go wrong. He'd leave or I would, and the pain would be too much to bear. I care about him way too much to go through with this.

My little bubble of happiness pops when my phone alarm cuts through the silence. I groan, rolling over to turn it off.

"Do you have to get going?" Miles says, trepidation in his voice.

"Yeah," I sigh.

Miles nods, pulling me in a little tighter. I wouldn't be surprised if he didn't know he was doing it.

"I hate goodbyes," I whisper. This is killing me. I feel like my heart is being ripped out of my chest and put onto a skewer.

"Me too."

He holds me in his arms for a while, both of us silent. My head is running through everything that has happened in the past three months. Arriving in Wyoming, seeing him again, the cows breaking the fence, Miles walking me home under the stars, kissing under the fireworks.

Him leaving for a week with no word. Finding out he was married and never told me. Standing next to him in the cabin in the middle of a rain storm as I broke both of our hearts.

Eventually, he rustles me to the side and sits up, grabbing his baseball cap from the side table. I toss the blankets off of my legs and gather my clothes.

We dress in a heavy silence, clearing up all evidence we were even here. It feels like we are erasing ourselves.

I hesitate by the door, looking back at him. Miles makes his way over to me, pulling me into a hug that feels like home. Tears leak out of my eyes and into his shirt as he holds me close.

I pull away first. "Miles—"

"Hey, it's okay," he interrupts. "You gotta go."

I nod, wiping my cheeks. I turn towards the door, stepping out onto the porch. The outline of the mountains is barely visible as the sky starts to turn yellow.

I can go over all of the reasons I should leave as many times as I want, but my heart still cracks as I step out into the morning.

Chapter 30

I Don't Know How

I TAKE A DEEP BREATH, making my way off the porch. Stepping off the last step and onto the dirt, dizziness fills my head. All I can see is swirls of gray with black spots.

Until I can see something else. Somewhere else. I know I'm not actually there, but it feels so real. So right.

I'm no longer on the porch, I'm in a place that feels *almost* real. Like a vivid dream. A little hazy.

I'm standing in a cozy living room with a big fireplace built of gray slate stones. A leather couch stands in front of me, covered in plush pillows and warm blankets. It's almost dusk outside. That special time of the evening when the sky is red and a couple of stars shine through.

A breeze drifts by out the windows, rustling red, orange and yellow leaves on the trees. It's the peak of fall, colors painting the hillside and golden grass blanketing the ranch. A small group of cattle grazes in a nearby field. The Tetons standing silent guard above it all.

Strong arms wrap around me and I'm hit with a sense of deja vu. It's a familiar touch, one that makes me feel safe.

Loved.

Then, I hear him.

"Hey," Miles's rough voice brushes my ear as he hugs me closer to his firm chest. His scruff brushes against the outer shell of my ear, sending shivers up my arms. "How about we take a ride up to Ember Meadow?"

Fireworks go off in all of my nerve endings. I'm wrapped up in his warmth, already burning up from his contact like a heat map everywhere our bodies meet. But, it's not the urgent need I usually feel when I'm close to Miles.

It's a comfortable feeling this time. Not rushed. I feel safe and secure, wrapped up in his arms, like I'm meant to be here. My heart bursts with an overwhelming sense of... something. It's a new feeling, one I can't quite put a finger on. Like light escaping from the darkest parts of me, bursting out into the air like a firework. I like it. I hear myself giggle, turning around to look at him.

Just as I turn to look into his eyes, the vision goes blurry, then gray again. I blink rapidly, willing it to come back so I can live in that life just a little bit longer. But, it doesn't.

My chest hollows out, the feeling leaving me so quickly I can barely believe it was there in the first place. I stand in the hot sunlight, feeling emptier than I've ever felt in my life. Tears well up in my eyes at the loss of that overwhelming, life changing feeling.

I'm back on the porch steps. It's the end of summer, and I'm walking away from Miles forever.

"You're extra quiet this morning," Hazel hums from the passenger seat of my car.

"I'm just tired."

She laughs, "I can practically hear you thinking. I've literally never seen anyone think as loudly as you. It's a talent."

Hazel is right. I've been lost in thought the entire drive, replaying the daydream in my mind over and over again. Or hallucination. Whatever it was.

It seriously messed with my head. My brain is self-sabotaging. Right when I've finally gotten up the courage to leave and move on with my life the way it was before, I start imagining what it'd be like to have a future here.

It's like my head knows that the logical thing to do is leave, but it's killing my heart.

"Is this about Angry Cowboy? Did he say something to you that upset you? We can turn back around and go kick his ass. Although I'm not sure that'd work out so well, but we could at least yell at him. Rough him up a little bit," Hazel throws a few fake punches into the air.

"No, he didn't upset me," I laugh. I shift around in my seat a bit, unused to talking about this kind of thing. For Hazel, sure, but never for me. "I'm just having a hard time leaving, I guess, and I don't know why. Maybe I spent too much time here."

"Kate. It's okay to not want to leave. Most people feel that way when they go to new places and have awesome experiences like you had," she says. I keep my eyes focused on the road ahead.

My voice is quieter as it comes out. "It's more than that. I feel like..." *I belong here.* "I just don't want to let it go. I don't want to go back to Juniper Ridge. This has never happened to me before and it's really freaking me out. I'm not even this attached to my own apartment."

"Is it Miles?" She asks again.

"No. Yes. I don't know. It's not *just* about him. I love my new friends here, I love the mountains and the town and the little coffee shop. I love the sunsets that make the entire sky glow. I love the people. I love the cabin and spending time on the ranch.

"Then there's him. I feel like I want to melt my body to his every time I'm around him. He drives me insane most of the time, and the rest of the time makes me feel like I'm the only person in the world. I'm just so angry. I was finally getting to know who he really is, spending time with him.

"It was scary, but it was addicting. And then, it all came crashing down. I'm just so upset it all had to end. I don't know, I'm not very good at describing all of this. I probably sound like a crazy person," I let out an awkward laugh, and glance over at Hazel.

"How was everything last night after I left?" She asks. I told her this morning that I stayed over at the cabin, but didn't mention Miles did too. I think I'm still processing everything that happened.

I sigh. "We kind of... spent the night together," I mumble.

"What!?" Hazel yells. "You were with Miles all night? Did anything happen?"

I feel my cheeks start to heat. Usually I have no problem telling Hazel about anything but this feels different. More real. "Of course something happened, it's Miles. I cannot be trusted around him. We agreed it was the last time. Well, last few times anyway."

"Katie!"

"What? I can't help it. He's just... him. You know?" I say, looking over.

She's staring back at me, wide-eyed with a smile bigger than I've seen on her in a while. "Oh my god," she spits out after a few seconds. "You're in love with him."

"I am not," I roll my eyes.

"You are."

"No, I'm not. I'm not a 'fall in love' type of gal, Hazel." My hands start to sweat on the steering wheel. Is Hazel right? Am I in love with Miles? There's no way.

"Seems like you are, for the right person," she sing-songs, turning back to face forwards.

My hands start to shake as I think about this summer. The way my heart beats faster when I know he's around. The fireworks in my stomach when he gets close, or winks at me from across the room. How dizzy I feel when his deep baritone laugh cuts through the air. When he touches me and it just feels unexplainably *right*.

"Holy shit. I think I might be in love with him." My jaw hangs open as the realization hits me like a truck.

"Hah! I knew it was about him," Hazel shouts. She takes one of my hands from the white-knuckle grip I have on the steering wheel, sandwiching it between her own. "Hey, it's okay. This is great. I'm so happy for you, Katie."

"This is not *great*. This is terrible," I yell. Hazel jumps a bit at my exasperation. "I can't be in a relationship, I'm not equipped for that. Look at my parents. One or both of us will get hurt for sure. Miles has a perfect, loving family, I don't fit in with that at all. He was married before, he definitely knows how to be in a long-term relationship. I'm just not that kind of person. Plus, we live in different places." I take a deep breath, trying not to freak out, but I'm not doing a very good job at it.

"Oh Kate," Hazel breathes. "I hate that you think of yourself like that. Of course you're capable of being in a relationship."

"How do you know? What if I'm not? Aunt Millie hasn't been with someone since I've known her and she's fine!"

Hazel sighs, and I can tell she's thinking about what she's going to tell me. Sometimes I wish I would slow down more often and think like she does instead of blurting things out as soon as they pop into my head.

"Of course you'd be fine on your own. You've always been independent, you can take care of yourself. But, you don't have to be alone all of the time. Just because Millie is alone doesn't mean you have to be. You can still be badass and be in a relationship. People do it all the time," she says.

I blink away the tears welling up in my eyes. "But what if I'm not good at it, Hazel? What if I end up like my parents? What if I hurt someone, or get really hurt?"

"Then you deal with it as it comes. There's probably going to be some hurt, even if it all works out in the end. You can handle it. I know you can."

"I just don't want to hurt him. He's been through enough. I don't know how to love him," I whisper. The words fall out of my soul and I feel a weight being lifted off of me. Deep down I knew why I was scared, but saying it outloud is freeing.

"Babe, no one knows how. You just do. You both try your hardest to work at being together and being decent humans. You'll both probably get hurt at some point, but that's okay, you'll get past it. Or you won't. But you know what?" Hazel smiles.

I nod, encouraging her to continue. I'm not sure I can get a word out without sobbing right now.

"It's all worth it in the end. My parents have gone through some rough patches over the years, but they bring each other so much joy it cancels out the pain. They created a beautiful life they love. They laugh with each other on the happy days, and cry together on the sad days. I want to have that. A best friend to go through life with, and a partner all in one. I want you to have it too. You deserve it, and you're capable of it," Hazel beams.

I pull into a parking spot at the small Jackson Hole Airport right as the tears start to flow from my eyes. Hazel reaches over from the passenger seat to pull me into a big hug I didn't know I needed.

"It's hard, Hazel," I sob, not sure she can even understand me.

"I know," she whispers.

Hazel stays with me until I finally dry my tears and manage a watery smile.

"Alright. Go," she urges, waving her hands at me like she's pushing me away.

I laugh, "Go where? I'm not the one with a flight to catch."

"Go get Miles, dumbass," she yells. "I didn't go through that whole speech for you to just drive home anyway."

My heart pounds so hard in my chest I'll be surprised if she can't hear it. "Right now?"

"Yes, right now, when else?"

"Well, I was thinking I'd head home and think about it for a few days."

Hazel laughs, gathering her purse and phone. "So you can talk yourself out of it? I don't think so. You're going to start this car once I'm out and head straight back to that ranch. I want a full report after. I'm holding you to this," she says.

My stomach tumbles over itself. She's probably right, if I don't go talk to him now while I've got the courage, I might not ever go back. Especially if enough time passes. By the time I get the guts up to do this again he could have moved on.

Wow. I don't like that thought.

"Okay, I'll go, I'll go," I concede.

Hazel smiles, stepping out of the car, "My work here is done." She grabs her suitcase from my trunk while I hop out of the car to give her a hug. I'm so glad she was here for my meltdown-freak-out. My heart feels just a little bit healed.

"Thank you," I whisper into her dark brown waves.

She hugs me a little tighter, then lets me go. "You don't need to thank me, that's what best friends do. You can repay me one day when I have enough time to date."

I giggle, "You'd have to spend time away from the ranch and Wade to date."

"Nevermind then, I don't want to date. I want to die a lonely spinster with only my horses to keep me company."

"If you insist," I deadpan. "Thanks for coming up to see the cabin, I really appreciate it."

Hazel's eyes crinkle at the sides as she gathers her bags. "I wouldn't miss it."

Then, she's gone and I'm left standing next to my car feeling like I could scream, throw up, cry or laugh at any moment.

Chapter 31

Bout Damn Time

SOMEHOW, I MANAGED NOT to talk myself out of this for the entire drive. I blasted my 90's country music playlist, rolled the windows down and let my hair fly all over as the fields, rivers and pine trees passed by. I was pretty happy with how easily I was handling driving back to Miles to see him again.

Until now.

Now, I'm standing at the door to the cabin. I know he's inside, his horse is still tied up to the porch railing. I can hear him shuffling around, probably trying to fix the electrical. This should be easy.

How many times this summer have I walked into this exact cabin to talk to that exact man? Countless. I've never hesitated for a minute. Not when I was sure he hated me, not when I was excited we were finally starting to talk, not when I was angry and confused when he broke my heart.

But, today, it feels different. Admitting my feelings to myself was exciting and terrifying at the same time. I know most twenty-five year olds have dealt with love and heartbreak countless times, but this is my first rodeo. I don't know what I'm doing, and I have to be okay with that.

So why is it so hard to move my arms and legs?

I take a deep breath, steadying myself as much as I possibly can. Before I can open the door, it swings open in front of me, startling me backwards a few steps. Miles starts towards me, then jumps back a bit, eyes wide.

"Katie. You're back," he says, surprise written all over his expression.

I clear my throat. "Yeah, sorry to startle you."

My ears buzz as I find my breath again. Why did I think I could come back? I can't do this. We can't be friends, we argue all the time. Why did I let Hazel talk me into this? I can't be in a relationship, that's ridiculous—

"That's okay," he breathes. We are both frozen in place, unable to make a move. "Did you forget something?"

I look into his fiery brown eyes, molten and warm and everything inside of me calms. I take him in; the way his hair falls across his forehead, the freckles popping up on his cheeks from a summer spent in the sun, the way his lips part as he waits for my response. The sparks of electricity between us are familiar.

The magnetic pull between us is still there, but now that I'm not pulling so hard against it, it feels like a comfort. Like an invisible string tying us together. It's been there all along. I'm not scared anymore, I just feel...

Home.

"Yes. I did." My voice sounds a lot more sure than I feel as the words roll off my lips.

"What?"

Moving a few steps closer to him, I close the distance between us. He doesn't step back. Instead, his arm instinctively comes to my waist, holding me against him. Sparks ignite on my side at his touch and I'm instantly craving more.

"This."

Standing up on my toes, I wrap my arms around his neck and pause just enough for him to pull away if he wants to.

Miles's breath hitches. "Bout damn time," he whispers across my lips.

I catch his mouth in a kiss as he presses his chest flush to me. I'm already melting into him. He's the sun and I'm a cube of ice on a hot day. His beard is rough against my fingertips as I pull him closer. I can feel my pulse everywhere. Hear it pounding in my ears.

One of his hands firmly grips my hip, pulling me in. The other tangles into my hair at the nape of my neck, gripping, combing through. Gentle and firm all at once. I sigh into him as a groan escapes the back of his throat.

He pulls away, cold air filling the space between us. My lips instinctively chase his until he's too far. My eyes flutter open as he tucks a few pieces of my hair behind my ears. I've never seen Miles smile so brightly. It fills me with the most amazing, warm light that I want to bottle up and keep forever.

"What does this mean?" His eyes twinkle as he asks the question I've been waiting for, as if he already knows the answer. I wouldn't be surprised if it's written all over my face. I'm not trying to hide it any more.

I take his hands in mine and take a deep breath. The words flow out of my effortlessly, as if they've been there all along.

"I'm in love with you, Miles. I'm not really sure what it means for us, but that's what I feel. I want to spend as much time as you'll let me by your side. I want to wake up and see your face, and fall asleep with a goodnight kiss. I'd rather fight with you every day than be just content with anyone else.

"All I know is I've never felt like this before, and I don't want to let it go. I can't let it go. The thought of driving back to Juniper Ridge alone just feels so wrong. And if it's too late, if you don't want me anymore, I understand. But if you're feeling any portion of what I'm feeling, I think we should give this a shot."

I take a breath, my entire body buzzing in anticipation. I don't have to worry very long.

"I love you, Katie. I want to be with you. I want you to stay," he smiles. His words are choked with emotion and it sends butterflies free in my stomach.

I laugh, pulling Miles into a hug. His arms wrap around me holding me tight as if I might disappear if he doesn't. "Oh thank goodness, that would have been so awkward if you had said no. Could you imagine?"

Miles's deep laugh vibrates into me as we hold on to each other on the porch. I've never wanted anything more intensely in my life, and feeling him want me back is euphoric. I don't ever want to leave this spot.

This feels like the start of something great. It's hard to let go of the little voice in my head telling me that it won't work out, that I'm not meant for this, that it won't last. But even if all of that ends up being true, I know it'll be an adventure. That's all I could ever want. A new adventure with Miles.

So, I follow my heart for the first time in a long time. I give in to him completely, staying in the moment. I can't remember the last time I've been so present in anything, not thinking about anything else at all but Miles and the way he sets my heart on fire.

He sucks my bottom lip, giving it the slightest nip of his teeth that sends shivers down my spine. His hands roam up and down my back, from my waist to my shoulders. I don't realize I'm gripping his shirt for dear life, pulling him closer even though we're already touching. I let go, wrapping my arms around his neck instead.

We've done this before, but it feels different now. There's a familiarity between us, but it still feels new somehow, too. Perhaps it's that we know each other's hearts. We've spent months around each other talking about life, our pasts, nonsense, and our deepest feelings. We've spent comfortable silences together just being near each other.

I may have spent all summer fighting the physical attraction between us, but somehow, the falling in love part happened anyway.

Miles pulls away, staring into my eyes as the fog of lust clears. I could look at him forever like this, lips puffy, hair mussed, staring at me so intensely I'm pulled into his orbit. There's a spell around us, thick in the air. All of my senses are heightened towards him, blocking out the rest of the world.

I love it.

"Does this mean you're staying?" he whispers so low I almost don't hear it. I think back to the perfect vision of the future I've seen twice now while I've been at the cabin. His soft voice and strong arms wrapped around me.

A grin breaks out across my face, "I'm staying."

"Well," he starts, breaking away from my arms and backing up a few steps, "maybe I'll see you around some time, Mac." Miles drawls, turning away towards the driveway. "I'll be sure to stay off your property, since cowboys aren't your type and all."

"Oh, shut up you big dork," I exclaim, catching his arm and pulling him towards me so abruptly we both fall back against the cabin wall behind me. His expression darkens, his laugh dying in his throat as his hips press against me. There's a new spark when his lips meet mine.

Miles does shut up. In fact, we don't say much to each other at all for a while.

Chapter 32

You Started It

SUN SHINES THROUGH THE spotless windows of the cabin in the morning and I wake up happier than I've been in... well, ever. I'm still in Wyoming, my vacation rental is finished and more beautiful than I could have ever imagined, and there's a cowboy wrapped around me keeping me warm.

A little too warm, if I'm being honest, but I don't dare move. His broad chest moves up and down at a slow rhythm.

I wait for the anxiety to creep in, for the freak out to start when I remember what I confessed to Miles yesterday but it never comes. Everything just feels so right, just like it did before. No rush in my blood to leave as soon as possible, no excuses running through my head of why this couldn't work out.

Just calm, and peace. It's a little weird, if I'm being honest, but I'm reveling in it. I'm not used to it. This brand new feeling I've never felt before. Not in relationships or family. Even with people I felt safe with, there was always the panic behind it all. The worry that it might all be taken away from me at a moment's notice.

But now, I can just feel the certainty of Miles.

The only sadness I feel is the loss of our time spent apart. Four years that we could have had together. Though, deep down, I know that we wouldn't have stayed together back then even if we had tried. Neither of us were ready. It had to be now.

My pulse jumps as Miles starts to stir, his arm that's wrapped around my side pulling me in closer to him. His breath skirts down the back of my neck, sending goosebumps down my arms.

I relax a little, melting into him to savor this moment. I've never had a moment like this with anyone. I wiggle in a little, snuggling up to him as much as I can.

"Mac." His voice sounds like sandpaper. "What are you doing?"

"Getting comfy."

He sighs, "If you keep wiggling around like that, I'll have to pin you down another way."

"You started it," I accuse.

"Yeah, and I'll finish it too," he says.

I turn around to face him, laying on my side. Deep brown eyes stare back at me, with just a little bit of gold. His hair is mussed and he looks just a little bit tired still. This might be my favorite version of Miles yet.

"Hi," I smile.

"Hey sweetheart," he says, intertwining our hands underneath the soft quilt. My stomach does a flip. I wouldn't mind waking up to Miles Autry calling me sweetheart every single morning.

"I bet you noticed that I'm still here," I tease, earning a laugh.

"I did notice that. I'm pretty happy about it."

"Oh yeah?" I run my hand up his arm until I get to his cheek. "How happy?"

He chuckles into my neck, pulling me onto him. Miles reaches up, running a hand through my wild hair. "I love you," he breathes. He says it reverently, like a spell falling over us.

"I love you," I whisper back. His answering smile is brighter than the sun. "I've never felt like this before, but I think I've loved you for a while." I lean down, my elbows on either side of his head. "I'm not very good at this whole relationship thing. I've never really done it before. But I want to try."

He laughs, his chest shaking beneath me. "Katie. I'm not good at it either. I'm divorced, remember?"

"You make a good point," I smile.

"You don't have to be good at it. We can both learn how, together. There's no rush. I just know I want you to be here, with me. That's all we need to think about for now. Sound okay?"

I nod, unable to speak. It takes a lot to render me speechless, but Miles Autry seems to do it pretty often. I fall into those deep brown eyes, drowning in him. My fingers reach up to his cheeks, tracing the few freckles the sun has darkened into his skin. Miles stares back at me through his lashes.

He's not just looking at me. He's *seeing* me. It's been a long time since I've let someone new this close to me. Close enough to see past the facade of a sparkling personality and tough exterior. Miles can see the vulnerability underneath it all. All of my jagged edges, all of the parts of me I keep tucked away, out of sight.

I should be scared. I should be running away by now, worried that he'll get too close and up and leave one day when he decides he doesn't want me anymore. But all I can feel is that burning light in my chest, wanting more and more of him.

I *want* to be loved. I want to love him. I want to stay here forever.

Leaning up on my elbows, I smile down at him, a curtain of rust colored curls falling between us. My gaze snags on a tattoo I haven't noticed before. Right on his left chest. It's an outline of a mountain. It looks so familiar, I swear I've seen it before.

"Didn't realize you were such a tattoo guy," I tease.

"I wasn't, until my divorce. Then I figured I might as well see what all the fuss is about. I always wanted them," he replies, never taking his eyes off me.

My hands roam across his light brown skin, grazing across the dark swirls of ink. Some I've caught glimpses of. There's the playing cards on fire on his forearm I see all of the time. A grove of pine trees, a longhorn skull, a deer.

"What's the first one you got?" I ask.

He chuckles, turning over so his back is towards me. "It's a little cliche, but I wanted the symbol of Wyoming to be my first one." There on his shoulder blade sits the Bucking Horse & Rider of Wyoming, filled in with beautiful swirls of color depicting what I assume is the ranch and the Tetons behind. "It's where I'm from, the place my family has called home for decades. It felt like I should honor it somehow."

I run the tips of my fingers across the symbol. So similar to the one I saw drawn in the window a few weeks ago. Same angles, same style.

"This one is my newest. Got it just this past winter." He continues, gesturing to a rectangle-shaped tribal tattoo on his connecting bicep. "It's a Chibcha symbol, a Colombian tribe my ancestors belonged to. Felt right having it near my Wyoming heritage."

"Are you sure you didn't have any of these when we met? They look so familiar," I say.

He smiles, "Yeah, Mac, I'm pretty sure."

I know I've seen that one somewhere. Not as a tattoo though. Just the design of it. Burned into wood like a brand.

My heart drops into my stomach. *All* of his tattoos are familiar, because I've seen them all around the cabin.

First, the deer I saw out the window that turned out to be the spitting image of the one inked onto his side. The longhorn skull across his back, the exact same as the symbol I saw in the fireplace. The pine trees of all different shades, wrapping around his bicep. Those were branded into a fence post. Now, the symbol I saw etched into the window sill upstairs on the night we kissed.

There's even an outline of the tetons, complete with snow capped peaks and a small forest of trees on his muscular thigh. The exact same as I saw on the window sill downstairs.

Ever since I started seeing symbols around the cabin, I thought maybe it was some sort of code. Or, at the very least, signs of the past popping up. But they were signs of Miles. Pointing me towards him. To our future.

He opens his mouth to say something, but stops, sitting up. "Do you hear that?" he says, voice low.

We fall silent and I can just make out a shuffling noise downstairs. Miles stares towards the door, eyes wide.

"What is that? Is someone here?" I ask, knowing he won't have an answer.

He rolls off the bed, pulling his sweatshirt back on, jumping into his jeans. "Might be some animals. Raccoons or something. I'll go check it out."

"I'm coming with you," I jump up before he can stop me.

"Katie, just stay here," he starts to protest.

"I can fight off raccoons just as well as you can, Autry."

Miles cracks open the door slowly, creeping into the hallway. The cold hardwood floors creaking just a bit as we walk. The shuffling has stopped. In fact, there's no noise at all. Just a smell wafting up the stairwell as we descend. It smells like–

"Did you start a fire?" Miles whispers.

"No, I was just going to ask *you* that."

Yellow and orange flames erupt from the stone fireplace in the great room, warming the cabin. Embers pop and float upwards as coals glow below. It's as if the fire has been going all night. The scent of smoky pine fills my lungs.

"I swear, that fireplace has a mind of its own," I laugh. Miles frowns, as if he's trying to solve a complicated math problem.

"One of us had to have started the fire last night, no one else has been here," he says, searching the room for any clues. He makes it over to the window, pushing open the crimson curtains. Sunlight floods into the cabin.

Vibrant hues of red, purple and orange glow in the light from the garden. The marigolds that were wilted, gray and dried up yesterday have blossomed to life overnight. They look better than they did when I planted them this spring. If I hadn't seen the state of them yesterday with my own eyes, I wouldn't believe they could have changed that quickly.

"Did you plant new flowers?" Miles asks, on the same train of thought as I am.

"No." I walk up to the windows to get a better view of the flower garden. "They were pretty much dead yesterday. How is this possible?" I whirl back around to Miles, who is standing in the middle of the kitchen as if he's frozen in place.

Those dark eyes burst aflame again as he starts to laugh. Before I know it, a giggle bubbles out of my throat too. We would look deranged to anyone that walked in, standing in the middle of the kitchen laughing at nothing.

"I'm sorry," he gets out, taking a deep breath. "I just used to call this the haunted cabin when I was a kid, and now all of this..." Miles shakes his head in disbelief. "Well, who am I to say it isn't?"

"Do you think Codie came back and did all of this? It couldn't have been Hazel, she's back home by now. And she's the only one who knows I'm here."

A smirk breaks out on Miles's face, "Hazel knows you're here?"

"Yeah, I kind of ran back here as fast as I could after I dropped her off. Why?"

"Does she know about me?" He sounds a little timid. Like if I give the wrong answer it would crush him.

I laugh. "If you're asking if she knows that you exist in this world, that would be a yes since you met her and talked to her a few times." He cocks his head to the side, giving me a pointed look. "If you're asking if she knows how I feel about you, well, she knows that too. She kind of... brought it to my attention. I hope you're okay with that, because it's a little too late to take it back." I walk towards him, wrapping my arms around his neck. His hands absentmindedly come to my waist, giving me a little squeeze as he pulls me closer. The invisible string between us pulling tight.

Miles smiles down at me, nothing but soft warmth in his expression. "Of course I am. It sounds like I should thank her. I like people knowing that you're mine."

"Yours, huh?" I tease, swinging my hips side to side. "We're going to get so much shit for this from Parker and Codie."

"Good." He leans down, pressing a kiss onto my forehead. "I've spent four years wishing I could call you mine, I'm not wasting another minute pretending this pull between us is nothing."

"Wow, Miles, who knew you were such a big softie. It only took me four years and a few months to finally get you to admit you like me."

"Love," he grumbles.

"That too," I giggle as his lips land on mine again. Another spark traveling up my spine.

A knock sounds at the front door, pulling us apart. We stare at each other wide-eyed for a few moments before jumping into action. I'm smoothing my hair down, thanking past Katie for putting on all of my clothes before coming downstairs. Miles is straightening his plain white t-shirt, walking towards the hallway.

Miles opens the front door before I can get to it and grumbles something to whoever is on the other side. The wooden door swings open further as I finally reach the front room, revealing none other than Walter Autry on the other side. His blue plaid flannel shirt drooping off his shoulders, cowboy hat crooked on his head.

Chapter 33

Sort Of Magical

"WELL, ISN'T THIS A nice surprise," Walter drawls, walking into the cabin. Miles steps to the side out of his way. I shoot a questioning look at him, but all he does is shrug. "I was on my way into town this morning and noticed that *both* of your cars were in the driveway so I thought I'd come check it out. Say howdy and all that." His eyes land on Miles, who has become the poster for neutrality, as if he's perfectly justified in being here. Like he does it every day. It's all I can do not to laugh at how obvious this is.

I don't really care what anyone thinks of us together, but it's still so soon. So fresh. I didn't think our comfortable little bubble would be popped less than a day after we created it.

"Isn't it a little early for you to be down here, Miles?" Walter asks, a hint of amusement in his voice. "You must have been gone before the sun was up, I didn't even hear you leave. Or come home yesterday. Didn't get much sleep last night?"

"Can't say that I did," Miles replies.

I choke back my reaction. "Miles was just fixing an electrical issue we found yesterday after the opening party."

Walter's eyes twinkle as he gives me a knowing smile. "I'm sure he was."

"Was there any other reason you came down here, Walt?" Miles saunters over to my side, but not quite touching me. His warmth radiates through the air. Why is he always so warm? I lean into him slightly, not realizing what I'm doing until Miles's hand comes to my lower back, steadying me. I practically melt into his touch, wondering how I spent these last few months not touching him.

Walter looks between us, practically beaming at what he sees. "I'd be lying if I said I didn't want to come and take a look at all of your hard work, Katie. I loved this place, after all. When I saw the two of you were around I figured it's my opportunity to have a look-see before guests arrive."

"Of course, come on in," I gesture to the living room. Walter takes off his dusty boots and wanders around the room, looking at all of the decor. Not a whole lot has changed since he was here last, but it's become more homey. I'm glad he gets to see this place thriving again.

We make our way around the first floor before heading into the great room. I breathe a sigh of relief when he doesn't look interested in going upstairs. It'd be pretty obvious exactly what's going on between Miles and I with one look at the primary bedroom.

Miles stays by my side the whole time, constantly touching me in some way. His hand on my back, his shoulder brushing up against me as we walk, his hand reaching for mine in the hallway. As if he can't hold himself back anymore.

Every time I glance at him, he's looking back at me with a smile. I can feel pride radiating from him every time Walter compliments another part of the cabin. Miles looks at me like I'm a wonder, like I'm a powerful force he can't take his eyes off of. I think he always has, in some way. I just couldn't see past the broken pieces of myself long enough to appreciate it.

The smell of the fire wafts up as we enter the kitchen. *Shit. I totally forgot about that.*

"Wow, look at this," Walter exclaims. "That's a damn nice fire."

"Do you know anything about this, Walt?" Miles asks, a lighter edge to his deep voice. "Seems to have been burning for quite a while, but neither of us started it or kept it going. The flowers out back are looking a lot different than yesterday, too," he nods to the window bursting with color.

"No, I don't know anything about— you said it just appeared today?" Walter's gaze snaps back to the fireplace, looking at it again. As if it could disappear at any second.

"Yes, it was already going when we–" I pause, searching for the words. "When we walked into the room. I didn't see anyone come in on the security cameras, and the only person I know who might possibly know I was still here is two states away."

Walter shakes his head in disbelief, turning back towards us. "This cabin always was sort of a mystery to me."

My brow furrows, "What do you mean?"

He takes a seat, leaning his cane up against the countertop. "You've been here for, what, a few months? Have you ever noticed anything out of the ordinary about this place?" *The fireplace, sparks of light, visions of fall, stairs moving beneath my feet.* "It's not a coincidence. This place has always been sort of magical. I've always thought of it as having its own personality. I may sound like a crazy old man, but I get the feeling you know what I'm talking about."

I nod, at a loss for words for the second time today. He's right, it does feel like the cabin has a personality. Not a scary presence, or someone messing with us. Just a little sparkle of something more.

Walter smiles with a far off look in his eyes, as if he's recounting a memory that's dear to his heart.

"Back when I first met Isabella, she came to stay in our cabin for the summer. It was her first summer working in the park as a ranger, and I suppose my parents told the ranger service they'd house some of the new rangers that weren't local on the ranch. We lived in this cabin at the time. My parents always made little comments about the cabin having a mind of its own, but I always figured it was a story to keep me in line as a boy.

"That is, until I saw some of it myself. Isabella didn't want much to do with me back then. Can't say I blame her. I was a reckless young cowboy, and she was starting her career at the national park. But all summer, we were thrown together more times than I can count.

"Now, listen," Walter shakes his head like he's remembering exactly how it felt. My heart skips a beat thinking about their wonderful love story I've heard in bits and pieces. "I can sign off a couple of them to be coincidences, but things started to get more and more unbelievable as time went on. Until both of us didn't have a choice but to give into it. I'm not saying we wouldn't have fallen in love without it, but it definitely sped things up between us. We were married a year after we met, haven't been apart much since."

"You can try to tell me it's just fate, but I know fate had some help and I believe it has something to do with this place." Walter looks out the window, smiling at the blooming marigolds.

My gaze snags on Miles, who like usual, is already looking at me with that same expression he's had all summer. I used to think it was annoyance, or even anger. But now I know, it's just Miles.

He winks at me before walking around the table. "I'm not sure I ever told you, Walt, but Katie and I actually met four years ago while I was in Salt Lake City for a cattle auction. Right after the fence broke for the first time."

"Is that so?" Walter raises his eyebrows.

My stomach does another one of those flips it's been doing all of the time lately when Miles smiles at me. Maybe it's because it took so long to get a smile out of him in the first place, or maybe it's because I know what he's been through to cause all of those frowns.

Chapter 34

Perfect Days

THIS TIME WHEN THE big wooden doors of the Alpine Rose swing open, there's a firm hand on the small of my back guiding me inside. The now familiar scent of pine and garlic fries puts a smile on my face as Miles leads me inside.

It's been two weeks of time spent just the two of us on the ranch. Catching up on all of the years we spent apart, riding up to Ember Meadow at sunset, navigating the new bookings at the Old Cabin. Most nights he stays at the guest cabin with me, huddled up by the fireplace as the fall temperatures set in.

One night, we went on a run up the dirt road just after sunset. The sky was red, still on fire, and the air was just chilly enough to give me goosebumps. We ran past fields of golden grass, groves of aspen trees turned yellow and oak trees turned red, cows enjoying the hay harvest of fall, and even a small pumpkin patch that apparently Isabella takes care of all year just to have pumpkins for a few of the kids on the neighboring ranches.

We stopped at the crest of a hill far enough away from the ranch house that it was just a small white spec in the distance, glowing with warm yellow light. The first stars of the night winking at us from above as the twilight settled in around us. I must have started to shiver, because the next thing I knew,

Miles's sherpa lined flannel was around my shoulders. I tried to tell him it'd be too hot for a run, but I suppose he was right about bringing it. I wonder if all along he brought it for me.

Miles and I stood there for a few minutes, with only the sound of our breathing in the air, our tennis shoes caked in dust from the dry dirt road. Until Miles pulled out his phone and clicked play on a song. Patsy Cline's "Walking After Midnight" played softly through his phone speakers as he pulled me into him, swaying back and forth.

We danced like that for the entire song, staring back at each other. Miles pressing his forehead against mine, and me drowning in those deep brown eyes I can never seem to look away from. It was one of those moments of peace you only feel every once in a while. When you wish you didn't ever have to leave, no matter how cold the night gets or how long the song is. I would have bottled it up if I could have.

We've had more times like that than I ever thought were possible. Perfect days.

"You ready for this?" Miles grumbles under his breath as we make our way to the back of the bar where a few familiar faces stand around a pool table. We're meeting Parker, Codie, and a few of our other friends here tonight. Only, they don't know I'm going to be here at all. Or that Miles and I are together.

Selfishly, I wanted to stay in our little bubble as long as we could to make sure that I wouldn't freak out like usual, even though I knew deep down that I wouldn't. I'm not perfect yet, but staying here feels right. Now, I'm ready to rip off the band-aid and see my new friends. Codie and I have some catching up to do, for sure.

"I sure am," I grin up at him, interlacing our fingers behind my back. I have to restrain myself from reaching up and running my hand through Miles's wavy black hair. This is the first time I've seen him without a hat on in a while. The corners of his lips curve upward just enough to form a classic Miles-smile. If you look close enough, you can almost see it.

Parker sees us first, standing up from the stool he's hunched over in with a grin on his face. Every time I see him, he looks like the happiest man on earth, smiling and excited to see everyone.

"What do we have here? Miss Katie is back in Jackson? I thought you were no longer with us." Parker booms, catching the attention of everyone else in the area.

"Jesus, Parker, you make it sound like she died," Miles says, rolling his eyes.

"I'm just surprised is all, didn't expect to see you tonight, Kate," Parker winks.

The air is knocked out of my lungs as Codie barrels into me, hugging me so tightly I'm pulled away from Miles. "Oh my god, Katie! Why didn't you tell me you were coming back? How long are you here for? Do you need a place to stay? We can have a sleepover! Did Miles tell you we were going to be here?" She takes a breath, looking at me as if I can answer all of her questions at once. "Why didn't you text me?"

I grin at her, unable to contain my happiness any longer. I'm not used to this whole 'content' thing but I love it. "We wanted to surprise you," I say, looking over to Miles. Like the past few weeks, he's smiling back at me with a warmth in his eyes that melts my heart.

"Who's we?" Parker says, looking between Miles and I as if he can't figure out a complicated math problem.

Miles grabs my hand, pulling me from Codie's embrace and against his chest. "Mac and I," he says, as if it's something everyone already knows. An everyday occurrence. I suppose it is, now.

I barely hear the gasps as he lowers his mouth to mine, kissing me in front of everyone. But, I do hear the hoots and hollers from Parker and the rest of the ranch hands when they've finally realized what's happening.

As I pull away giggling at Codie's shocked expression and Parker's endless questions, I feel overwhelmed. I can't believe this life is actually mine. That I'm standing here next to my favorite person in the whole world, with our friends, in this beautiful town in the mountains.

Even if we go up in flames, I'll still have this moment. The first time I've ever felt that life-altering feeling that I never want to let go of no matter what.

I feel like I belong.

Epilogue

Miles

WHEN I WOKE UP this morning and saw the date on the calendar, I knew it'd be a perfect day. October twenty-first. The day Katie chose to stay one year ago. The day the best chapter of our lives started. And today, I've planned a ride to Ember Meadow for the two of us. I'm hoping it'll become sort of a tradition for us on this day. Pack some snacks, and enjoy the day outside until the sun goes down and the grass lights on fire.

Metaphorically, of course. There hasn't been a real grass fire on the ranch in at least three months.

This year, we had more to look at than the glowing orange field at sunset. In the spring, we started construction on our future house up by the meadow. We've been living in the big house since I finally convinced Katie to move in with me two months ago, but the big house never really felt like ours.

After a while of deliberating, Katie and I bought the piece of land that contains the meadow and butts up against the Old Cabin property over the winter. We started on it right away, and it's just about halfway done. We're nothing if not quick.

It took Katie about six months after staying in Wyoming to break away from her parents' company, MacPherson enterprises, and start her own short term rental business. Her first purchase was the Old Cabin, which just so happened to be fully booked during peak season, and pretty busy in the winter as well. Spark Rentals, her new business, is already looking at a second location in the valley.

The stairs of the Old Cabin creak as I make my way down to the living room. I blocked out the cabin this weekend as part of my plan to create a sort of anniversary tradition. Luckily, I was able to get an open spot.

Katie's copper curls shine in the fireplace light as she stands behind the couch, looking out the window. The fall leaves have turned, painting the ranch in shades of yellow, orange and red.

"Hey," I say, hugging her close to me as I breathe in her familiar scent. Lavender and something warm. My short beard brushes against the outer shell of her ear as I feel her shiver in my arms. "How about we take a ride up to Ember Meadow?"

She turns towards me, giggling and pulling me into a hug. "You say that as if we haven't planned out the day to do exactly that."

"Hey, I'm trying to at least pretend to be spontaneous here. Let me have this."

"Fine," she gives me a quick kiss, but I pull her right back in. "You know," she says onto my lips, "this is totally a deja vu moment. It's so weird, but when I was leaving to go back to Idaho, I swear I saw this exact moment playing out in my head. Everything is the exact same, the leaves, the fireplace, you."

"What I'm hearing is that you were daydreaming about me, and I gotta say, Mac, that's a little obsessive." I give her a wink as she smacks my arm.

"Your ego is bigger than this ranch. I'm being serious, I can remember it like it was yesterday."

"I don't know what you saw, but if it brought you back to me, I'm on board with it."

I can't help but think of what could have been if things were different all those years ago when we first met. Would we have made it to where we are now? Would we have been ready to love each other fully? I think everything happened the way it was supposed to. We had to run into each other four years later for our hearts to be ready for this life.

All it took was an old legend and a cabin where love and a little bit of magic flow through the walls. That's why we celebrate this day by visiting the place where it all started. No matter where we are, we'll always come back here.

An ordinary day, doing something we do pretty often living on a ranch, but no part of it feels ordinary to me.

This life we've created is extraordinary.

Acknowledgements

Every book begins as a spark, and Ember Meadow was no exception. What started as a 'what-if' idea grew into hours-long conversations, late nights at the computer, countless cups of coffee, shaped by the people who believed in it every step of the way. I am endlessly grateful to those who dreamed alongside me and reminded me why I started this journey in the first place.

First and foremost, this book was written because of my sister Sami. We spent days on the lake, nights in the woods, phone calls, and pretty much every moment we could dreaming up this world and the people in it. There would be no Miles and Katie without you. Thank you for being the best idea man in the entire world. You'll always be the very first to read anything I write, and I'm so grateful for that.

To Daylen - thank you for being my real life romance book. And for all of the nights I sat at my laptop in a drafting cage with my headphones on. I appreciate you more than you know.

To my Mom - who supported me in this venture since day one, and always asks for updates. Can you believe it's done?? I'm so grateful for everything you do for me.

To Kellianne, Lauren, Savannah and Brooke - I have the coolest friends ever. I cannot believe how much you all were willing to do to help me out with this dream from sending in edits to type-setting. Thank you for being some of my first readers and confirming that Miles is, in fact, hot enough. I owe you each, like, ten cups of coffee.

To all of my Beta and ARC Readers - your support from before day one means so much to me. Sometimes I just sit around and think about how lucky I was to have such a wonderful group of early readers. I do not deserve you!

To my book club - the coolest group of girls west of the Mississippi.

And finally, to you. Thank you so much for picking up this book. It may seem like just another romance novel, but it's my heart and soul in writing. Thank you for supporting my dream.

Abigail Morgan writes stories with her boots in the dirt and her head in the clouds. Usually the kind drifting over the Rocky Mountains. Her romance novels mix the wild west with cozy charm and always carry a dash of mountain magic. When she's not writing or reading, she can be found chasing golden-hour light with her camera, sipping coffee that's almost too pretty to drink, or swimming in the lake. *Ember Meadow* is her debut novel.

author.abigailmorgan

authorabigailmorgan